STOCKHOLM NOIR

EDITED BY NATHAN LARSON & CARL-MICHAEL EDENBORG

AKASHIC
BOOKS

Published by Akashic Books
©2016 Akashic Books

The cost of this translation was defrayed by a subsidy from the Swedish Arts Council, gratefully acknowledged.

Series concept by Tim McLoughlin and Johnny Temple
Stockholm map by Sohrab Habibion

ISBN-13: 978-1-61775-297-1
Library of Congress Control Number: 2015934072
All rights reserved

First printing

Akashic Books
Twitter: @AkashicBooks
Facebook: AkashicBooks
E-mail: info@akashicbooks.com
Website: www.akashicbooks.com

ALSO IN THE AKASHIC NOIR SERIES

PARIS NOIR (FRANCE), edited by AURÉLIEN MASSON
PHILADELPHIA NOIR, edited by CARLIN ROMANO
PHOENIX NOIR, edited by PATRICK MILLIKIN
PITTSBURGH NOIR, edited by KATHLEEN GEORGE
PORTLAND NOIR, edited by KEVIN SAMPSELL
PRISON NOIR, edited by JOYCE CAROL OATES
PROVIDENCE NOIR, edited by ANN HOOD
QUEENS NOIR, edited by ROBERT KNIGHTLY
RICHMOND NOIR, edited by ANDREW BLOSSOM, BRIAN CASTLEBERRY & TOM DE HAVEN
ROME NOIR (ITALY), edited by CHIARA STANGALINO & MAXIM JAKUBOWSKI
SAN DIEGO NOIR, edited by MARYELIZABETH HART
SAN FRANCISCO NOIR, edited by PETER MARAVELIS
SAN FRANCISCO NOIR 2: THE CLASSICS, edited by PETER MARAVELIS
SEATTLE NOIR, edited by CURT COLBERT
SINGAPORE NOIR, edited by CHERYL LU-LIEN TAN
STATEN ISLAND NOIR, edited by PATRICIA SMITH
STOCKHOLM NOIR (SWEDEN), edited by NATHAN LARSON & CARL-MICHAEL EDENBORG
ST. PETERSBURG NOIR (RUSSIA), edited by NATALIA SMIRNOVA & JULIA GOUMEN
TEHRAN NOIR (IRAN), edited by SALAR ABDOH
TEL AVIV NOIR (ISRAEL), edited by ETGAR KERET & ASSAF GAVRON
TORONTO NOIR (CANADA), edited by JANINE ARMIN & NATHANIEL G. MOORE
TRINIDAD NOIR (TRINIDAD & TOBAGO), edited by LISA ALLEN-AGOSTINI & JEANNE MASON
TWIN CITIES NOIR, edited by JULIE SCHAPER & STEVEN HORWITZ
USA NOIR, edited by JOHNNY TEMPLE
VENICE NOIR (ITALY), edited by MAXIM JAKUBOWSKI
WALL STREET NOIR, edited by PETER SPIEGELMAN
ZAGREB NOIR (CROATIA), edited by IVAN SRŠEN

FORTHCOMING

ACCRA NOIR (GHANA), edited by MERI NANA-AMA DANQUAH
ADDIS ABABA NOIR (ETHIOPIA), edited by MAAZA MENGISTE
ATLANTA NOIR, edited by TAYARI JONES
BAGHDAD NOIR (IRAQ), edited by SAMUEL SHIMON
BOGOTÁ NOIR (COLOMBIA), edited by ANDREA MONTEJO
BRUSSELS NOIR (BELGIUM), edited by MICHEL DUFRANNE
BUENOS AIRES NOIR (ARGENTINA), edited by ERNESTO MALLO
JERUSALEM NOIR, edited by DROR MISHANI
LAGOS NOIR (NIGERIA), edited by CHRIS ABANI
MARRAKECH NOIR (MOROCCO), edited by YASSIN ADNAN
MISSISSIPPI NOIR, edited by TOM FRANKLIN
MONTREAL NOIR (CANADA), edited by JOHN McFETRIDGE & JACQUES FILIPPI
NEW ORLEANS NOIR: THE CLASSICS, edited by JULIE SMITH
OAKLAND NOIR, edited by JERRY THOMPSON & EDDIE MULLER
RIO NOIR (BRAZIL), edited by TONY BELLOTTO
SAN JUAN NOIR (PUERTO RICO), edited by MAYRA SANTOS-FEBRES
SÃO PAULO NOIR (BRAZIL), edited by TONY BELLOTTO
ST. LOUIS NOIR, edited by SCOTT PHILLIPS
TRINIDAD NOIR: THE CLASSICS (TRINIDAD & TOBAGO), edited by EARL LOVELACE & ROBERT ANTONI

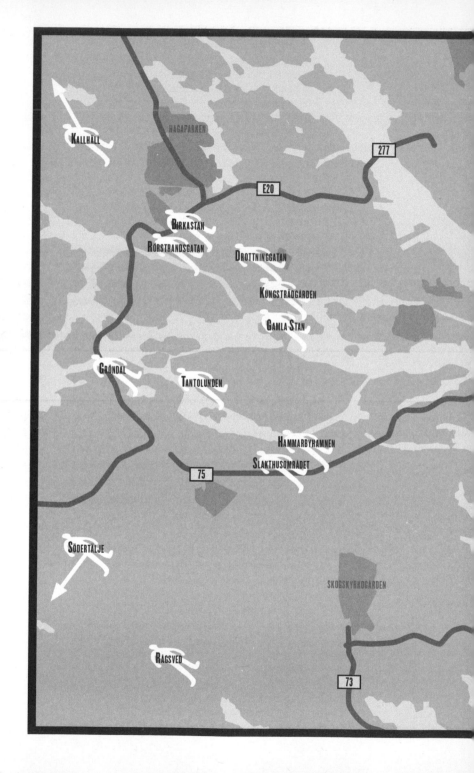

STOCKHOLM

222

RÄTTSHÄLLEDEN

SALTSJÖBADEN

229

TABLE OF CONTENTS

PART III: THE BRUTALITY OF BEASTS

INTRODUCTION
WHILE THE CITY SLEEPS

To the tourist, the city of Stockholm appears a shimmering dream. Laid out on a series of islands, it is verdant, clean, and surrounded by crystalline water. On paper, Stockholm is paradise. And in some respects, it truly is. But in most respects, it is anything but.

While Stockholm is Sweden's capital, crown jewel, and the seat of its monarchy, it's impossible to understand the city without taking a closer look at the country as a whole. Its citizens are largely happy to prop each other up, paying taxes into a theoretically fantastic system of free health care, education, generous maternal and paternal leave, an expectation of six-to-eight-weeks paid annual vacation. Culture and the arts are valued and heavily subsidized. Government-sponsored graffiti contests, concerts, crafts fairs, and municipal skate parks abound. If born into this system, you can expect a very high standard of living.

Yes, there is much to be proud of and thankful for as a Swede. It's a great country, a second home for one of us, the birthplace for the other. There's a lot to love about Sweden.

Naturally, all is not so simple. Sweden, a famously neutral country, is one of the world's biggest arms dealers. The Swedish role during World War II was . . . *complicated*. The extreme right wing is on a meteoric rise, as expressly isolationist/anti-immigrant groups steadily gain a foothold in the country's government. While the myriad political parties create coalitions in order to survive, Sweden edges ever closer to a two-party political system, with the once-colorful spectrum of political voices narrowed and watered down.

Sweden is the home to multinationals like drug giant Astra-Zeneca, Spotify, Volvo, and, of course, IKEA—that benign beacon of modest conformity, still unable to shake the faint but persistent whiff of fascism that has surrounded it since its inception.

Like nearly everywhere else in the world, American exports such as McDonald's, Starbucks, etc., are creeping in. There exists a shockingly vicious tabloid culture, and Swedish television is dominated by American films and TV shows, or homegrown versions of Fear Factor, Survivor, and The Voice—though this is a relatively recent development. Until the late 1980s, there were only two (state-run) TV channels. Programming was sourced as much from the East—Finland, the Soviet Union—as it was from the West.

Swedes, being modern Westerners, very naturally want their lattes, the occasional Big Mac, streaming Netflix, and their position on the world stage, whatever the field. Swedes want to make money and compete in the global marketplace. The end result is something like free-market socialism. And why not? But can the two "extremes" (capitalism, socialism) coexist in this way? With the appearance of "private" health clinics, bringing stratification to the system, the trend toward overseas boarding schools, and the pervasive lure and abundance of all things material . . . well, it challenges the myth of a classless society, as only the elite will be able to indulge in these "enhancements." Naturally, this inspires a simmering anger amongst some of those less well endowed.

Returning to Stockholm itself—while this town is admittedly

not a gnarly, crime-infested metropolis, the city is still plenty dark. Stockholm has two very distinct hearts that beat, each absolutely dependent on the other. One heart is lodged deep in the moneyed streets of Östermalm and Vasastan. The other beats deep in its suburbs, essentially an inversion of the inner city, an external growth of the old Stockholm that serves to triple its population.

This is the front-and-center issue of our age.

A Christian Democrat might describe this outer urban growth as a tumor, or a fungus, a deadly threat to the Swedish social system, to be surgically removed if possible. The left, on the other hand, would be at pains to express its view that this growth is an evolution, to be nurtured like the development of a new fantastic limb with which the entity called Stockholm can do exciting and new things.

Politics aside, we could be talking about Stockholm, London, or New York City when we observe that these dual trajectories can be classified as *monied*—indigenous, blue-blooded, white, comfortably settled; and *aspirational*—newly arrived, generally nonwhite, ready to work hard and climb the class ladder. In other words: the immigrant.

Pragmatically, all systems would fail without the aspirational heart. It's this segment of the population that keeps the wheels running, the kitchens of fancy restaurants staffed, the hospitals functioning, the garbage collected. And in a country like Sweden, with its tremendous tax-driven health care system, you need a lot of folks pulling levers to keep everything upright. There should be nothing controversial about this observation.

Complexities arise when we acknowledge an obvious trend: increasingly, the dominant group (the indigenous white) no longer wants these core jobs. We can observe this worldwide.

To understand the nature of Stockholm's outgrowth, we

must examine the Miljonprogrammet (the Million Program), the Social Democrats' staggeringly ambitious 1965 housing blitz, with its aim of constructing a million new homes within a decade—free from misery, bad air, and the disease of the inner city.

The architectural style employed here, almost by necessity, was termed modernist, but the end product seems to bear a closer to relation to functionalist style. To be more direct, most of these structures would not be out of place in the Soviet Union or the former German Democratic Republic.

The earnest, wide-eyed social plan to create "good democratic citizens" was clearly and happily stated as part of the public works project. The predominate living unit was called a *normaltrea*, a three-room apartment of about seventy-five square meters, designed to snugly contain a family of four.

The last elements of the Million Program—the construction of world-class schools, libraries, playgrounds, and areas of greenery—proved far more difficult to achieve. And the lofty if noble vision to integrate diverse groups of households was, it could be safely said, an abject failure. This was due in part to awkward, hasty construction . . . and in terms of the utopian vision of world citizens mingling, cross-pollinating—it was not to be.

Two coinciding factors in the late 1960s scuttled these plans, at least in the sense that their architects had intended. First of all, middle-class (mostly white) Swedes might pay lip service to the ideals of the Million Program over drinks—oh, absolutely! But they wouldn't dare to actually live in these unfortunate places. This dynamic dovetailed with the steady arrival of more "New Swedes" from North Africa, the Middle East, subcontinental Asia, and later the former Yugoslavia, all in immediate need of housing.

A large percentage of Sweden's Iraqi population resides in the suburban Södertälje, and it's notable that Sweden has taken in more Iraqi refugees than the US and Canada combined. This arms-open-wide immigration policy is certainly commendable, and is a remnant of the Olof Palme administration: its solidarity with anticolonial struggle and general anti-American posturing. But many Swedes are perhaps not so comfortable with what the fruit of these policies actually look like.

By design, these new communities were self-contained, isolated from the outside world. As such, the immigrant communities of the greater Stockholm area were efficiently (if unintentionally) cut off from the rest of the population.

Walking through these areas today, spots like Husby and Tensta, you will see the Swedish equivalent of one of America's most notorious housing projects—Chicago's former Cabrini-Green Homes. The recent riots of May 2013—needless to say, an extremely rare occurrence in a town like Stockholm—are perhaps a taste of things to come. Class hatred has always been an issue, even in a supposedly classless society, and now a racial element has been introduced that was not there before, simply because the society had been too homogenous to support it.

Look again at the term "good democratic citizens." Or the term *normaltrea*, with its Latin root *normal* ("conforming to common standards"), implying that the ingredients of "normality" involve a happy couple, two children, and a modest apartment. This is the same type of utopian/uniform thinking that led to the growth of the American suburbs in the 1940s, intended largely to house returning soldiers and their families. In *Stockholm Noir*, the city is presented as a gaping maw ready to devour your soul should you wander down the wrong alley . . . but it doesn't limit itself to the urban, even in the earliest incarnations of the form. The city can represent a place to reinvent yourself, to duck out on your history, to begin again and rise like a phoenix.

Even so, as early as the late 1940s—with the American suburbs a model for the upwardly mobile, for those seeking escape from the shadow of the urban—even as they were being constructed, the suburbs were recognized as places of immense spiritual corruption. Put a twenty-two-year-old male with extreme post-traumatic stress disorder fresh from the battlefields of Europe in a remote box with his family. Put an unhappy wife next door, looking to escape her hellish life. Add yet another angry, damaged man to all of this, and put a smattering of children in everybody's path. You have on your hands material for countless problematic situations.

In this volume, Johan Theorin's "Still in Kallhäll" takes place in the "suburbs" of Stockholm, and his tale astutely reflects the violent envy felt by those on the periphery. Anna-Karin Selberg's "Horse," as well as Inger Frimansson's "Black Ice" and Malte Persson's "The Splendors and Miseries of a Swedish Crime Writer," similarly take place on the outskirts. These areas are as indicative of the true nature of Stockholm as the neighborhoods depicted in Torbjörn Elensky's "Kim," set in the central, beatific Gamla Stan, one of the best-preserved medieval sectors in Northern Europe. Or in the piece by coeditor Nathan Larson, where the events take place in the tony upmarket shopping district of Stockholm, among the haute clothing racks of Swedish designers.

Wherever there is existential dread, where there are shadows, where there is money in the hands of some and not in others, where there is lust, wherever a human can try and fail, there is noir. All that is required is the insight that we will not make it out of this life alive, and we are damned to chaos. Everywhere misery and hatred live, there is noir. Where there is fear and despair, there is noir. This is where literature steps in and gives voice to that creeping sense that there is a deep disease, a rotten core within all this shiny economic growth.

Everywhere is noir. Even, and especially, in a paradise like Sweden, where the citizen is given every tool to go out and become a great success but is paradoxically held to an almost subliminal expectation to fall in line . . . and never shine so brightly that you disturb your neighbor.

Even as crimes rates remain extremely low, Swedes love scaring themselves . . . and above all they love their crime fiction. Traditionally, Swedish crime novels have been verbose, realist stories about good-hearted, weary cops, faced with all the things the country has in truth never seen: mass murderers, rampant mafioso, and overall mayhem. The public devours this stuff, needing stimulation of the fear center that is so rarely disturbed in Sweden. Tired, flaccid police procedurals, often overly long.

Swedish crime fiction hasn't always been Liza Marklund, Stieg Larsson, and Leif G.W. Persson. In the early days, the politically incorrect Gustaf Ericsson wrote hard-boiled fiction, most famously *The Man You Killed* (1932). Many of the early Worker's Movement writers, like Jan Fridegård, explored the darkest edges of Sweden at night. Remaining within the safety of the harmless parlor-crime genre, authors like Stieg Trenter and Sjöwall and Wahlöö churned out material in the vein of Agatha Christie or Ed McBain—well-meaning but formulaic, social democratic stuff. From this rose the Mankells and the Marklunds, coming to full flower with the Dragon Tattoo series, and thus the Swedish crime fiction miracle was realized.

The rest is best-selling history. But it is emphatically not noir.

In this anthology it's our aim to showcase the darker, grittier, more intense world of Swedish noir fiction. Here the dangers lurking beneath the IKEA lifestyle are given free rein, and words are given to the ambivalence and despair of a model society. We have invited only a handful of the finest crime writers; the other contributors are poets, uncompromising literary fiction writers, hard-core literary beasts.

Crime is frequently a vehicle for noir rides, but it needn't be. Noir is unfailingly realistic in the sense that there is always moral and narrative complexity—if you're a sociopath, you can fuck someone's partner, take everything he or she is worth, and get away with it. No problem. And if you're a sociopath, there's no universal law. You can get close to success, but dread will always follow, and there's always the possibility of total collapse. It transcends gender, race, or political system. Noir is not nihilism; it is exaggerated realism. In this sense there can never, ever be a truly happy ending.

Kinda like life.

Nathan Larson & Carl-Michael Edenborg
Stockholm, Sweden
January 2016

PART I

CRIME & PUNISHMENT

STAIRWAY FROM HEAVEN

BY ÅKE EDWARDSON

Birkastan

Translated by Laura A. Wideburg

The sun in the window behind me was starting to set over Stockholm. Like a freshly powdered corpse, it's always most beautiful in the twilight. Stockholm can't bear the day; it lives at night, like a vampire.

The light shone into the eyes of the woman walking into my office. She could see me as nothing more than a silhouette, but I could observe her in detail.

She didn't wear much makeup. She sat down in what passed for an armchair in front of my desk. Well, neither the armchair nor the desk were worthy of the name, but they were what I owned and obviously she decided they were enough.

For what? For help?

That's what goes through my head each time I meet a new client. Self-esteem is not one of my strong points. I'm still fairly good at my job, but my grip on things is growing more tenuous by the day. The signs are all there—sentimentality, compassion, thoughtfulness, all those complicating emotions tied to goodness—but I can scarcely help myself these days, especially that day, as I was hungover and had already downed the hair of the dog, a bad sign for sure, but of late my life has consisted of one bad sign after another, my job of bad news, really bad news. I had tried to lighten my depression by reading the book on the desk in front of me, but the words made no sense, even less than usual.

Human beings, in the shape of angels or demons, come into my office in Birkastan somewhat randomly. The woman sitting in the armchair in front of me, now crossing her legs, resembled an angel who had determined to forsake the light of heaven to glide down the stairway to the dark, to the earth. To me. But her eyes were cold, as if she'd already seen everything, been everywhere down here.

"Can I get right to the point?" she asked.

"Sure."

"I need your help to find John."

"Who's John?"

"A man I know."

"I'll need more than that."

"He's disappeared," she said before looking at something out the window behind me—but there was nothing there, just Stockholm dying her death in beauty. The woman shifted her gaze to the bookshelf just to the left of my window. It was filled with crime novels. Dostoyevsky, Gogol, Borges, Stendhal, Yates, Burroughs, Hemingway, Strindberg. She examined the open book on my desk.

"What are you reading there?"

"*Finnegan's Wake*," I said. "James Joyce."

"Is it good?"

"I've just started."

"You're at the end," she said, nodding toward it.

"I always start at the back," I replied.

"Is that how people read Joyce?"

"That's how people should read this book. I've solved the riddle."

"I see," she said. "I never read."

"Reading is good for the soul."

"So what should I read? Any suggestions?"

"*The Red Room* by August Strindberg," I said. "It's about Stockholm."

"I'm tired of Stockholm."

"If you're tired of Stockholm, you're tired of life," I said.

"So you're a philosopher."

"You get that way in this job."

"You look tired," she said.

"Not that way."

"Can you philosophize some help for me?"

"Is John your spouse?"

She stared at me as if she didn't understand the word. *Spouse.* Sounds a little old-fashioned, but I'm an old-fashioned man. I keep a bottle of Dewar's White Label in my desk drawer. I wear a suit and tie. I was about to lighten the bottle a bit when she came in. I listen to Led Zeppelin and Black Sabbath, in that order. When evening falls, I like to remember my youth, 1969 and 1970. I can say I had a year of real life, which many people don't even get.

"Are you married?" I asked to clarify.

"Yeah, but not to each other," she said, elegantly fluttering her wrist.

I considered my ghostly memory of her long after she'd gone. She'd told me her name was Rebecka, and it could be true enough—I didn't ask for her ID, I'm not the police. And, well, my name could be Jimmy Page or Tony Iommi, for example, or even Peter Kempinsky, which is what it says on the office door. It's a nice name. I chose it myself.

I sat as the electrified darkness shone in through the window from the street below. Birkastan. My part of Stockholm. I wasn't born here, but I've come to call it home. Lost in my reflections, my hangover intensified and I suddenly needed my medicine, so I opened the desk drawer and pulled out the bottle, poured two fingers in the glass that had been set in front of Malcolm Lowry on the bookshelf. I lifted the glass and drank, feeling the warmth go through my chest as it burned my throat. The water of life. The devil's drink. The devil's music. I held the glass up toward the window. The alcohol was clear and it shimmered in the night, pure and true—it wasn't grubby like the rest of life. I took another swig. My desk drawer also held my other medicine; I knew that the only place I'd remember to look for it was next to the whiskey bottle. Venlafaxin Hexal and Dewar's, an extraordinary combination to battle depression, a cure not unknown but condemned by psychiatry. The pills have no taste.

John, John, John, I thought. *Follow John,* I thought. *Where are you, buddy?* I'd taken the job. I'd told her it wasn't going to be easy. People who want to disappear can manage it pretty well. I glanced at the photo she'd handed me. John stood against a neutral background. He seemed neutral himself, good-looking, friendly. It would have been better if he'd looked like an asshole.

"He hasn't been accused of a crime," she'd told me, recrossing her legs.

"How do you know that?" I'd asked.

She didn't answer. I believed her, naive as I am.

"He could be anywhere," I said. "Here in Stockholm, out in the countryside, abroad."

"No, he's in Stockholm. I'm sure of it. In fact, I'm sure he's still in Birkastan."

"How do you know? Lots of people leave Stockholm, not to mention Birkastan."

"Not him. Not John. He can't."

"Why not?"

She didn't answer this question either. Perhaps she would later on, but I hoped we wouldn't meet again. I had no desire to see her again—it wouldn't be good for either of us. Her beautiful legs looked artificial, as if they'd been carved from an endangered wood.

She paid and left. Five hundred thousand royal Swedish kronor, cash, in an envelope. Half my fee. Too high a sum? I needed it, and she was ready to pay. I knew who'd told her how much I charged, and I planned to spring for a glass of Glenfarclas, the forty-two-year-old bottle, the next time I saw him. She had been absolutely certain that I was the right one for the job, and she was right, but for the wrong reason.

There were hints of spring in the air as I walked down toward the Atlas wall. The promise of light. Stockholm would soon melt into another summer. It was the same miracle every year. The city was bigger than life in that way, bigger than all of us; it had been here before we arrived and it would be here when we were gone. I had no plans to leave this mortal plane anytime soon, but I wasn't so sure about John. I had a hunch, but I could be wrong. It's been known to happen. I'm just a sinner with a bad conscience.

On the other side of the inlet, Kungsholms strand glittered with gold. I hardly ever walked over the bridge. Kungsholmen is a part of the city that nobody with brains would ever trust. It's always smiling but its smile is false. Even now, it winks with its red and yellow cat's eyes, but nobody who comes from the northern part of town is fooled.

It smelled like charcoal and fire and thyme inside Degiulio's. They'd left two tables out on the sidewalk, as if some tourist would want to sit there and dream of spring. As if Italians eat outside when it's forty degrees Fahrenheit.

I took my usual table at the back of the room. Maria had set flowers on the table, as she always did. That day they were yellow tulips, my favorite. I leaned toward them and drew in a deep breath, feeling like a real person for a moment.

Maria was at my table already. My only human friend in this world.

"You look tired, Peter," she said.

"A glass of that red varietal you had yesterday," I said. "A large glass. Thanks."

"It's called Alba," she said.

"Yeah, that's the one."

She walked over to the bar and poured the wine, returning with a large glass. The flames inside the oven refracted the red color. There are so many shades of red. I've seen most of them.

"You have any lasagna with mushrooms tonight?" I asked. "No meat."

"You can have whatever you want," she said.

"Then I want a grappa too."

"You drank too much grappa yesterday, Peter," she warned.

"That's why I need another glass today."

She gave me a look that triggered a long-forgotten memory: someone had leaned over me once when I was a small child; a good person, but not my mother. It was my first memory. I could never catch it and hold onto it, but I knew it had been the happiest moment of my entire life.

"Then get me a second glass of the Alba instead."

"You haven't finished the first one yet," she said.

"I'll drink it while you're getting the second glass. I thought I could have anything I wanted."

"You seem really unhappy this evening," she said.

"I have to find somebody."

"That's not news."

"I think I'm losing my grip," I said.

She paused. "On what?"

"I'll try to figure that one out while you're getting my second glass." I lifted the Alba. The color was deep red. "Tell the cook not to use too much cheese. Cheese is the corpse left over from milk."

"What's that supposed to mean? It sounds terrible."

"It means just what I said."

"Did you think that up yourself?"

"No, Bloom did."

"Who's Bloom?"

"*Ulysses*. James Joyce. Bloom eats cheese. The cheese eats itself. It's self-consuming. Just like dogs. They eat themselves, they vomit, they eat themselves again."

"Cut that out," she said.

"I can't, Maria."

"Then stop talking. I don't like it."

"But it's true," I said. "Everybody eats everybody. The city eats itself."

She left me alone at my table after that. I looked around, but there was no one new to observe. I was the only customer at a table. Most evenings I'm the only one. Birkastan people usually just pick up their brick-oven pizzas. Nobody sits while they wait. I drank and closed my eyes. Maria was playing nineteenth-century opera at a low volume. Opera and pizza were a perfect combination. Large gestures, large promises, large voices—but most of it empty and superficial, followed by a heavy, greasy feeling in your belly, as if your body has been weighed down with concrete.

A young woman came in from the twilight and I overheard her ordering three pizzas: one Margherita, another Margherita, and . . . Margherita. She was clearly a creature of habit, as am I, simple is best. She was beautiful in an old-fashioned way and the kind I like, as if she'd stepped out of a Swedish film from the forties. Her round face, her pageboy haircut, that certain style of trench coat. Jussi Björling could have been singing in the background, although there weren't any pizzerias in Sweden in the forties, let alone takeout places. Though perhaps in my decade, the fifties, you could find boiled hot dogs in paper, or fried herring. I was born after the war, in 1953, part of the smallest generation of children ever born in Sweden. I wonder how many of us are still around. Maybe I'm the only one. Though the Met in New York City was Jussi Björling's main stage for decades, he died of a broken heart in Stockholm's archipelago. He was forty-nine years old, ten years younger than I am now. It's not right. He was a true artist in a false profession. He drank . . . but who doesn't? He always had a black dog following him . . . but who doesn't?

The woman looked in my direction. I lifted my glass in greeting. It was *numero due*. Not much was left in it either. She glanced away, without nodding or smiling. To her, I was a lone drunkard—that's a good old-fashioned word, *drunkard*—sitting in a lonely pizzeria in the loneliest part of town. But she'd be wrong. I'm a thinker. Right then, I was thinking about my own youth, when I was two months shy of my sixteenth birthday and Led Zeppelin released their first album, on January 12, 1969. That was the life, then. And I was one month shy of my seventeenth birthday when Black Sabbath released their first album, on Friday, February 13, 1970. Led Zeppelin changed rock music forever and Black Sabbath picked up their riff and created heavy metal. The sound existed on Led Zeppelin's first album, but the evil heaviness had been lacking. It was born with Sabbath, and everything since then has been nothing but repetition, just like my life. Like here, at Degiulio's, where the woman had picked up her pizzas and was heading back out into the darkness without looking in my direction. By now, I was working on my third glass of Alba and my lasagna was in front of me. A perfect portion. I inhaled the aroma. It was slightly bitter from the portobellos, chanterelles, and black pepper.

My phone vibrated in my breast pocket, like a pacemaker with a low battery. I pulled it out: the client.

"So?"

"Somebody saw John," she said.

"Where?"

"Karlberg station," she said. "He was leaving."

"Where was he heading?"

"I don't know. God, time is running out!"

"Who saw him?"

"Does it matter?"

"It matters to me," I said.

"It's not important."

"I'm hanging up now," I said. "I'll call back later tonight."

I ended the call and got up from the table. Maria glanced at me.

"I have to go out for a while," I said.

"Take care of yourself," she said.

Night had fallen over the city. I heard noises above my head and looked up. A dozen ravens were flying in loose formation toward the west; the flock looked like a Rorschach test against the electric sky. I didn't want to interpret what I saw, it would just scare me. The ravens were cawing, hoarse and scoffing, as if they knew everything.

I followed Atlasgatan to Sankt Eriksgatan, then took a right and went south to Norrbackagatan.

Everything was quiet in front of Karlberg station. It was the time of day where normalcy rules, where healthy humanity draws inward, does the dishes, puts the kids to sleep, works on the crossword, all those things I've longed for all my life.

No John there. Nobody had seen him. To me, it seemed that the client knew who'd spotted him. Perhaps she had. She was nuts, really, which was why I was standing there uselessly.

I walked back the way I'd come. I met no one.

Maria nodded when I stepped back into Degiulio's.

"Let's start over from the beginning," I said. "Including the wine."

I sat at my table and called Rebecka.

"Nothing," I said.

"Did you really go there?"

"Yes, and now I'm having my dinner," I said.

"But it could be too late!" There was a note of desperation in her voice, raspy like a file. I'd heard it before. The client comes to me with a practiced cool air, with practiced replies, but those soon collapse and blow away just like bad rock music or bad literature. Only naked panic is left.

"It's never too late," I said. My own practiced reply, superficial and false.

"I trusted you!" she said.

"Congratulations."

"He might take off again!"

"Then I'll find him again," I said. I put my fork into the fresh lasagna Maria had set before me. It was new, not the old portion warmed up in the microwave. The food steamed, just like it should, you could burn your tongue on it if you wanted; you ought to at least have the option.

"You didn't find him!"

"No."

Maria brought the wine. It had the same refracted color as before.

"But I will," I continued. "Was John seen anywhere else?"

"No, just here in Birkastan."

She'd tripped up. Earlier, she'd said she lived in Östermalm, that she was heading back there straight from my office.

"Give me something more specific," I said. "Besides the station."

"Have you been drinking?" she asked.

"Answer me," I said.

"It sounds as if you've been drinking."

"I'm trying to eat my dinner."

She said something I didn't catch, and I hung up and dropped my phone back into my breast pocket so I could eat. I remembered when I was a child, I'd gone with an uncle to the woods around Nykvarn to search for mushrooms and we found a glade that shone like real gold from the chanterelles, and that was the last time I was ever happy, actually happy, like the people in magazines and on TV. I thought about John. I thought about the song "Good Times Bad Times," the single from Led Zeppelin's first album.

The train station was once again as silent as the sky above Karlberg Lake. If John had been here earlier in the evening, he was certainly gone now, sucked into the glittering city. *There's a lady who's sure all that glitters is gold.* I thought of this other Led Zeppelin song as I glanced over at the bike rack with its long row of locked bikes with stolen wheels. Can't trust anything or anybody these days. It resembled an art installation, a commentary on something about which I ought to be aware. This is true art as far as I'm concerned: pictures sent directly to my insides, lighting them up, something pure and clear and simple.

I saw a missed call from Rebecka and rang her back. A commuter train slowly pulled out of the station, a lit worm on the way north.

"I need to know who saw John this evening," I said.

"Are you out in the city now?"

"I'm at the station. Who saw him?"

She didn't respond. She knew the answer; actually, this meant my assignment was over. Everything depended on silence. If she had broken that silence, she'd be in big trouble now. I wonder if she understood this, really understood what it meant.

"I'm going home," I said. "Nice to have met you."

"Wait!" she shouted.

"For what?"

"John was the one," she said.

"Excuse me?"

"John was the one who called."

"So you're telling me that your missing John called and let you know where he was?"

"Yes."

"Why?"

"He was worried."

"Ha-ha."

"It's not a joke. Somebody's after him. Somebody's looking for him."

"I'm looking for him."

"He doesn't know about you."

"So what made him think this?"

"We didn't . . . he didn't have a chance to tell me. He hung up. He'd called from a prepaid mobile phone. It's dead now."

It's always the past, I thought. Nobody can ever escape the shadows of the past. It was a banal thought, but still true.

Perhaps she really was crazy, my client Rebecka. Perhaps John only existed in her mind. But if there were a real John wandering around the streets of Birkastan and somebody else was following him, I'd be out half a million Swedish kronor.

"So I won't go home," I said. "Where are you?"

"A pizzeria on a side street. The only place that's open."

"Degiulio's. You've been following me."

"No," she lied.

"I'll meet you there," I said.

John lived on Drejargatan, on the second floor. As soon as Rebecka had left my office I'd gone straight there and rung the doorbell. Nobody opened. The last name *Beijer* was on a sign on the apartment door. Nothing else. Now I was standing there once more. I rang the bell again. It was pretty late. John's wife ought to be home if she were in Stockholm, but nobody opened the door.

I took out my skeleton key. The lock clicked and I pushed the door open. The lights of the city illuminated the hallway like a spotlight. I could smell the silence. I took my gun from my shoulder holster, followed the artificial light down the hallway into a room, glimpsed the contours of something, walked closer, saw it was a body. She lay on the sofa with an arm over the side as if she were resting, waiting for nightfall, but night was over for her, and day too, and all the other days forever and ever, amen. One day we all will die, but we have to live those remaining days and nights still left us. Her big day had already arrived. I touched her arm and it was cool, not cold; she'd died today, shot in the throat. The wound resembled a scarf which should protect from the cold, but it was warm in the room. From the heat, I saw condensation collecting on the window facing the street; I saw the woman's face, still beautiful even in its death grimace, and I didn't even know her name.

John, I thought. John, did you do this?

In the small V-shaped park between Drejargatan and Birka-gatan, I saw a shape sitting on one of the benches. I knew there were ten benches altogether. They were green in the daylight.

"Who's there?" the silhouette asked. I recognized the voice.

"Kempinsky," I said.

"What are you doing out here this late?"

"And what are you doing, Arne?"

"Just waiting to go to bed."

I walked closer. Arne was one of the homeless guys in our neighborhood. He was visible now, under the light of the streetlamp, the skin of his face already showing the tightness that makes alcoholics in the last stage of the disease start to appear Asian.

"If things ever calm down around here," Arne said. "No privacy."

"What are you talking about?"

"I'm staying up here," he said.

"What do you mean by *if things ever calm down?*" I asked.

"People coming and going," he said. "Damned traffic."

"Under the bridge?" I asked.

"Where else?"

When I got back to Degiulio's, Maria had already placed the chairs on top of the tables. She was alone in the restaurant.

"Was there a woman here?" I asked. "She was supposed to wait for me."

"Nobody's come in since you left," she replied. "Since you left the last time, I mean."

"Yeah, I come and go." I called Rebecka's number. No answer. I didn't leave a message either. I stepped outside again.

The arches beneath the Sankt Eriksgatan Bridge are a popular spot for the homeless to sleep. Walking twenty yards in, I was overwhelmed by the stench of urine and shit and filth, dust and damp cement, illness, death. I saw not a single person; only God and the devil knew what was hiding in the shadows. Nothing moved. The place was lit by naked bulbs from a few fixtures built into the walls; the cast was blue like a dead iris. A toilet of broken porcelain—Rörstrand—stood in the middle of the shitty cement floor. Yet another incomprehensible tableau that spoke to me. In the distance, I could see discarded gym equipment twisted in awkward positions.

Graffiti covered the bare walls. Rough pictures, rough words, messages from a world beneath the underworld. *There's a sign on the wall but she wants to be sure, 'cause you know sometimes words have two meanings.*

A word can have more than two meanings, I thought, words are just the surface layer. I walked over to read something resembling a headline: *EXTRA! EXTRA! Entire Cat Family Missing! Has the Collector Struck Again?* It meant nothing to me. It was a joke or maybe it wasn't a joke. It was a headline that fit this environment. The Collector existed in the real reality's unreality. Everything smelled like paranoia here, fear, desperate words, desperate situations, but the answers were not there, just the insane questions. Ozzy Osbourne had searched his entire life and what did he find? *I can't see the things that make true happiness, I must be blind.* He was singing my song too, one of the blind seers.

I thought I heard something to my left. I turned. Could be a cat, could be the Collector. Hundreds of painted faces covered the walls over there, like a Warhol work, all black-and-white, men and women. It was as if I had stepped into an art gallery, and perhaps I had, as it had been months since I was down here last, and everything around me might have been classified as art while I was aboveground. They all seemed to watch me, their eyes following me, the old optical trick painters have played with for thousands of years. I walked closer. One of the faces farthest to the right was a little bit smaller than the others; it had a different black-and-white nuance. It was still, but not as still as a painting. I saw the outline of a body and a pair of shoes on the ground.

"John?" I said.

No answer. The eyes stared at me. They seemed less real now, as if they were part of the collage. I blinked, and the face was still there when I glanced again. I felt the weight of my Colt Peacemaker in my holster, as I always did when my senses were on full alert, when things were reaching their end. Perhaps this was not the best weapon for my purposes, but it was the fourth version of the SAA, adapted to a new world.

"Peter Kempinsky here," I said. "You can come out."

"Who the hell are you?" the face asked. It flowed out from the shadows. "Why are you persecuting me?"

He was a few yards away. A man my age, about my height, wearing a suit like mine, nice features, we could have been friends if it weren't for Rebecka.

"Why are you persecuting me?" he repeated.

"Why are you running away?" I asked.

"I'm not running anywhere. I have the right to be anywhere I want to be in this city."

"So you chose this place," I said.

"I'm afraid," he said.

"Afraid of me?"

"Of whoever is following me."

"Why would anybody follow you?"

He ran his hand across his chin, a desperate gesture. His eyes darted, as if he'd just realized where he was. He looked at me.

"She's the one," he said.

"Who?" I asked.

"Rebecka. She sent you. She can't take no for an answer. So she's sending you, whoever you are, a policeman, private detective, friend, or whatever the hell you are, to convince me to go back to her."

"You're wrong, John," I said as I drew my Colt. "She sent me to kill you."

The fear in his eyes was as real as life and death, I'd seen that black light many times in the seconds before I killed someone. But this guy was not done with life. I don't know what I was waiting for.

"You're making a mistake," he cried.

I'd heard that many times before too. A professional killer hears all kinds of excuses. But the mistakes were never mine; they were from the past lives of my clients or my victims.

"It's my job," I said.

"No, no! You don't understand! She's as dark and as dangerous as the water under the bridge down here! She wants revenge! Then she won't let *you* get away."

"Interesting," I said, lifting the revolver. The place was perfect, a ready-made cemetery for professional killers. In the best of all possible worlds, I would be back at Degiulio's tomorrow evening, Rebecka would give me the rest of the money, I'd drink a well-earned grappa, and perhaps go home with Maria—it had happened before—or maybe with Rebecka; anything is possible in this city.

"She'll knock you off too!" John yelled.

I didn't reply. I'd heard that before as well, but I liked that old-fashioned expression, *knock off.*

"She killed my wife!" John yelled. It sounded like the last lie of a drowning man.

Try to show a little dignity, I thought. *And as we wind down on the road, our shadows taller than our souls.* I'd always liked that part, often wondering about what it meant. The soul for me is something like the back side of the moon, something everyone knows and talks about, but that nobody has ever seen. I try to see if the soul flies out of people when I kill them, but I've never succeeded. A tiny, flying shadow would have been enough for me. A tenth of a second of a breeze. But no.

"Why'd you call her tonight?" I asked.

"What?"

"You called her from the Karlberg station and said someone was following you."

"Jesus Lord God," he said. "She's really fucking you blue."

"Watch your language, please," I said.

"Don't you get it?" he screamed, his voice echoing as if it were the soundtrack accompanying the graffiti on the walls, perhaps Velvet Underground, music for the black-and-white scene we found ourselves in. "I ended it, but she can't accept that. She's crazy! She won't accept it from you either."

"What do you mean by that?"

"If you kill me, she'll kill you."

He abruptly calmed down then, as if revealing this truth would comfort him on his way to heaven. I glanced back at the stairs behind a crooked apparatus for training on a trapeze. The stairway led up into the darkness and perhaps to the light of heaven. John would reach it, with my help.

"So what did she pay you?" he asked. "Half a million? She'll just steal it back. Think! Think! Why would she tell you that I called her? Why'd she lie about it? Why don't you ask about my wife? Why don't you ask me about Maud?"

"I didn't have the chance," I said.

"So you know?"

"Just like you do," I said.

"No, no, *she* did it!" he yelled. "I came home too late!"

"She paid me a million, actually," I said, caressing the trigger like a lover, my only friend, but before the explosion killed the silence forever in that disgusting place, I glimpsed a shadow up where the stairway disappeared into darkness.

She moved down the stairway like a seraph. The gleam I'd seen was a pistol in her hand. Looked like a Glock 17, semiautomatic, dangerous in the wrong hands. The light from the walls made her shimmer like a blue angel. I still held my revolver, and it was still aimed at John's head.

"Shoot him," she demanded. "Do your job, Peter Kempinsky."

"Not under orders," I said. I let the barrel drop slowly so it now pointed at the broken porcelain toilet—the color as white as Rebecka's face. Her mouth was a black wound, reminding me of Maud's throat. She stood one step up from the ground.

John froze. His face was in shadow again, as if he'd stepped back, but he hadn't moved an inch.

"I paid you to do a job," she said.

It's an expression I like very much, *do a job,* and I'm good at *doing my job,* but I'd made my decision, really made a decision: I didn't like her.

"Did you murder John's wife?" I asked.

Her laugh sounded like ice cubes hitting cement.

"What's it to you?" she asked.

"I don't work for murderers," I replied.

"You've been drinking too much," she said. "You don't know what you're saying. You're a murderer yourself."

"I'm a killer who takes jobs only from the innocent," I said, and I shot her in the throat—just once since I'm a good shot.

Her Glock slid to the ground, not breaking when it hit the cement—there are those who say a Glock is mostly plastic, but that's a myth. Rebecka fell and became a part of the stairway that would lead her neither to the ground nor back to the darkness above.

"You just lost half a million kronor," John said.

He still sounded calm, as if he were under the influence of something strong, perhaps the taste of death, its smell.

"She didn't have the money on her anyway," I said. I slipped my revolver back into my holster and walked away. I felt nothing and it made me sad, a longing for something I'd never had.

The moon was huge and strong up over the Atlas wall. It was much brighter outside than from where I'd come. I turned onto Völundsgatan and stood next to the James Joyce International Literary Society, just a hole in the wall with one window. The room inside was lit up, a nightly séance.

I pushed open the door and walked inside. It smelled like coffee and ink. Some people were sitting around a table. They looked at me, two men and two women, all middle-aged. I knew them. One of the men wore a plaid cardigan. I liked it. The room smelled like whiskey too; I breathed it in. I saw the bottle, a forty-two-year-old Glenfarclas.

"How did it go?" the man asked me.

"Relatively well," I replied.

"It did?"

"I owe you a drink," I said, nodding toward the bottle.

"That's why I brought it," he said, and the others laughed. I laughed too. It felt good to laugh. There were books lying on the table. I lifted one of the volumes in my hand.

"So this is the one we're working with tonight?" I asked.

"*Dubliners*. Have you read it?"

"Just once," I said, and turned to the last page.

STILL IN KALLHÄLL

BY JOHAN THEORIN

Kallhäll

Translated by Kerri Pierce

The murder plan was perfect, Klas knew—after all, his intended victim was old and in a wheelchair. The plan was simple. The murder easy. The only problem was getting out of Kallhäll alive.

The thing was, a person could die a slow death in Kallhäll simply by living there, as Klas himself had done for the last six months.

Still in Kallhäll, he thought every morning when he woke up in the suburb—in the one-room apartment on the fourth floor, in a large concrete building that doubtless had slumbered for fifty years like a giant on the bedrock, just waiting for something to happen, which never did this far out from downtown Stockholm. Kallhäll was located where once there had been forest and isolated cottages, until the capital really began to expand.

The Ditz snored gently beside Klas, deciduous trees sighed outside the window, and birds sat in them and sang, undisturbed by roaring traffic—all of which reminded him that he wasn't in the city's center.

He hated his girlfriend. He hated trees. He hated birds.

Most of all Klas hated how the fuckers who called the shots in Kallhäll desperately tried to make him comfortable. Did they actually think they could simply build longer jogging trails, more residences, and new health centers and keep him here forever?

Klas had no intention of staying in Kallhäll. He was resolute, and on Thursday he'd take his tight leather gloves and a wool cap with him to the city—that way, he wouldn't leave any evidence behind.

Klas Svensson was good at covering up his tracks. He'd left Falun the year before, forced to break all ties with his home-town because of some stupid petty debts he owed to the wrong people, and a hysterical bitch who had threatened to report him for assault. It felt natural to head down to Stockholm; all the young men went there and there was plenty of work to be had.

Within a week he'd snagged a job at Sailor Store in Östermalm. With its wide glass windows, it was only a few blocks from Stockholm's most exclusive street, Strandvägen, where imposing stone buildings towered over the Nybroviken Bay. Plenty of boaters lived there; they waltzed into Sailor Store with sunburned faces and dazzling white teeth and shamelessly fished out their fat wallets. Klas thrived in Sailor Store.

A place to live was another matter. In the beginning he stayed in a hostel on Fridhemsplan and hunted for a rental flat in the city's center, but there was nothing—no available apartments in Stockholm. A number of his Sailor Store colleagues still lived at home with their parents despite the fact that most were at least thirty years old. Others subletted apartments, or lived in some hole-in-the-wall for which they shelled out at least five thousand kronor. Some had taken out several million in loans to buy a studio apartment.

Without any money, Klas was forced to look for an apartment farther and farther away from downtown—all the way out in Kallhäll. There he found a furnished studio and moved in.

In the beginning, he was overjoyed that he'd actually managed to find a place. After all, Kallhäll was close to the water, maybe he could buy himself a sailboat. At work and in bars in the city he told chicks about his new place, but all he got were empty stares.

"Where do you live?"

"Kallhäll."

"Kallhäll? Where the hell is that?"

"Northwest," said Klas, "past Jakobsberg. It's not too far, you just hop on the commuter train and . . ."

But as soon as he began to explain, the woman he was talking to had already stopped listening. No one pays attention once they realize you live in the suburbs.

In the center, your life matters. Outside the center, you're just a loser.

During his second week in Kallhäll someone slipped a brochure through the mail slot. He read it before ripping it up.

Welcome to Kallhäll! Located right on Lake Mälaren, Kallhäll is a thrilling place to be, with plenty to offer to both inhabitants and visitors. Fresh air, new housing opportunities, and a fast and smooth commuter train ride into Stockholm . . .

The commuter train into the city—it quickly became the only thing Klas liked about Kallhäll.

Though it wasn't on the train that he'd met the Ditz, it was in Stockholm. On a break from Sailor Store, he'd gone, as usual, down to Strandvägen to wander along the dock and take in the boats and stone buildings. Wishing and dreaming.

Out of one of the wide doors, number 13B, came a young woman in white jeans and a black quilted jacket with a large suitcase in her hand. The suitcase was a horrible color, hot pink, and seemed heavy. She carefully closed the door and left.

Klas wouldn't have given her another thought if he hadn't seen her again that same evening after work. It was the hot pink suitcase he recognized, only this time he saw it in Kallhäll. The chick from Strandvägen was carrying it, only now she also had a paper bag of groceries. She schlepped everything over the bridge from the station toward Kallhäll's small center, past the shops on Gjutarplan, before continuing along the rows of apartment buildings.

What was she doing out here?

Her ass wiggled nicely as the struggled with the suitcase. Klas smoothed his bangs, put on his best sailor grin, and approached her.

"Do you need help?"

She turned around, smiled, and nodded, just like a grateful ditzy girl. Her ass was more attractive than her long, pale face, but the face would do.

The suitcase was heavy; Klas struggled with it up the stairs.

"It's filled with books," the Ditz explained, laughing nervously. "Just some heirlooms."

"Heirlooms?"

"From my grandfather. He lives in the city, on Strandvägen. He gives me things in advance, before I can inherit them. He's alone, the poor guy . . ."

Klas nodded and thought about the wide doorway: 13B. He helped her home and accepted a coffee in her small kitchen. The rest of the evening he listened to her sob story: how her grandfather, an old major general, was the only one she had left. No parents, no siblings. She'd been two years old and strapped in a car seat when her father had tried to pass a truck outside of Varberg. The family was killed—her father, mother, and older brother—but she'd remained firmly stuck within the protective casing and had survived without a scratch.

Klas listened. He accepted a vegetarian dinner, and watched while she sliced and diced with intense energy as she simultaneously flipped on the TV. Turned out her evening entertainment was cooking programs, and her major passion was root vegetables. Chopped beets, sliced carrots, diced rutabagas.

Klas thought about the hot pink suitcase and realized he wasn't in love. She told him her name, but he knew he'd always think of her as the Ditz.

Still, three weeks later they were a couple. Six weeks later he moved in with her.

It was the apartment he'd fallen for.

Not the one in Kallhäll, obviously, but the big one on Strandvägen. Her grandfather's apartment, which the Ditz was going to inherit. And after two months Klas got to see it himself when the major general invited them to dinner.

It was magnificent. Five large rooms on the fifth floor with gorgeous stucco work and a wide balcony that looked over the docks and the water. A century-old parade apartment. A bit dark and dusty, but that was easy to fix—just a matter of tossing all the old furniture, polishing up the parquet, and painting the walls white.

Klas wanted to live there, absolutely. He saw himself walking around the apartment in a Turkish robe, alone (the Ditz was missing from this particular fantasy), saw himself standing out on the balcony with a cappuccino and studying the street life down below. In the center. High above the rest of the world, far away from Kallhäll . . .

He opened his eyes and studied the Ditz's grandfather. The major general sat in a wheelchair at the dining table, looking like a tattered crow in a cardigan with a bent neck and a croaking voice. His hand trembled as he lifted a large brandy glass. Now and then he threw a severe glance at the wall clock. Did he want them to leave?

"No, Grandfather's just a little time crazy," the Ditz told him on the train ride back to Kallhäll. "His routine is always the same, year round. At half past eight he rolls out on the balcony to make sure the Swedish flag has been hoisted up on Kastellholmen, so he knows that we aren't at war. At ten the home help comes and drops off lunch and at twelve he eats. At one he has a glass of brandy. And he listens to the news on the radio all day . . ."

"Does he ever go out?" Klas asked.

"Only out onto the stairwell," the Ditz said. "He rolls out at three thirty to water the fig tree."

Klas remembered that tree—it stood in a large limestone pot outside her grandfather's door. He nodded at the Ditz and pondered.

He decided to become more punctual.

Every morning, after having met the Ditz's grandfather, he went into the city earlier than he needed to and headed down to Strandvägen. Just before eight thirty, he stood on Strandvägen in the shelter of some trees and observed the windows of 13B.

The Ditz was right: her grandfather was like a cuckoo clock. At exactly eight thirty the balcony door opened and the major general rolled out in his wheelchair. Five minutes later the door shut again.

Like a fucking cuckoo clock. And this suggested that he was equally punctual the rest of the day too.

With his eyes locked on the apartment's high window one morning, Klas decided what he was going to do.

* * *

It was a Thursday like any other that he took the cap and gloves to work at Sailor Store. Later that afternoon he complained of a sudden migraine and went into the staff room to rest. He carefully locked the door, but didn't make it onto the couch; the store had a back door and he used it to sneak out.

Out on the sidewalk he glanced at the clock; it was 3:18. The day was cloudy, but there was no rain in the air.

He started across the dry asphalt. He didn't run, but took long strides. Down to Strandvägen.

Six minutes later he was at the door of 13B. It was locked, but he had memorized the code the Ditz had punched in.

Half a minute later he stood inside the dark stairwell and pulled on his gloves and cap. He listened anxiously for any sound. Everybody was at work, everything was still. And so was he, after he'd snuck up the wide marble steps.

At 3:28 Klas reached the second floor and listened again. The stairwell was silent, all the apartment doors were shut.

A minute later he stood in the dark on the fourth floor. Waiting.

At exactly 3:30 he heard a door open on the fifth floor. The old man coughed. A soft creaking noise, the sound of rubber wheels rolling across the stone floor.

Klas clenched his jaw. He summoned the old rattling elevator up from the first floor so that the racket would cover any other noises. Then he started up to the fifth floor.

Now he could see the wheelchair on the landing right above him; the back of a naked head visible. The Ditz's grandfather was hunched over in his chair, facing away from Klas.

The major general mumbled to himself as he fiddled with his fig tree. The chair's back wheels were only a few inches from the top step.

The elevator continued to rattle. All the doors were shut. Klas was set.

Now.

He stepped up with an outstretched hand, grasped the wheelchair's steel rim, and quickly jerked it back in one sharp move. The wheels went over the marble edge, the whole chair tipped back. Klas stepped aside and saw the major general's hands flap like startled birds in the air. He fell down, the back of his head first, his body somersaulting down the stairs, landing with a low thud at the bottom.

Klas didn't even glance at the old man. He stopped the wheelchair's fall so it didn't make a loud clatter, climbed the stairs, and dragged the heavy stone pot toward him.

Turning around with the pot in his hands, he saw that the major general was still alive. He'd landed on his back with his head to the side. Klas bent over him, balancing the stone pot on the stair right above the old man's wrinkled brow.

The Ditz's grandfather recognized him; when their eyes met he understood exactly what Klas was about to do; he opened his mouth and let out a terrified breath of cognac. However, no cry for help could escape before Klas let the stone pot fall. The pot's edge struck its target perfectly, causing the major general to shudder one last time.

Klas was finished here. He stood and fled. The elevator had since stopped on the fourth floor, but he took the steps in long strides. The stairwell remained empty the whole way down to the bottom floor. No one had heard or seen a thing. He stripped off the cap and gloves on the fly.

Out through the door, out onto the street. Look relaxed now, not hounded.

He was back at work five minutes later—it was only 3:43.

He entered through Sailor Store's back door, stepped into the shop, and told the boss that he felt better.

His boss looked him over. "Are you sure? You seem sweaty."

Klas smiled quickly and wiped his forehead. "Just a slight fever."

At five thirty that evening he headed home to Kallhäll, where the Ditz stood slicing beets.

Klas closed his eyes and kissed her neck. Then he sat next to the TV, awaiting the vile veggie meal. And, obviously, anxiously waiting for the telephone to ring with a call from Stockholm.

And so it did late that evening. It was a death report, a tragic fall down the stairwell, an accident that sometimes happens to old men, especially when there is alcohol in their system. The police didn't suspect any foul play, and Klas wrapped his arms around his sobbing girlfriend and sighed.

The reading of the will was held eight days later, and the Ditz took the commuter train alone to the lawyer's office. She had several handkerchiefs with her, she was still grieving.

Three hours later she arrived back in Kallhäll, her eyes red-rimmed, and immediately began slicing and dicing in the kitchen.

Klas joined her at the sink and quietly asked: "How did it go, sweetheart?"

"Good," she said softly.

"Did they read the will?"

"Yes."

"And you're inheriting . . . ?"

"Yes . . ."

Klas closed his eyes in the narrow kitchen and felt nearly intoxicated by success; he was tired, he'd slept poorly this last week, but he saw an enormous apartment with a broad balcony before him. *Mine*, he thought.

". . . and my cousins."

"What did you say?"

"My cousins and I are to inherit everything," said the Ditz. "It was cool to see them again." Her voice actually sounded a little happier now. The beets were chopped, she began to mash them in a glass bowl.

"What cousins?" asked Klas.

"My mother's brother's kids," she replied, smiling.

He stared at her, didn't smile back. "You said he was alone. That you were all he had."

"Grandfather? Yeah, he was totally alone. I mean, my cousins are only teenagers . . . Obviously, they didn't come by so often. They were too young for that—"

"Where do they live?" Klas interrupted. "Here in Stockholm?"

"Live?"

"You have to tell me where they live. I want an address."

Just teenagers, he thought. Teenagers don't sit in wheelchairs and they hardly drink cognac, but they can still meet bad ends. Get run over by a car, or pushed from a ferry.

Klas stepped closer to the Ditz. "I'll take care of it. We'll make it out . . ."

"What are you talking about?"

He nodded toward the kitchen window, toward the forest beyond. ". . . out of here. We'll move into the city. You'll inherit everything, the whole apartment . . . just like I planned for you."

The Ditz stared at him, confused. "Grandfather fell," she said softly.

"It was no accident," Klas said. "I was there . . . Don't you get it, you fucking ditz?"

She shook her head blankly.

Finally, Klas snapped. There was no reason to smack her—but suddenly he'd done it, right across her face so that she fell back against the sink. No reason, but it felt good. Klas stepped forward and raised his hand again.

The Ditz shrieked, lifted her hands protectively, and reached for something. At first Klas didn't know what it was, but then he saw that it was one of the knives from the counter, the chef's knife.

"Drop it!"

He threw himself at the Ditz, tried to twist the knife from her hand; they danced around the long kitchen sink and knocked over the bowl of beets. Klas slipped on the mash with his arms around the Ditz and hit the floor beneath her—hard.

He tried to push her off him and get up; the only thought in his brain was: *Where the fuck did the chef's knife go?*

Then he felt an icy weight in his breast and knew the answer.

Anna Nyman couldn't have been happier in Kallhäll. She loved the forest and the birds and the close proximity to Mälaren. She appreciated the health center and the senior get-togethers at the Munktell Museum and the little square with all the shops. She'd lived on Bondegatan in Stockholm for many years and had moved out here to retire, away from the noise and congestion, and it felt like the powers-that-be in Kallhäll had done all they could to make her comfortable.

Her only problem was with some of her neighbors. Sometimes they played their music too loud, and some weekends you could hear fighting. Up until now, the young couple in the apartment right next to hers had been quiet; but this evening loud voices came through the wall.

Then it got worse; Anna heard an insane shriek and the sound of shattering glass. After that it was quiet for a few seconds and then the outer door opened. Heavy steps staggered out into the hallway. Someone summoned the elevator up from the ground floor, but didn't get in.

Anna cautiously opened her door. She glimpsed someone in the hallway. It was the young man from the neighboring apartment, slouched against the wall. He stared at her with heavy lids, and then stumbled toward the elevator and slowly lifted his hand, but seemed unable to open the steel door.

Anna went outside to help and it was only when she'd opened the door fully that she saw the neighbor's white shirt was shredded. Red splotches were spread across the breast.

"What happened?" Anna asked.

Without answering, the man stumbled into the elevator and collapsed onto the floor.

Anna followed and bent over him. He looked around, slowly opened his mouth: "Where am I?"

"You're home," Anna said. "In Kallhäll."

He coughed blood and began to laugh to himself, and almost immediately the floor beneath them shook. The elevator began to descend.

"There now, stay calm." Anna took the man's hand and tried to comfort him, but he closed his eyes like she didn't exist.

"Still in Kallhäll . . ." he mumbled, and laughed and coughed blood onto the elevator floor, the entire way down into darkness.

THE SMUGGLERS

BY MARTIN HOLMÉN

Rörstrandsgatan

Translated by Laura A. Wideburg

Twilight comes on quickly.

The pub is housed in a small shed in the back courtyard, not far from Rörstrands porcelain factory. The dank premises measure barely thirty square meters. Black smoke is thick on the walls and across from the door a scratched wooden bar runs down the long side of the room. On the far end of the counter, a tiger-striped tomcat with scarred ears sits cleaning his fur with slow strokes of his tongue.

Behind the counter, there is a man wearing a soiled apron over his protruding stomach. He runs his hand through his enormous walrus mustache. One of his thumbnails is missing.

The fire crackles in the cast-iron heater in the corner. From the building across the Vikingagatan comes the furious song of the riveting machines from the porcelain factory. Their monotonous clatter is broken by the dull thump of four bronze candlesticks hitting the surface of the bar counter.

"Light is on the house."

The bartender strikes a match and lights the candles. He's set the candlesticks down between two men sitting at the bar. They both wear blue shirts and the heavy vests of rock blasters. The older man is carrying a trowel in his belt as if it were a weapon. Their wooden clogs are spattered with white mortar. The younger man nods listlessly, his elbow on the counter. He's holding a three-cornered schnapps glass in one hand. It's empty.

The back door creaks, and a girl, her blond hair in a bun, enters. Cobwebs stick to her knitted cardigan. She wears wool socks with her clogs and carries a wicker potato basket filled to the brim with sawdust.

"Make sure you do a better job than last time! Spread the stuff out all the way to the corners!"

The bartender shakes out the match and puts it back into its box. The girl nods and with a rustling sound she shakes the sawdust over the floor. She works methodically from one side of the room to the other. She kicks the sawdust under the tables and chairs. The men at the bar follow her movements in silence. The scent of resin and fresh shavings fills the room.

In the corner, beneath a warped rectangular window, a woman sits at a table and the grease stains on her wide-brimmed hat gleam in the grainy, fading light that comes through the dirty, lead-rimmed panes. She's darkened her eyebrows with burnt cork and black flecks have fallen onto her eyelashes. Her lips are painted red. She holds a cigarette between her fingers. On the table, there's a pack of Bridge and a broken white enamel cup holds a number of cigarette butts stained with red lipstick.

As the girl with the basket of sawdust approaches, the woman shifts her skirt aside and lifts her high-heeled, worn-out, lace-up boots—she's not wearing stockings. A large bruise shows on her pale calf. The girl looks away as she kicks the last of the sawdust beneath the woman's chair.

"Well, what a shrinking violet we have here! Don't worry, soon she'll be making a living with her legs in the air too, just wait and see." Slurred, but loud, the woman's voice cuts through the clatter of the machines. The men at the bar hold back their laughter, but their shoulders shake. The younger man slaps the older one on the arm. The girl says nothing. She makes her way quickly over the sawdust and sets the basket by the back door. She looks down, smoothing her apron with both hands.

The front door opens and the leather curtain made of pig-skin is pushed aside with a swish. The flames of the candles flicker in the draft. The men at the bar turn around. The tom-cat pauses in his cleaning, his tongue halfway out of his mouth.

The sawdust crunches under heavy soles as the youth walks into the room. He's wearing a sailor's cap that seems to be a few sizes too large. He hides his mouth behind his hand as he glances around. Fish scales glisten on the frayed sleeves of his jacket.

He chooses the table farthest from the door and pulls out a chair. Beneath his slight blond mustache, his upper lip has a cleft that stretches halfway along his nose. The edges are pale pink. His yellowed front teeth show through the gap.

He sits down with his back to the wall, facing the door. The girl comes to him with a schnapps glass and an unmarked bottle. She shows him the bottle and the youth nods. The girl quietly fills the glass to the rim. The oily surface of the liquid glimmers as she strikes a match and lights the candle on the ta-ble. She is already turning away when the youth raises his hand. She stands silently, holding the bottle in the crook of her arm.

The young man grips the narrow stem of the glass with three fingers and lifts it up a few millimeters before setting it back down on the table. He closes his eyes. His chest heaves twice. Then, in one swift movement, he brings the glass to his lips and drinks it all down. He grins crookedly with his mangled lips. The girl pulls the cork from the bottle with a plop and he nods. She fills it to the brim again before he waves her away.

The front door opens again; the leather curtain is drawn

aside and the breeze makes the flames of the candles dance. One flickers out. A black line of smoke drifts toward the ceiling. The cat jumps softly down onto the sawdust. He lifts one of his forepaws and shakes it slightly before he heads toward the door. He slides between the newcomer's well-polished leather boots and disappears outside. The constant clatter of machines stops suddenly when the whistle of the factory signals the end of the workday.

The new arrival bends his head slightly to avoid hitting the top of the doorframe with the bowler hat that sits atop his head. He has a rolled-up newspaper under one arm while in his large hand he carries something wrapped in an oil-stained piece of sackcloth. With his free hand, he fishes out a watch with a gold chain from his vest pocket. He checks it and looks around. The bartender nods toward him and he nods back. The woman in the corner hastily stubs out her cigarette in the enamel cup. She gathers her skirts and disappears out the door behind the man's back. The door slams shut behind her with an echoing thud.

The burly newcomer slips his watch back into his pocket. He glances around the room one more time before he moves forward to the table where the youth with the cleft palate is sitting. In the total silence in the wake of the stopped machines, the other people in the room can hear the young man inhale deeply. The large man smiles broadly and sits down across from him. There's a clunk of metal as he sets the sackcloth on the table. The youth nods in greeting and stares down at the full schnapps glass in front of him.

The bartender goes over with a filthy rag and wipes down the table, avoiding the sackcloth bundle and newspaper between the two men. He brushes crumbs into his cupped hand as he speaks.

"Good that Belzén sent you, Hickan. I sent word to him two days ago that I—"

The man called Hickan holds up his hand. "I'm here for another reason."

"I understand, I understand! Do you want the usual?"

Hickan nods. "The usual."

The youth glances up for a second. Both of the men at the bar are counting coins. They put their money on the counter and head out the door without waiting for change.

The bartender comes back with a bottle of Estonian vodka. He fills a schnapps glass for Hickan as Hickan stares at the youth. The bartender sets the bottle on the table and walks away. Hickan smiles as he lifts his glass.

"For better luck next time!"

Both men throw back their heads and let the schnapps run down their throats. Hickan shrugs his shoulders and shudders. The youth runs a finger over his thin mustache as he glances at the package in front of him. Hickan takes out cigarette paper and a small silver box, placing both on the table.

"So, how are things on the islands?" Hickan removes the lid from his silver box. There's a slight whisper as he drops tobacco into the cigarette paper he keeps pinched between his fingers.

The youth clears his throat: "The windstorm last week got up to gale force eleven." His voice is high-pitched, and he has a slight lisp.

"And?"

"The gale hit when we were out. The boathouse, where we live right now, lost part of its roof. Lindén up on the hill was able to loan us some sheet metal to keep the water out for a while."

"There was a bit of wind here in the city as well."

Hickan rolls the tobacco in the paper, licking the adhesive side, sealing the seam of the cigarette tightly. The youth keeps stroking his sparse mustache.

"I was with Lindén and we had to anchor that night with a defective engine. We drifted a few hundred meters and then the chain broke. I put together a sail from a bunk to guide our drift."

"And that worked?"

"With Neptune's help, as Lindén put it."

"You archipelago fishermen have always been resourceful."

"You take what you have and you do what you can."

"I have a story about Olsson, the Berghamn pilot. You know him?"

"Only by name."

"Oh well, I'll leave it for another time, then."

The match scratches against the tabletop and flares as Hickan lights his cigarette. He rolls it between his fingers and watches the smoke curl and make its way to the soot-covered ceiling.

"I used to smoke that English brand Mixture but it got difficult to get ahold of. During the war, I started smoking Windsor, but it was too harsh for me. Now I keep changing brands, but I can't seem to find one I like. This one is Perstorps Prima." Hickan nods toward the silver box. "You're welcome to roll one of your own."

"No thanks. I prefer to chew."

Hickan smiles and brushes some ashes from the tabletop. Behind him, the bartender is putting clean glasses on the shelf. They clink as they touch.

"So I hear your engine broke down the day before yesterday." The end of Hickan's cigarette burns through a full centimeter of paper.

The youth nods and looks away. "The coast guard was after me."

"Yeah?"

The youth clears his throat. "Yeah, they were after me. I was pushing the engine hard and thought I'd gotten away when it started dying just outside of Yxlan. Pund-Ville was on the island and saw what was going on so he fired a couple of shots into the air to distract them. But it didn't work. A few minutes later, the engine died completely."

"I had two men waiting for you in Gröndal."

"The boat is ready to go. I fixed it. The fuel looked like coffee grounds when I pumped it out. I took the whole motor apart and cleaned it. I even paid for a new filter."

"And the barrels of alcohol?"

"The engine works just fine now, even better than before. It purrs like a kitten."

"The barrels?"

"I had no choice."

"Can you search for them in the water?"

"Not in Norrviken. It's too deep."

Hickan stubs out his cigarette in the mug. There's a slight glug-glug sound from the bottle as he refills their drinks. He lifts his own glass while putting his other hand on the sackcloth package.

"If the coast guard caught you with the alcohol, at least there'd be a written report. Now we have nothing but your word."

The youth stares down at the table. The back door creaks and then slams shut, as the bartender and his helper slip out. Someone inserts a key from the outside and there's a thud as the bolt slides home. Hickan nods toward the young man's glass.

"I imagine you're too young to remember that pub called Hamburg Cellars? They closed about seven or eight years back."

The youth lifts his glass with a shaking hand. Hickan smiles.

"It wasn't much bigger than this place here, but it had an

interesting story. You could find it at the crossroads of Götgatan and Folkungagatan not far from Södra Bantorget. The horses would stop there on their way to the gallows at Skanstull. In this country, we've always thought a man deserves one last drink. A nice custom, don't you think?"

Drops of liquor spill between the fingers of the youth's shaking hand. Sweat slides down his face beneath his sailor's cap.

"They had a special cupboard there. All the glasses were on display. They engraved the name and the date."

The spilled liquor collects in one of the grooves in the table, making a small pool.

"They say one of the condemned refused his drink and told them he'd come back for it. Of course, he didn't."

"My wife . . . she's in that way." The youth's voice could hardly be heard.

"How far along?"

"Seven months."

"Let's drink to her health. *Skål!*"

Both men throw back their drinks. Hickan pulls at a corner of the sackcloth and opens it, revealing a revolver. It's black with a grip made from light wood. Right beneath the drum there's something stamped in Cyrillic letters as well as the year: *1915.* Hickan places his huge hand over it.

"Do you know why Belzén trusted you with this job?"

"Because I know every bay and inlet in all the islands and know all the good hiding places."

"Like pretty much every other inhabitant of the archipelago."

"So why did he trust me?"

"Because your brother vouched for you. He's worked for us for years. It's the only way to get into our little organization. Would you say that you've let him down?"

"Perhaps I have."

"As well as us?"

"Maybe so."

Hickan runs his hand over the hard contours of the revolver. Outside it is starting to rain. The first drops hit the dirty pub windowpanes. Night has fallen.

"I have two daughters myself. The youngest just started elementary school. It seems like yesterday when I held her in my arms for the first time."

Hickan holds up his huge hand. Between the middle finger and the ring finger, a wide scar runs all the way down his palm. He laughs.

"There's nothing I wouldn't do for them. A man who can't take care of his family is not a real man at all."

The rain is picking up. It hits the tar-papered roof with an intense clatter, like the riveting machines had made earlier. The revolver scrapes against the tabletop as Hickan pushes it toward the youth.

"Don't you agree?"

The youth smiles quickly and he puts his hand on the revolver. Hickan nods.

"It's a Nagant. You have seven bullets, no more, no less."

The youth nods eagerly. He takes the revolver and stuffs it under his belt, pulling his shabby jacket tight around his body. He clears his throat. "I won't disappoint Belzén again."

"Make sure you don't."

"Who's the mark?"

"One of our own. A piece of crap brazen enough to steal an entire truckload right from under our noses. We'll send you his name in a few days."

"I don't know if I—"

"As we see it, you don't have a choice."

The youth nods and pulls his wallet from his pocket. Hickan raises his huge palm.

"No, it's on the house."

The youth nods, pushes the chair away from the table, and stands up. The two men shake hands.

"So, you'll hear from me in a few days."

The youth pulls up his collar and with his fist outside his coat he leaves the pub. Hickan fills his glass and rolls himself another cigarette. He doesn't notice the cockroach climbing up one of the table legs.

Almost immediately, the bartender and the girl come back in through the back door. The girl is carrying the tomcat in her arms. The rain has left dark patches on their clothes and has plastered their hair to their heads. The bartender runs his hand over his walrus mustache, shakes the liquid from his hand, and then makes his way across the sawdust. He has a slight limp. He sits down across from Hickan and brushes his hand over the table before he starts to speak.

"You scared away all my other customers!"

"They'll be back."

"So, did you tell him the Hamburg Cellars story?"

"Works every time."

The bartender's laughter echoes throughout the bar. He's missing a few of his upper teeth. He runs his hand through his hair. The cockroach climbs over the edge and stands on the table, its long antennae sweeping back and forth.

"As I told you, I contacted Belzén a few days ago. We're running out of inventory and I need a delivery as soon as possible."

"I understand. Unfortunately, we have a break in our supply lines at the moment."

Hickan picks up his newspaper and rolls it tightly and laughs. "That kid?"

He raises the newspaper over his head. "We can stand to lose a few hundred liters overboard. But his brother is a piece of crap . . ." Hickan smashes the cockroach with his newspaper, then turns it over to survey the mangled remains. He wipes them off on the edge of the table as he lowers his voice. "Did he really believe he could make off with one of our trucks? And get off scot-free?"

The bartender laughs and twirls his mustache. "So they'll both learn a lesson."

"It was Belzén's idea. Business is business."

The bartender nods, pulls the cork from the bottle, and fills both glasses.

Outside the bar, the youth sees Rörstrandsgatan is nearly deserted. The factory workers have all hurried home through the rain. An old woman with a scarf over her hair waddles out of the general store at the corner of Birkagatan. She peers up at the rainy sky. From the wicker basket under her arm the necks of milk bottles with their patent corks and rolled-up cones of newspaper poke out.

The youth with the cleft palate walks along, his collar up and his shoulders bent. A horse and open wagon go past. Empty beer bottles rattle, while the ragged hooves plod along on the cobblestones. From down near Sankt Eriksgatan Square, a streetcar bell rings. The youth glances around as he crosses the street. A train blows its horn on its way to Central Station.

Behind him, the city is cloaked in darkness from the rain and smoke from kitchen fires. He comes upon a lamplighter, an old man wearing a moth-eaten military coat and carrying his long pole over his shoulder. The guy stops by one of the square gas lanterns to light it. The gas socket hisses and its tongue of flame flares in vain against the glass, unable to escape. The yellow light reveals the old man's wrinkled face, reflected in the puddles below.

The youth lets his gaze follow the row of streetlights that look to him like lighthouses out in the archipelago leading the way into the city. He puts his hand into his coat, clutches the cold revolver, and sticks out his chest before continuing south.

His upper lip, cleft in two, gapes as he smiles.

THE SPLENDORS AND MISERIES OF A SWEDISH CRIME WRITER

BY MALTE PERSSON

Gröndal

Translated by Laura A. Wideburg

I was busy with another murder when my cell phone rang unexpectedly. In media res or in flagrante delicto or whatever the proper technical term may be. The victim was a young woman, yet another of all these young women who have to die, and unfortunately she also had a rather striking resemblance to my famous ex, Anette. I had my priorities, so I ignored the call. Not answering the phone makes one look busy and important these days, I told myself, and kept my hands hovering over the keyboard. I'm a writer.

That's another thing I kept telling myself. A crime writer. I knew that status was far from reality. At the moment, I was a minor criminal who'd worked in advertising. I was nobody.

Still, these were my words on the smudged laptop screen:

The victim was a woman of around twenty years old. Commissioner Almqvist studied her naked body, and thought she was, or rather had been, everything a modern man could reasonably, or unreasonably, desire in a young woman. She was thin, but not unnaturally so, and her breasts were larger than you'd expect with a body like hers. Large, light-blue eyes, which could no longer see. Oval face, narrow nose, small mouth. A bit above average in height, in good shape, but not too muscular. The paleness of the corpse was the only flaw, except for marks from one or more hard punches to her left cheekbone. Otherwise, light-blond hair which you could tell was natural from both her partially shaven pubic area and the roots of her hair. Someone had cut off the victim's long hair and used it to tie her to a wooden chair—the chair was an Eva design by Bruno Mathsson, something Almqvist knew, since his wife had an expensive interest in classical Scandinavian functionalism. A catheter was inserted below her left breast, which appeared to have been used to empty the blood from her body. Almqvist had, as the expression goes, never seen anything like it.

I changed *light-blue* to *forget-me-not blue*. I deleted *small mouth* and put in a different sentence: *Her mouth was covered by police tape.* I added, *In her lap, a volume of the Swedish law book,* Regulations Concerning Property and Buildings, *was open to the famous Chapter 12: How Pigs Should Be Let Loose in an Oak Forest.* This I deleted again. It was too ridiculous, even by the standards of Swedish crime novels.

The whole scene was nothing but a piece of shit. Deader than the victim it described. Nothing left to do but start over; but I couldn't concentrate. When you stop answering the phone, after a while people stop calling. The only ones who keep on trying are people who believe they are too important to be ignored. And so my thoughts immediately turned to . . .

I picked up my cell phone. Just as I suspected. Anette.

Of course, I had no intention of calling her back, but as I was about to put it back down, it buzzed with an incoming text message. Anette again: *Am in town. Want to get together?*

Get together? Did I want to get together?

I looked out from my office window: the factory buildings, the rusty water towers, the glittering water . . .

After an aborted attempt at reflection, I texted back: *If you want to meet me, you'll have to come to my end of town.* I don't know why I used those exact words (I was thoroughly interrogated about them later on), but my idea, in addition to playing hard-to-get, was probably the chance to meet like we used to— at a bar in Hornstull. Those were my best years, when I held down both her job and mine. I was a copywriter, and I hadn't started to think so damned much.

It was now just about a year since we had broken up, ending our own personal party, which had gone on, with few interruptions, for thirteen months. We'd hit the town, mostly as part of Södermalm's promiscuous and sorrow-free—or perhaps soulless—art and media circles. Her ambition then was to be a fashion designer, a dream of so many young women.

Anyway, we met at work and soon went on to happy hour, which merged into parties and weekends at bars and clubs, including gatherings on apartment balconies during the light summer nights. Events. Retro raves. Pretend-bourgeois dinner parties. Microbrews and MDMA. Sex in bizarre places. That idiotic conviction of youth that everything you hope for will come true.

Not long after she left me, I lost my job. Hit by depression, I self-medicated with uppers and downers, and it seems I said a few things to my boss and coworkers, things I didn't have enough talent to get away with. I was also the last hired, and then the economy tanked, so I was the first to go.

But I'd bounced back.

Or so I told myself.

This past summer, I'd been spending many late nights by my wide-open window in the cramped office. I watched the guard dogs running around off leash on the grounds of the ce-ment factory across the street. Often, when I would hear the bass booming from one of the nearby clubs, I'd think of it as the rhythm of a life that was no longer mine. A life retreating farther and farther away.

In retrospect, I'm amazed that I ever met a woman like her. She was way out of my league, even back then, or should have been. She was always the center of attention. The kind of person people say could be a model and who later actually becomes one, moving up and away from their lives and toward other parties in other cities. (I assume you've seen a photo of her somewhere. By then, I was already out of the picture.) And what did I have? Besides a reasonable face and a reasonable fashion sense?

So if I was going to go out and see her again, I wouldn't hurt my reputation to have our acquaintances see us together again.

But that's not how it turned out. She interpreted my text message more literally than I'd intended. Or perhaps she was hit by childish inspiration. She wrote: *Playing hard to get! Still, I have an errand close by. Let's meet at the swimming dock, 6 p.m., okay? I'll bring wine!* ☺

She meant the little floating dock down by the lake so quaintly named the Triangle. You can find it between Liljehol-men and Gröndal. Just a few hundred meters from my tiny of-fice. I thought it would be embarrassing—we'd skinny-dipped there one late, drunken evening, shortly after we first met—but I couldn't see how to get out of it. So I agreed. I didn't believe her about that errand in the vicinity. Either she wanted to relive her teenage years (I knew she'd attended a Waldorf school not too far from there) or she was working on her image of being spontaneous and crazy.

I sighed and started a new crime scene, one a bit less far-fetched. *They found her naked body, cut to pieces, in the water . . .*

The hum of a sewing machine came from the office next door. It was three hours until six. I had time to think about the details.

Details matter to losers. I really wanted to see myself as a careful, rational, and methodical person that year—sitting, as I was, in a tiny office between Liljeholmen and Gröndal, wanting to become a crime writer. I had read interviews with successful crime writers. According to them, all it took was a bit of discipline. The only thing that mattered was regular work hours and a strict schedule. Don't deviate from the conventional narrative arc, follow it without sentimentality, and you will reach the pot of gold at the other end. I had also read countless articles on "How to Write a Best Seller." The pathways to achieving this miracle differed only slightly. A story that worked always began with presenting the protagonist, preferably in a different situation from what he finds himself in at the end. Step two is introducing a conflict that forces the protagonist to act. And so on, until all seems lost before it eventually reaches a perfect conclusion—neatly tying up all loose ends.

That was the plan. And how hard could it be if you had enough pens and Post-its, a computer and a sick imagination, and a tiny office in an old rundown building?

Wanting to become a crime writer was not the most original or even greatest of ambitions. In Sweden, there are police officers and lawyers and criminals and psychologists all writing crime novels; poets and intellectuals all writing crime novels; hundreds of journalists and doctors and teachers and house-wives all writing crime novels. This was a country where even the minister of justice wrote crime novels!

So the general impression was that *anybody* could write a good mystery, and once you'd written one, you'd become an international success. Who gives a shit that there are fewer ho-micides in all of Sweden in a year than in any large American city in one or two months? That's exactly what makes Swedish murders so tantalizingly exotic and symbolically loaded. And if your prose is a bit lacking, your foreign editors would improve it. Yep, you didn't even have to write well to write crime novels. An equitable business worthy of the world's most equitable so-ciety: the Swedish Model!

Even I wanted to write a detective novel, of course. Then I'd make some money and gain some status and—not the least important thing—I'd be able to revel in macabre scenes of vio-lence in a socially acceptable way. Which, when you get down to it, is exactly why so many people *read* these books.

Perhaps it's not surprising that I soon got tired of my pa-thetic plots and wound up in a never-ending cycle of creating new descriptions of crime scenes and murders. Not being all that rational of a person, I seldom came up with a good method.

Oh, I forgot to mention how I supported myself. Inspired by my own drug use I had set up a modest and discrete mail order business. It was based on the ability to receive mail under a false name at this old rundown office building, where nobody kept track of who was renting which space. The same dynamic also got in the way at times. It meant a lot of running up and down the stairs and new faces all the time, who were, as Stockholm people are in general, often hard to tell apart. But I thought of this business as just something temporary until I achieved my dream of being a real writer, and, of course, that's why I had this tiny office in the first place.

A common piece of advice to aspiring authors is to write about what you know. It was just about six when, reinforced by a few well-chosen pills, I left my office and walked into the heart of what I knew best. In front of me, the street with the streetcar tracks. To the left, the tracks went past the barracks-like building of the City Mission, and then on past the new, very sterile Liljeholmen—the shopping mall had just been completed and the square was decorated with benches designed to keep people from sleeping on them. To the right, the tracks swung past Gröndal's small fifties-style center and past the marina with its derelict boathouse—a special place, where you can still find some of the last old eccentrics side by side with the well-off newcomers, polishing their old mahogany boats as if they were sarcophagi getting ready for their last trip down the river to the ruler of the underworld . . .

I felt an irrational loyalty to this place. But if I were going to impress the international audience I was dreaming of, I would certainly be forced to change this last remnant of an unexploited side of Stockholm to a darker, more derelict, and more dangerous place than it actually was. Isn't that what they all do? Sure, somebody had been shot here a few years back. Sure, everybody heard that some pizzerias were really fronts for the cocaine trade. But not even the mafia from the Balkans could stand against the incoming tide of middle-class families. Soon the only poor people in this part of the city would be members of the so-called artistic class—my neighbors in the office building. Then, soon enough, they'd all disappear too. Real estate moguls were looking for locations like old factories and harbor areas for renovation. The building where I had my tiny office was doomed to be turned into luxury condos or offices. The reason none of this had happened yet was that it was very difficult to move the cement factory docks.

I didn't walk to the left or the right, but straight across the street past the assisted-living building. I'd worked there one summer when I was a teenager. There were old folks who remembered how things used to be: when both this side and the other side of the water were working-class neighborhoods that people looked down on. The jail on Långholmen had still been open, and there was an infamous workhouse for the poor somewhere in Tanto . . .

I headed toward the Triangle past the pest control company Anticimex, to the swimming dock. They say the water still has large concentrations of heavy metals: one of the few reminders that this area once harbored an entire complex of workshops and small manufacturing plants. Bo Widerberg had used some of the decrepit factory buildings when he directed his film *Joe Hill* in the seventies. To find any traces of this activity these days, you have to know what to look for.

It was that time of year when summer turns to fall. Not all that warm anymore. Still, the sky was clear and the sun had not yet set.

She was perched on the edge of the dock and, at first, I didn't recognize her. She had a new look, more mature. She wore a coffee-with-too-much-milk coat and her hair was done up in a retro-forties look. She greeted me with a huge smile, which I did not like one bit. I thought, *She's trying to be extra nice because she's feeling sorry for me. She doesn't know how, so she's overdoing it.* Then I thought, *She's still stunningly beautiful.*

"You're not mad at me anymore, right?" she asked.

"Of course not," I replied.

"Good," she said. She pulled two small bottles from her coat pocket. White wine with screw tops, the kind you get on airplanes or from a hotel minibar.

The swimming dock was deserted and totally pointless if one didn't want to go swimming. Neither of us said anything, we just started walking together, following the path counterclockwise around the lake.

I held my bottle in my hand and tried to act nonchalant. I commanded my brain, *Make small talk.*

When she asked me what I was up to these days, I told her I was writing a mystery novel.

"How original," she said. "So what is your mystery about?"

"Well, murder . . ." I shrugged and continued: "It's tougher than I thought. I want it to be really noir. But look around you! The sun is glittering on the water and we live in the world's safest and most secure country. The worst crime is if a few immigrant kids get caught smoking pot and the police break a minor law or two hauling them in."

"I disagree," she said.

"Why?"

She glanced around nervously. I followed the direction of her gaze: a dark-skinned guy in sweats leaned against a fence not far away. He was looking at us, and then he turned away. Nothing special about him.

Then she seemed to calm down again and surprised me (in the way that still surprised me when she abruptly shifted from being childish to being highly articulate) by giving me a mini-lecture on Stockholm's past. Its *soul*, as she put it. She reminded me that during her lifetime both the prime minister and foreign minister had been assassinated in this very city.

"What? Were you even born when Olof Palme was killed?" I asked.

Apparently she'd been conceived by then.

I looked her over and tried to imagine how she'd appear dead in one of my crime novels, but it was hard. She was so alive right beside me. All I could imagine was fucking her. With a certain bitterness, actually a great deal of bitterness, all things considered, I remembered our last time together. She had been on top, and right after I'd come, she stood up in a no-nonsense way and walked to the bathroom to clean off the semen that was already coming out of her. She was beautiful right at that moment too. Efficient and beautiful at the same time, just like that damned midcentury modern furniture I'd let Commissioner Almqvist's wife collect.

"Are you in Stockholm for a reason?" I asked.

"Every chance I get, I come back. I've been offered a part in a movie. It's a small one in some kind of horror or fantasy film. What do you think about that?"

I'd heard that fantasy was going to be the next big thing after crime but I thought it was just a temporary trend. I shrugged. "You could always play the dragon," I said.

"I wish! That would be a great part! But no . . . more like running around and showing skin . . ." She turned her head, and I could see her white neck.

I asked why she'd even wanted to see me.

She said there was something she needed to ask me. She'd remembered the photos I'd taken of her. Mostly innocent enough—photos from the parties we attended and the like, but there were a few nudes and a few more, well . . . unusual ones. Some taken in a cemetery, for example. I wished I had been able to forget about them. Not easy, when every single day I tortured myself by looking at them.

"Oh, the photos," I said, "I'd almost forgotten them."

"Anyway," she said, "I just wanted to check in with you to make sure you weren't still angry with me and that you had no intention of doing something stupid."

Stupid? I'd never do anything like that. I used them for myself, masturbating and crying and keeping them as inspiration for my artistic ambitions. "I'd never do that," I said.

"It'd be great if you just deleted them."

"Sure. Trust me," I lied.

We stopped by the fence. A jogger ran past us.

"How's it going with the drugs?" she asked.

"Pretty much quit," I said, but I noticed that even as I said it, my speech was slurred.

She asked me if I had a few "test products" on me. I'd expected her to ask and I handed over—after checking behind my shoulder to see whether the dark-skinned guy was still hanging around and looking at us, but he was gone—an envelope. What she was interested in was a medical product not available to just anyone. A niche drug.

"How much do I owe you?" she asked, reaching for her purse.

I stopped her by grabbing her wrist.

"Ow," she said. I have strong hands. I'd grabbed harder than intended.

"I'm not going to sell to you," I said. "And if I ever sell to you, I won't do it like this." Then I let go of her wrist.

As I walked back, it was starting to get dark. The sun peeked though the pillars of the highway bridge, as it got ready to prepare another beautiful sunset over Vinterviken Bay. If things had been different, we could have walked back together to watch the sun set.

They found her dead in the water the next day. She was right where I had left her. The scene did not match any of the ones I'd imagined: She was in the water with all her clothes on and no obvious wounds. Her hair was loose, the best fashion for drowned people. (A hundred years ago, someone would have written a poem about the scene, and it would have been just as perverse as anything crime novelists write today.)

The cause of death was drowning—but not a typical suicide. In addition to the psychological improbability of the whole thing, it was just not possible to jump into the water and drown right there without rocks or weights in your pockets or a great deal of sleeping pills in your system. Neither of those was found. Yes, a small amount of alcohol, but nothing else, no foreign substances in her blood. How carefully did they check, though? Did they know what to look for? Her purse was missing, and with it, the small envelope I'd given her.

The scene was suspicious—not just because of the missing purse, but also the bruises on her wrists and neck. This could indicate that her head had been held underwater. Or something else. But when the police traced the text messages between us, which they'd gotten from the phone company, and realized I was her overemotional and disappointed ex, it did not look good for me.

I had no alibi, of course. When the police took me in, I pointed out she'd told me she had another errand to run nearby. I told them about the dark-skinned guy who'd been hanging around. What did he look like? "Dark-skinned" and "sweats" were not much to go on. I don't think they worked very hard to track him down, either. Shortly after that, they confiscated my computer, which, stupidly enough, I hadn't erased any documents from. The photos of Anette, the detailed descriptions of murder, the records of my side business—it certainly did not look good for me.

So you can imagine how it went. First she appeared in the headlines: "Fashion Model Found Dead." Then I came into the picture: "Model Murder: Police Suspect Ex-Boyfriend." And on and on: investigation, arrest, jail, court case. Everything has been written in such detail that it makes me sick to write another word about it. I was no longer a nobody. I was either a killer or a man wrongfully accused. I got hate mail and letters of admiration. There are so many idiots out there.

I was convicted, by a divided court, over my protestations of innocence. Yes, yes, I was guilty of trading in illegal substances, there's no doubt about that. In Sweden, that's just as bad as murder anyway. But as far as Anette's death goes, there was hardly any real evidence—a disturbing lack of it—and my lawyer and many other people knew this. Perhaps I did too.

So we're in the midst of an appeal, a process that's slowly moving forward. I've begun to serve my sentence. I'm a great prisoner. My cell reminds me of my tiny office, even if it lacks a view of the water.

Prison is not a game, but it has done wonders for my work ethic. I've finished my crime novel, such as it is. I now have some new experiences I can use. It also helps that describing murder scenes is no longer an obsession of mine, and I've found that I no longer believe crime never happens in Stockholm.

It was easy to find a publisher. I was infamous, hardly a disadvantage. The book is coming out next year. I'm already writing a second. That's what crime writers do: they write one book and then the next.

Still, my appeal is coming up. My lawyer is convinced I'll be set free, if I don't do something stupid (he's not all that happy about my devotion to the written word). Whatever happens, the dead are still dead, and people will continue to believe whatever they want about the living. Whether the court decides I'm innocent or guilty is just a small detail in the bigger picture.

Only losers care about details.

HORSE

BY ANNA-KARIN SELBERG

Rågsved

Translated by Rika Lesser

I've pursued her for months. Waited. Waited for tracks she
must have left behind, signs. People think they can be in-
visible moving through the world, but they always leave
something behind. Sooner or later, if you wait long enough. If
there's anything I've learned, this is it.

At first, all I could do was sense her, a slender shadow in the
investigation, she scarcely existed, but gradually she assumed a
body, and finally all her names collapsed into one.

I hold it in my hand. *Kim.* There's something about her
that almost arouses jealousy in me. Her face in the passport
photo, the narrow marked jawline, the serious expression. And
then something in the eyes that doesn't go with the rest of her
expression, a slight feminine nonchalance almost creating a touch
of condescension around her. Natural, inborn contempt. I can see
how she uses it, how with only a glance or gesture she dismisses
anything in her surroundings that doesn't suit her. She knows the
art of disdain and I can sense the feeling of being its target. The
resentment that would call for revenge. But I'm not someone she
can dismiss. She chose me such a long time ago, she waits for me as
patiently as I do her. As if our lives sought each other out from the
first moment. In retrospect, everything we ever experienced will
appear as inevitable steps, slowly closing the distance between us.

I check the address again, Sköllerstagatan, and then the map.

When Erik reported on the case to his colleagues that morning—it's months ago now—I instantly knew what kind of case it would be. In certain investigations something breaks into me, hits me, and starts to communicate with something deep in my body, forever forgotten. Draws out a nasty, stirring anxiety and forces it forward. Forces me to return to the place I never want to come back to. The place I always return to, in every investigation that draws my attention. Some inexorable magnetic power. Pushes me back to the day that turned me into who I am, the day that repeats itself in my life, a repetition I have transformed into a profession, into a hypersensitive instrument. Shivering, it searches its way into each case that awakens my sleeping unease with vague promises of something I cannot understand, something I can sense but not see, brute patterns and indistinct connections on their way to forming. A raw anxiety that gives no rest until every possibility is reviewed, every opening is searched out, and the evasive tracks of a perpetrator are decoded and identified. It is an instrument I bear like an imprint of the past, of the hours I cannot recollect: the lost hours my thoughts grope for in the investigations, but will never comprehend. As if a part of me should exist there, somewhere in the cases.

I can see my parents, I can see them perfectly clearly, although I was only one and a half years old when they found us and I know what I see is my own creation, something I've gleaned and put together from scant reports and the four photos the social services sent with me. I can see their eyes when he leaves them, their eyes in death. He killed them for the five grams of heroin my father hadn't yet shot up his veins and some cash. I've never returned to the place we lived, have avoided it all my life, I never went back to that side of the city.

When they found us I was lying beside my mother, she had been dead the whole night. A night that forever induced a distance to my feelings and cut them loose from my thoughts: cold, raw, and harsh, my thoughts live their own lives, grope about in the investigations like an alien machine. A night that made me inseparable from those I hunt. By chance we are each on opposite sides of the law, predestined to devote our lives searching for each other, as if searching for our lost half.

"Hey," Leila says and runs her fingers through my hair when I come home in the evenings. "Don't worry, baby, everything will be fine." Our daughter Mia looks at us with the face of a three-year-old who already knows she's not quite like either of us, and knows just how lonely that makes her. Her unfathomable gaze on my face, as if she can touch me with it. She's always had that gaze, since the moment she came into the world, lying on Leila's stomach in the delivery room. She lay there and observed us with her dark, enigmatic eyes, not making a sound. She struck me speechless, as if setting me in a scene I couldn't grasp; for hours she would just lie there looking at us. "Everything will be fine," Leila says, but she doesn't know that the force coursing through my veins is my element and the water I drink, owning me so profoundly I might not survive if it were to suddenly disappear. Like Epaminondas's spearhead, the spearhead he kept stuck in his heart, knowing that as long as it remained there he would live, but if he pulled it out he would die.

Leila strokes my hair, but knows nothing of who I am, what moves in my interior; she is lighthearted. Or perhaps she does, in her own remarkable way. With Mia it is different, everything is there between us, as if she saw straight through me from the very beginning.

* * *

I hold Kim's picture in my hand, in the emptiness that ensues when a case is solved, when all tension disappears, the emptiness I never know what to do with. I get up from the desk and slowly collect my things. I look at her address again; it tells me nothing, nothing but a closed case.

I phone Erik. I can tell he's sitting in the car as I hear the police radio in the background. There's a moment's silence when he absorbs what I'm telling him, that I've found her, that I know who she is.

"*Her?*" he asks, bewildered.

"Her."

I give him the address, still holding the photo in my hand, my fingers close around her face.

"Okay, I'll meet you there."

We hang up and I sit back down for a few minutes until I pull myself together and stand up again. Sköllerstagatan. I don't even consider taking the official car there, as if this isn't a place I can get to by car, drive to myself. As if somebody else must take me, but Erik is in Norsborg, so I must go by subway. I pull my pistol out of the holster, insert a new magazine, stuff the gun back into the holster, and strap it on. It rests just under my armpit, close to my body, like a metal-and-leather protuberance, concealed from the world by my jacket. It's autumn outside on Surbrunnsgatan, the air is clean and clear, the colors so beautiful, and the cold bites my face. When I walk down toward Sveavägen, there are loud noises from children playing soccer in the empty basin of the fountain next to the Stockholm Public Library with the Observatory Grove above. Two of them stand a bit apart from the group, near the edge that separates the shallow basin from the street. Two girls, maybe nine or ten years old, they look like they're whispering about something.

One of them lays a hand on the other's shoulder, studies me as I walk past; they make me think about Mia, make me wonder what she's doing. I close my eyes for a second; she's somewhere in the preschool, maybe in the room with building blocks and Legos, sitting on the floor with the other kids, lost in a game. When I drop her off there in the morning, she throws off her coat, runs in to join the others. It's her own world, a world to which I'm not admitted, which is hers alone, and I find myself standing outside with her brightly colored coat in my hand, following her with my eyes before I slowly hang up her coat on the little hook that bears her name in the entrance hall. Sometimes I stand awhile outside in the courtyard, peering through the window, watching her play without her knowing, before I tap on the windowpane and she looks back at me and waves. Some mornings she's sad, I see how she keeps herself together, trying not to show it, she sucks on her fingers while something in her eyes distances her from me. As if it's she and not I who finally says: Go now.

I feel the weight of the pistol as I walk down to the subway at Rådmansgatan in the chilly air. Passing through the turnstiles, I choose the stairs, not the escalator. The 19, the line I catch every day I don't take the car, although never in this direction. I stand on the platform and wait. Something makes me nervously feel for the pistol, touch it lightly with my hand, as if its weight isn't enough to reassure me of its existence. The train arrives and I take a window seat, see my face reflected in the glass in front of the tunnel's darkness, and feel her presence, feel the inexorable motion that makes the distance between us shrink, melt together to nothing. Hötorget passes on the left, then Central Station, and when the train exits the tunnel at Old Town the city is gorgeous, stunning, the colors of the trees in the south are mirrored in the water, yellow and bloodred; the beauty makes something well up inside me, almost like tears. There are a few women around me, a young girl, and a man in a suit. I get the feeling that they're staring at me, that they see something inside me, and sweat penetrates my T-shirt, like I'm losing control, like they're sucking it out of me in complete silence. We pass Slussen, Medborgarplatsen, and at Skanstull I can't stand it any longer, have to get off with blood rushing to my head, the cold sweat like a film on my skin when I lean against a pillar on the platform.

After a while everything clears, I head to Åhléns department store on Ringvägen, go to the cosmetics department, as if I need time, as if I want to drag it out. I walk around between counters of perfume and makeup, nod at some of the saleswomen, ask a few questions; this is routine, but it's a tactic that always works while my eyes wander over the products behind them. I know what things are worth, I've learned to pick out what's expensive and reject what's cheap. I decide on a fragrance from Jimmy Choo.

In the ad behind it, a woman leans her head so far back that you can scarcely see her face, her collarbones catch all the light, the dress's plunging neckline forms a V between her breasts. I test the scent on my hand, cedar and something floral I can't identify; when the salesgirl turns her back I pull out one of the drawers below the samples, find the right product, and take it with me. I smile in her direction and nod at the guard by the exit; he follows me with his eyes as I take a few turns, holding the small paper box in my hand. The faint, pleasant scent of cedar accompanies me among the shelves, just a hint of it, and I let the box drop into my pocket. Then I select an inexpensive bottle of shampoo from the shelves, and walk toward the cashier. The calm that spreads out when the salesperson wraps it, it's like a drug, I hand her my credit card and she slides it through the slot. The small sum burns in the card reader, and she tiredly returns the card with the bag, not looking at me. It's a movement she repeats, mechanically, over and over again, hundreds of times a day.

I let my gaze glide over the guard's face without settling, as if he were an object, before I exit onto Ringvägen. The crystal-clear fall air shoots its way into my lungs and I don't know why I keep doing this. I give away the loot as gifts to Leila. As if I want to be discovered, punished, but I don't know what for, as if nothing but risk can eradicate the guilt and bring rest.

When I take the elevator at Götgatan down to the lower level, five o'clock is approaching. The 19 appears in the tunnel again and I board the train. When it shoots out on the bridge between Skanstull and Gullmarsplan a few boats float by in the bay, these are their last trips before winter and I can see straight through the glassy walls of Eriksdal's indoor bath thirty meters below; the small solitary figures in the swimming pools, dark unprotected silhouettes against the light blue water. We pass Gullmarsplan, Globen, the rest of the stretch I've never traveled. Sockenplan, Svedmyra, Stureby. I check my phone, send a text message to Leila, telling her not to expect me for dinner, then look at the display for a few minutes, but she doesn't reply. She's busy, I know she's picking up Mia. I wonder what they'll eat, think about all the things Mia wants to bring home: the pacifier with the octopus cartoon, the big brown-and-black dog she carries around everywhere, the drawings she's made. How they cross the little courtyard with the baby carriage. I feel the straps of the holster around my body, as if they're holding it together. Högdalen comes up on the left, a sign above the housetops reads, *Högdalen Center*, and a few fathers with small children and two drunks get on before the train starts again. We glide past a park with ramps, teenagers skateboard on them in the autumn sun, and then I can see Rågsved in the distance. My eyes search for two places among the houses, although I know it's just a coincidence. Hers and mine. Hers must be somewhere among the clusters of apartment buildings on the right side of the tracks, mine on the left. I suddenly realize that maybe she's not at home or won't open the door; I haven't anticipated such a situation, have prepared nothing in advance. But deep inside I know she won't disappoint me.

I go through the turnstile, to the left are some wide stairs with narrow iron banisters. Behind them trees in brilliant colors, and above them towering houses, but I don't recognize them, they could be any houses. I walk in the other direction, away from the past, down through the tunnel under the road, and emerge on a small square. It's surrounded by two semicircular buildings with shops—Ammouris Livs, Dina's Pirogues and Sweets, Medihead Home Care, Rågsved Games and Tobacco, an ICA supermarket. In the middle there's a fountain and a few men sitting on benches, each one by himself. I check the address again on my phone, it must be somewhere on the other side of the square, one of the buildings on the hill visible from the subway. Nervously I check the time, wonder if Erik is stuck in traffic somewhere on the highway. I calculate how long it would take from Norsborg, he should be here already.

In the beginning I didn't know she was a female—I assumed she was a man, about my age, just under thirty and completely outside the usual networks, number unlisted but known in other ways. I'd heard her nicknames, *Kimsha, Kimmie, Kimo*, heard them so many times. Something in the way the junkies pronounced it, it got into me and began to do its slow work. *Kimsha, Kimmie, Kimo*. At first she was just a series of question marks in a few investigations, investigations that weren't even related to her, brief notations, before we understood that she was big, that she was the spider in a heroin flowchart, a heart shy of light which at the same constant rate, minute by minute, supplied the central arteries with a substance, a substance that sought out thinner and thinner blood vessels, shot itself into users and made their jerky excited movements subside, their eyes fill with a glassy tranquility. I'd imagined an older man, lean, wiry, and for some reason wearing a black leather jacket, his face radiating a special, peculiar intelligence. Someone who worked alone, who didn't rely on others, who never revealed to his customers who he was, but who'd succeeded in earning enough respect in the bigger networks to be left alone. Someone who saw it all as a job, any job, and brought in a lot of money, but in some remarkable way without upsetting organized crime, as if it weren't worth the effort it would take to do something about him.

Someone who was his own boss.

Their faces often come to me, their bodies and character, vague but still with distinct features. Sometimes they coincide with reality, sometimes their real features surface later like a shock that tears down everything I've built and strengthens my desire to find them. Avenging the scene that made me who I am. Again and again, as if I live in a frozen time, encapsulated in sheer mechanics.

I sit down on one of the benches, restless. Just opposite from where I sit—within the body of semicircular buildings that extends around the square and ends just in front of Capio's health center—there's a pub. The Oasis Restaurant. Three men and one woman sit outside in their jackets, it must be one of the last days for outdoor table service; they sit in the shade with their beer and cigarettes, freezing, they look worn out and are deep in loud conversation. But out here on the square it's surprisingly warm, maybe the semicircular row of buildings provides protection from the wind. I try to figure out when they were built.

It's a lovely square, you get the idea, the benches, the foun-tain. I get up and check the time again. The Oasis Restaurant. Abruptly I cross the square—I need to get something.

The men in the sidewalk café call something out when I go in, as if they immediately see that I'm a stranger, that I don't fit in, but I don't catch what they say. More people are sitting in-side, some men who look like alcoholics are drinking at the bar, two or three guys stand by themselves at the slot machines, a larger group sits at one of the tables. I stand at the bar, without making any eye contact, but I can feel their eyes on me. I never drink on the job, I'm surprised at myself. The bartender comes over, says nothing, just gives me a questioning look. There's something guarded about him, as if he doesn't understand what I'm doing here. He takes my order. There are no other single women here, absolutely no one my age. He dries off the glass with a towel in his pocket, sets the beer down in front of me on the counter. I hand him my credit card. My phone says it's almost quarter to six, Leila hasn't texted back and I take a few deep gulps of the ice-cold liquid.

Then I get a look at her—she must have been sitting there the whole time on the other side of the bar, looking at me with-out me seeing her. She's wearing a red T-shirt, I try to read the faded gray words printed on her chest, something with *Plugged*. She's thin and sinewy, has two tattoos on one of her upper arms, two bands in the same black, stylized tribal design, which run around her biceps, separated by a few centimeters. She doesn't look much like the photo, and she's not the enigmatic figure she ought to be, given the circumstances, and yet I know this is right, this is her, it can't be anyone else. Suddenly I wonder what she's doing when she's not taking care of business. I see her in an apartment, alone, how she sits there during the day and plays video games. She studies me calmly, almost curiously.

Shame and eagerness stun me for a few moments, and I wonder if she can see this, when one of the drunks staggers toward the bar, close to me.

"You're cute," he whispers, and I remove his fat hands from my body, take a swig of my beer without looking at him.

After a while she gets up and comes toward us, shoves him aside with her arm and a hard, weary expression on her face. When he goes, she puts her beer down on the bar: I can't figure out whether she's amused or contemptuous.

"You don't live around here," she says, and I don't know how to reply, as if nothing I can say would be right.

"No," I finally answer.

Her forearm against the bar counter, it's covered with thin strands of hair and I can almost touch the attraction that binds us.

I check the time on my phone again. "Could you wait a minute?"

She nods.

Outside the autumn sun disappears behind the roofs. I dial his number, walking back and forth in front of the restaurant while the call goes through. When he finally answers I tell him that he doesn't need to come anymore, but I can hear that my voice sounds too harsh.

"What's happened?"

"She's not there."

"Have you already been there? Yourself?"

I see the contours of her body inside, leaning slightly forward, her arms resting against the counter. I don't really answer him, only repeat that she isn't there.

"You've been there? What the hell are you thinking? You broke into the apartment? Without a warrant?"

"She's not there. I know where she is. We'll talk tomorrow, okay?" I answer, fatigued.

It's cold, and I've left my jacket inside—I see it hanging next to her on the barstool. When I walk in again she looks at me quite openly, all the way from over by the bar.

Her apartment is dark, I sense that it has two rooms, that it's completely symmetrical, one room on either side of the hall and maybe a kitchen between them. When she takes a step toward me I seize her wrists and put her hands around my neck.

"The bathroom," I whisper in her ear, holding her wrists gently; she doesn't try to free herself. I lower her arms and put them around my waist, concerned that she'll place her hands on my shoulders if I let go of her and feel the holster straps through my jacket.

"There," she nods toward a door behind my back.

I let go of her and walk into the small bathroom, closing the door carefully behind me. I hear her take off the jean jacket and hang it up, then she goes out to the room on the right. I remove my own jacket, the pressure in my chest, as if it belongs to someone else, a cry that isn't mine. I unbuckle the holster and look around. It's clean and impersonal, like a hotel bathroom, the only signs of her are the laundry basket in the tub and her clothes inside it, underpants, T-shirts; I want to open the medicine cabinet, but stop myself. Turn on the water instead, wash my face before I carefully bend down, protected by the running water, until kneeling on the floor, and I shove the holster with the pistol as far as I can under the bathtub. The feeling of pressure, as if I'm going to vomit. When I turn off the water I don't recognize my face in the mirror, it is closed, locked, and I don't know what's going on behind it.

It's still dark in the apartment, she hasn't turned on any lights, I hesitate, enter the room on the right, and stop in the middle, not knowing where she is. Suddenly she's close beside me, quiet and agile like an animal. We kiss softly and carefully, the sharp, cutting taste of alcohol and her thin, sinewy body turns beneath my hands. I pull up her T-shirt, she's not wearing a bra, her breasts are so small they fit in my palms. Her nipples, big as raspberries, are hard between my fingers, she draws me closer, breathless I inhale her scent, feeling her angular hip bones against my own.

"Who are you?" She pushes me back at arm's length, her eyes searching in the darkness. Black as coal against her pale face, her dyed hair reaches just below her shoulders and I know from the photo that her eyes are green, but it's too dark to see their exact color.

She strokes my cheek gently. "Come," she whispers, taking my hands and pulling me toward the bed. She removes my clothes, turns me over like a baby, strokes my back, touches me with firm, open hands, kisses the nape of my neck, takes one of my breasts in her hand, and with the other, presses an open palm against my cunt. It's like being caressed by a pro, someone who knows my body by heart, someone trained in shooting it straight up. The serenity, the substance that brings everything to rest.

Afterward I try to make her out in the darkness, she's lying on her side of the bed, naked, but I can barely see the outline of her body. She sits up, reaches across me, and gropes for something beside the night table, gets hold of her T-shirt and a pack of cigarettes, an ashtray and a lighter. She smokes slowly with her back against the wall and I recognize her from the photograph. There's something self-sufficient in the way she smokes, in the discrete, defined movements distinguishing her body from its surroundings. I can understand why they leave her alone.

"I saw a performance," she says slowly, exhaling the smoke. "A day or two ago. I never go to such things."

She leans her head against the wall, waits and peers down at me in the bed. For a second I see Mia's sleeping body, the nightmares that chase her, how sometimes when she wakes up she doesn't understand that they're over until several minutes later. The terror that shines in her eyes before the dreams flow away, until everything clears and grows still.

"A man ran from one corner of the stage, jumped high up, and fell straight to the floor. Then he got up and did it again. Again and again." She slowly lowers one hand toward the blanket. "How can that be called a performance?"

Something warm shoots up behind my eyes and I smell her cunt through her crossed legs; she's only wearing the red T-shirt. *Plugged Recording.* I wonder what it means, where she got it from. She exhales again, suddenly indifferent, before she stubs out the cigarette, gets up, climbs over me, and disappears into the bathroom.

When I wake up she's sleeping beside me. I gather up my clothes, head to the bathroom, fish out my holster, and fasten it tightly under my arm. Quickly put on my jacket in the hall, then I stand for a while in the doorway to the bedroom and look at her before leaving; sleep smoothes out her face, as if she were dead or a newborn baby.

When I leave her, I choose the street down the hill toward the center of town, and before reaching the small square I sit awhile on a bench in front of a soccer field, beside a home for the elderly. I pull out my phone and call the task force. It doesn't take more than fifteen minutes, they must have been nearby, I recognize them when they appear in the rotary where the slope ends, in unmarked vehicles. No sirens, just two big vans, one light, the other dark. I get up and go, hear them climbing the hill behind me, I push my hair out of my face, can smell her sex, she's still there in my hands. Her jawline burned into my retina, just as lovely in reality as in the photo.

She'll keep her beauty for a long time, long after our contemporaries have lost theirs to old age.

PART II

Fear & Darkness

FROM THE REMAINS

by Inger Edelfeldt

Tantolunden

Translated by Laura A. Wideburg

Curled up in bed with my old-fashioned composition book, I'm finally feeling warm after the ice-cold night. And after such a strange encounter. She wants me to write down her tale. That's all. A tale of winter and chill; an ice-cold saga. How fitting, that we are now in the middle of winter, with an unbelievable amount of snow covered by a shiny hard crust.

Everything was strange from the start—I mean yesterday, after I returned from my vacation and went out to see how my garden cottage had fared in the bitter weather. I wrapped myself in warm clothes and walked down to Bergsunds Beach, and then along the footpath by the edge of the expansive frozen water, toward Tanto.

The entire hillside seemed to be covered in a thick layer of white frosting. On the rock wall, at the first, lower wooden staircase, icicles hung like huge organ pipes. The second staircase, the one I usually take up to my cottage, had turned into an icy ramp, with barely visible steps. Still, I managed in spite of my slippery boots.

Once at the top of the hill, I could see out, over the encrusted surface of the water, the bridges, and the skyline with its glittering windows on the far side of the ice. The massive buildings on the horizon stood close to each other and seemed to exist in another time, a science-fiction future that appeared unreal and far removed from the garden colony—this special realm of small cottages painted in bright colors and their small yards with benches, tiny gazebos of glass, and other dreams embodied on their sloping plots. In the summertime, the whole effect is beyond idyllic, but now it seemed full of some fateful magic, as if a powerful winter sorcerer had bewitched it with frosting.

I'm describing all this because it all belongs. In the movies, characters never suspect that something unusual is afoot, but I *felt* it then. Everything was a premonition, a forewarning, but of something beautiful. As if something was calling to me. A crystal-clear, silent song vibrating in everything. Or am I reconstructing this after the fact? No, that I doubt.

The day had been sunny and clear, but the blue sky was beginning to darken as twilight approached; everything was breathtaking. The only thing that troubled me was the fear that the harsh weather might damage my cottage. This beloved small building, just one of the numerous playhouses for adults on the hillside, was my oasis during spring, summer, and fall. Mine was light blue like old-fashioned baby clothes for boys. The weather vane is less cute; it's a rusty vulture. In addition, there's a ceramic Poe raven nailed to the lowest branch of the apple tree.

I like to write in my little house, my refuge, now frozen solid. The snow lay heavy on its roof, the window panes were covered in strange, blossoming frost patterns. The ceramic raven watched me stolidly from the apple tree. I had to use a shovel to hack at the ice along the little door to open it.

An unpleasant smell struck my nostrils. *Dead rat*, I thought, *but in this cold nothing dead should be able to give off such a stench.*

With a bit of shock, I realized that someone had been in here. Nothing was damaged, but I was sure someone had been rummaging around.

No. That premonition I'd had on the way over had not been hinting at something beautiful. What I saw made me catch my breath. The instinct to vomit choked my throat. I saw a *shape* on the other side of the room—the thick plastic mat had been pulled up to cover something shoved right against the little bench, with its view over the spirea bushes, where I typically sat in the summer to drink my coffee.

Call someone. The words flew through my mind. *Get out of here. Don't check this out all by yourself.*

But yet, a moment later, I still stood there, looking at the figure under the mat. The *girl*, this word came to me, as if she were all the girls in the world, as if there were no living girls, happy girls, girls eating ice cream in the sunshine.

She was curled in a fetal position. Her skin was bluish white, her limbs oddly thin. The body, frozen almost solid, wore nothing but a thin, dirty summer dress which had, perhaps, once been white. That the dress was trimmed in romantic, innocent lace made the sight especially creepy.

I couldn't see her face. Her long dark hair curled over her features as if she herself wanted to hide them as a last gesture to spare any future gawkers. Or perhaps the killer had done this, covered her face, her stare. *Trafficking*, I thought. *Crime scene, police.* I felt so faint I had to sit down, powerless, but still unable to look away from the little naked foot. Repugnance and horror ran through me as well as wild tenderness, sorrow, and anger—as if I should be able to hug her and comfort her! Yes, that's what it was like, what it was actually like.

The light in the cottage shifted into a darker blue, as if it emanated from her, oozed out of her. I was entirely alone in this cottage on the frosted hillside during twilight with the frozen body of a girl. *A nightmare*, said the voice in my head. And then I noticed a dead rat beside her body. A number of dead rats, actually. Had they chewed off her face? *Don't even think about that.* A dark, trapped cry throbbed in my head, my throat, my chest. It carried no coherent thoughts with it; both the ability to think and the ability to act had fled.

Then a quick movement. Unexpected, incomprehensible. A rustle, an exhalation, and she sat up. I was so shocked I didn't have time to be afraid, but I felt I had been thrown into another dimension, a kind of dream state, where this could happen.

I saw a tiny heart-shaped face. Her eyes were totally black, like bullet holes, with no whites. Her features shone gray-white, haloed by her black hair. Her lips were moving slightly, an almost silent sound reached my ears, but I could not make out what she was saying—was she speaking a foreign language?

Then came something resembling a laugh behind a closed mouth, and she said, "Welcome!"

Perhaps she'd already hypnotized me. At any rate, she seemed to be, in some inexplicable way, already familiar.

"Don't be afraid," she said. "My name's Alma. I'm just sleeping here. It's good that it's winter. The days are short. And I never freeze."

I had nothing to say to that.

"You realize what I am, don't you?"

When I silently shook my head, she smiled briefly and I could see her sharp teeth, white as pearls and glistening. Yes, I must have been hypnotized. I didn't even shudder.

"I've been finding places to sleep here and there," she said. "Ever since it happened." Her black, eternal gaze bored into me as she cocked her head. "You're a kind person, aren't you?"

Well, what was I supposed to reply to that? I shrugged and forced a smile.

She said, "I don't kill people." She fluffed her hair the way girls do. "I've been sleeping in different cottages until I came to yours. Yours was the right one. You're a writer. I love books. Rather, I love to disappear into them. Brontë. Oates. Atwood. And, of course, Poe. I love your raven, by the way! I thought I would just wait here until you showed up. And now here you are."

"Can I help you in some way?" I managed to say. I really hoped I would not have to help her die. I didn't want to deal with a cross and a stake or old black blood. I didn't want to hear her pleas for eternal rest.

"Sure, you can help me," she replied. "I've been praying for you to come! You want to use words to scare people, so let me inspire you. You'll hear my story, you'll give me a few nights of your time, and I'll be your Scheherazade. Yes, you will be the one to write my winter tale. You will make it beautiful. You will write it so that whoever reads it will want to weep. Their tears will become diamonds in the cold; they will be stars and shine forever in my memory. And what you will do for me, you will do out of love."

Alma's Winter Tale

I was sixteen years old then. You think I might have been younger, but I had just turned sixteen, I am sixteen, I will be sixteen. How long has it been? I think it's been three years now, but five hundred years from now, I will still be sixteen.

My mother and I had argued. We often argued. She'd throw me out of the house, and then she'd call me on my cell phone and apologize: *Come back, Alma, I didn't mean it! I didn't mean to say that, I didn't really think that, just come back and everything will be good. I'll stop drinking and bringing home stupid men. I'll become an angel, the moon is made of cheese, there's peace on earth, the climate issue is resolved, the world is all candy fluff, just come home.*

This time it was also winter, and she threw me out without warning. Just because. I was locked out in the falling snow and wind, late at night, no coat, just a long sweater, no phone, no keys. *You whore, stealing Lasse from me.*

You see, we lived in this neighborhood, in one of those huge tower blocks on Flintbacken, the ones shaped in a half-circle. In the same building, next to our entrance, were a school and a preschool for English-speaking children and I often wished I could live there instead. A sign said: *Welcome to the Suns.* If you took the stairs on the left side of the building, through the groves, you went down to the beach. The path along the beach always had joggers on it in all kinds of weather, but halfway up there was a bench not far from the stairs and I sat down on it in spite of the cold and the snow. I hoped I would get pneumonia or a urinary tract infection or something. Maybe even die. And it would be *all her fault.*

I sat there for a while, the falling snow muffling all sounds, although I could still hear the frenetic pace of the runners training for some marathon and a dog barking in the distance. I could hear the sound of a train crossing the Årsta Bridge—a train going *away*, I've always loved that sound.

Die, die, die! I kept thinking, and I don't know who I wanted to die, me or her. Perhaps I wanted everything to die, sucked into a black hole and gone, like in *Donnie Darko.*

I hadn't heard any footsteps, but a guy suddenly appeared in the snow in front of me. My first thought was he must have come from a costume party. He wore a tall black hat, sunglasses, and a tuxedo. A little like the Sandman. I remember thinking that he was trying for the creepy look and he'd succeeded, but in my state of mind, I was not afraid. I felt he was very attractive, extremely attractive, even sexy. Unfortunately.

"May I sit down?" he asked, and I said, "Sure."

He sat down and we were silent for a while. Then he said, "Look, you're freezing. You don't need to freeze." He was all over me in an instant and I remember his sickly black eyes as he whipped off the sunglasses and then everything faded.

I woke up with snow on me everywhere, in my mouth and eyes and nose; I was lying stretched out on the bench, completely covered in snow; he must have left me in this odd position. I sat up. Everything felt strange, shifted, changed, as if I'd had some kind of memory loss or had fainted. But the strangest thing of all was I wasn't freezing. I had no idea what time it was. I didn't have my cell phone. The air was so still, however, that I thought it must be very late at night. No sounds of running from the walkway, no day sounds at all. Had anyone seen me as they walked by? Do people bother to look around at all?

Then I heard a dog barking shrilly from the top of the stairs. It sounded like a tiny, terrified dog, and the voice of the owner trying to calm it was female.

I got up, reassured that someone was out and about, and a woman too, and I walked up the stairs to ask her what time it was.

I will never forget the expression on her face. She was as terrified as the dog. She told me the time—one thirty in the morning—and then she pulled the Chihuahua, still barking at the top of its tiny lungs, as far away from me as she could, while striding down the path in a different direction. Her reaction terrified me too. I knew nothing but had the urge to go home. Mama would ask me for forgiveness, I thought, and she'd make me a cup of hot chocolate. She is nice to me as soon as she regrets what she's done, which usually happens after a few hours.

I couldn't get the door code to work. I pressed the call button for our apartment, again and again, until she answered over the intercom. The connection was bad. She said hello a number of times and couldn't seem to hear what I was saying, but she must have realized it was me, because she let me in. Once inside, I pressed the elevator button, but it didn't work that night either, so I ended up taking the stairs three flights up. The elevator was waiting right by our door, so why hadn't it come down? I rang the bell at the door to my home.

She opened it and screamed, then slammed the door shut. I hoped no neighbors had heard her. I pushed the mail slot open and said in as friendly a way as I could, "Open the door, Mama, it's me, Alma!" No answer. I slumped against the door, ready to cry. I decided I would wait it out until she opened it again. Instead, the mail slot opened and she pushed a piece of paper out. She'd written a message: *Whoever you are, go away! I'm calling the police.*

Whoever I am? Had she gone completely psycho or had I?

I thought I heard a noise from one of the neighboring apartments and my first reaction was to hide in the elevator, which was, of course, waiting right by our—or should I now say *her*—door.

The next shock of the night—I was looking straight into a mirror and there was no reflection of me. Only the inside of the elevator. I put my hand on the glass. No matter what I did, I was not there. I can't begin to describe how terrifying that was. You're used to checking yourself in the mirror, right, to see how you look? I thought I'd found myself in the middle of a nightmare, but I could not wake up.

I tried to press the down button and heard a crackling sound, but the elevator refused to work. I went down the stairs and into the basement where I found a moldy blanket. I hid under it, shaking like an animal, but not from cold, because I could no longer feel the cold.

Terror short-circuited my thought process and saved me from realizing, at that moment, what my existence would be like from here on out.

Yes, and what *is* my existence, you wonder? Think of rats. I live on rats, pigeons, rabbits. A blood hunger is now a part of my being, and I soon discovered that small animals are drawn to me. I can hypnotize them the way snakes hypnotize their prey. I realized fairly soon that I couldn't remain long in the light of day, not because it kills me immediately, but it makes me weak and ill. As long as it was winter and the days were short, I found it easy to sleep. But my first summer was unbearable . . . so many nights in subway tunnels and the hidden rooms by the abandoned train line below South Hospital, in culverts and caves and other places where I encountered darkness and rats. I spent my time searching for the man who had been my transformer, but he was gone without a trace. He'd told me nothing about what was going to happen to me, nothing at all about my new existence. But there was one thing I had decided on my own: I was not going to kill human beings. I would not become that depraved.

Are you laughing now? No, I see you're not laughing. That's good.

The loneliness! Of course, I'd believed I had been lonely and abandoned and bullied when I was a human being, but now I was so completely cut off from everything and everyone. In addition, something electromagnetic about my new being short-circuited cell phones and computers, so that I couldn't use the Net. I was something completely *other*, something with another kind of electric charge, something of another dimension but still requiring nourishment from the normal dimension of the living. I'd become something that could not die and yet was no longer alive.

Obviously I frightened most people, but those who were not afraid of death were not terrified of me, and at times they found me tempting. Those were the ones who wanted to die, who wanted me to kill them! I'd run away before I could fulfill their desire, even though it was against my new nature. Perhaps it was my dignity that mattered.

I spied on Mama, and it hurt when I saw her, but I didn't dare show myself. I had seen my image—a bullied girl's school photo—beneath the newspaper headlines: *MISSING! MUR-DERED?* I have to admit I was happy to see Mama sad and depressed; it was my only comfort.

I hung around my old neighborhood until something happened. I've just returned—I've been away for a long time and there's a good reason for that. Here's what happened: Then . . . then it was fall again and I was crouching beneath a thicket near my apartment building. A girl crawled in. She looked tired and worn out, and she didn't see me at first. She shot up. People do that in my neighborhood. She took out a makeup kit and tiny mirror to paint a new face onto the tired one. I hadn't thought to make my presence known, but something forced me to.

"Sorry," she said. "I don't have any more."

She was not afraid of me at all. It seemed she mistook me for a friend. She called herself a "crack whore" and seemed to believe I was one too. She told me I was too young to shoot up; she said that a few times. She also told me my eyes were strange. I said I was almost completely blind.

This girl seemed to like me. She was acting like a big sister.

She offered to make up my face. She said I felt cold and she took pity on me. She shouldn't have done that. We stood too close, much too close, and I lost my dignity. Something came over me and all went black until I returned to myself to find I was next to a body drained of blood. I was overwhelmed by what was happening to me. Probably it was not just the blood, but the drugs. I felt in shock but also filled with dancing fire, a pure and delicate but grim blessedness. Grim, yes, powerful and shameless. At least as long as the effect lasted. I sat there beside her body and waited for her to transform like I had. Then I would have a friend, someone like me! Now that I'd done what I'd done.

I sat there for hours. Nothing happened. Dawn started to break, so I needed to find shelter somewhere else. When darkness fell again, I returned, but the police were there and the thicket was taped off; they were bringing a body bag. I realized she'd died a real death. I fell into an abyss of shame and torment. I had killed another human being!

All I wanted was to hide and get away from everything. Oh, I was good at not being seen, of course, at pulling the hood of my sweatshirt over my head, hiding my face beneath my hair, sneaking past security guards and everyone else.

One night I took the last subway all the way out to Hässelby strand, where I'd lived when I was younger, before my mother inherited the apartment in Tanto. I knew that there was a grotto in Grimsta Forest, near Maltesholm Baths. I wanted to go into hibernation and disappear.

I felt sad when I got to the beach where I'd swum and eaten ice cream as a little girl. The food stand, with its ugly graffiti, now shuttered. The fire pits for grilling hot dogs. The playground with its green wooden cars. Nobody was swimming now.

There were a few dog walkers and I stayed away from them. Like a hunted animal, I took refuge in the hidden grotto. I covered the entrance with branches. I stayed there for some time, crying, feeding myself with squirrels and small birds, staring at a glassy, swollen moon which seemed to me like a large breast filled with heavenly shining milk, unreachable but still so beautiful it broke my heart.

What could give me any comfort, any grace? Only my dreams. I dreamed I lived in the country of the moon, a pearl princess in a mother-of-pearl castle on the white plains of the moon, free from shame, from feelings, from hunger, from guilt. There in my lair, I dreamed many beautiful dreams. It was painful to awaken—drawn out from them by my blood hunger.

Winter arrived—the cold was harsh and few people came to the beach. The nights were almost completely empty. A raw beauty animated nature. Frost covered everything. I walked along the beach beneath the moon and peered out over the frozen waves: when I looked at my own hand, I saw that frost covered my skin and made me glitter and shine like a blessed, beautiful being. Loneliness, ice-cold, exiled, but also a kind of freedom, a place to breathe, as far from human beings as possible.

By chance, I discovered that the human blood I'd drunk had given me new skills. One night, as I sat on the stairs of the food shack enjoying the moonshine, a couple of loud guys came walking along the beach. I pressed back tightly against the shack and wished I could hide inside it when I found myself going through the wall. It gave way and let my body in bit by bit until I was entirely inside, with the outdoor furniture and umbrellas. I found I could now go through other walls too, force myself through solid materials. My amazement caused me to laugh out loud, but the gang outside just continued on to the closest fire pit where they made a huge bonfire with all the trash they wanted to get rid of.

Were there other things I could do that I was not yet aware of? Yes, I found I could hover in the air, like in a dream where you find it easy to fly once you decide to try. I could move very swiftly, almost teleport myself short distances, if I concentrated hard enough. I tried to tell myself I'd had those skills from the beginning, but I knew that these gifts arrived only after I'd drunk the blood of the dead girl.

I remained in exile, mostly in the forest. One night, in the season between winter and spring, the moon was shining so very brightly that for some reason I wanted to celebrate it, or honor it, as if it could help me. The full moon is a cold and harsh parent, but still somehow I felt I could communicate with it, even if it was only pretend. And now I wanted to show it my respect. During my walks on the beach, I had found things left behind by others; the nicest was a necklace of rock crystals. A child had forgotten a plastic handbag with a pattern of stars. And once I found a long strand of Christmas garland on a bush; I draped it in my hair. And I had my white dress that I'd found in a bag behind a thrift store in the city.

Dressed in these pretty things, I walked down the path to the edge of the water until I reached the swimming beach. The warmth of the day had melted most of the snow that had been on the sand and the ice was gone too, but the night was still cold. I'm mentioning the cold because it has to do with what comes next. When I'd left the edge of the forest, I saw a young man in just jeans and a T-shirt, standing barefoot on the beach. The rising moon gave him a long, indistinct shadow. As I came closer, I saw his teeth were chattering. He didn't see me at first; he was staring at the water. He took a step into the surf.

"Where are you going?" I yelled. He turned toward me with no fear at all.

A second later, I was by his side. "Don't do this," I said. "You have no idea what death is like."

He stared at me, shivering, and tried to say something, but he was freezing so much he was no longer able to speak. His lips had a blue tinge. His eyes were large and beautiful, *he* was beautiful.

"Wait here," I said, and in a second I was back at the food shack where I'd seen some blankets were stored. I brought back two. In the meantime, he'd taken a few more steps into the water.

"No, you must not!" I exclaimed. I wrapped him in one of the blankets and took the Christmas garland from my head and set it on his. This earned me a timid smile, more like a grimace, really. His eyelashes were long, like a child's.

"Put your shoes on," I ordered. "Go back home." For a fraction of a second, I thought we might be able to be friends, the young man and me, though who knows how I could even think this as my eyes were drawn to his throbbing jugular vein where his blood pulsed, and the hunger welled up in me like a shock to my body, and I could barely hold myself back. I stepped away from him, shaking as much as he was.

"Forget me," I managed to say. "Tomorrow you will find someone else, someone who will listen to you and understand what you're going through. I promise."

He reached out a thin, shaking hand.

I ran to the edge of the forest, up among the trees, I had to reach my cave, my lair. My entire body was in revolt. Luckily, I came across a hare, which I sucked dry, but it took a long time for me to calm down.

Later, I retraced my steps to the place where I'd seen him.

Both his clothes and the blankets were gone. The Christmas garland was arranged in a circle on the sand, with the words THANKS. DAVID scratched inside.

I had saved him. I had prevented him from drowning himself. I wept with happiness, sorrow, and other human feelings, as if I was still human, over that which was still possible and that which was not.

David! His name alone, and the memory of his eyes—it was enough to make me happy. I snuck up among the human houses until I saw him again. I followed him until I knew where he lived. In the yard by his house, I formed a heart with the last bit of snow, and I hoped he would see it before it began to melt.

I did not dare stay near where he lived. Not even in the neighborhood, by the beach, or even in the forest. I went back to the city, to human beings. My life there was much easier now that I knew how to use my new skills. I could always find somewhere to sleep. And at first I thought it was exciting to go wherever I wanted, observe secrets, research people's lives. It was like reading books or watching movies, but in real time. Unfortunately, I could not influence them very much. Mostly I watched as I swayed in the darkness outside people's windows. Much of what I saw shocked me. Many people find themselves in difficult situations that are not their fault, but there are so many others who make life difficult for themselves and others even though they aren't poor, sick, oppressed, or even damned, the way I was damned. *If only you knew!* I wanted to scream. *You need to value your lives!* But I realized that most of the time they would only hear my voice as some frightening sound. It became ever more clear that only those who are not afraid of death will experience me as something other than a monster.

I observed happy people too, the ones who could value themselves and other people. I did not understand where they'd received that gift. They were not always beautiful and rich. They were often fairly lonely people, but still able to enjoy their lives, as if they were honeybees with an inexhaustible supply of internal nectar. When I saw these happy people—and I mean *really* happy people, not those who pretend they're happy—when I saw them with my depthless eyes, I saw that they had a golden shimmer around them that seemed to come from within. It might sound sentimental, but they were like little lamps. Seeing them made me both happy and endlessly sad, a pain that was simultaneously as beautiful as it was unbearable. I don't think I'll tell you any more about it. It hurts me even to talk about it.

Thinking of David was just like that—a bright blessing and a stinging pain simultaneously. Something alive to protect and value, but with no fulfillment for me. Yet, better to be nourished by the thought, the dream, than to be destroyed by reality. Or so I thought.

Eventually I started searching for others like me. I wanted to know more about who and what I was, but when I finally did find one, I regretted it immediately.

I'd started hanging around in Tanto again so I could spy on Mama. And winter finally returned—my third winter as one of the undead—so I walked over the ice to Årsta Island to sleep in one of the abandoned boats there. I was getting tired of human habitats.

When I woke up and crept out on deck, *he* was sitting there, hunched like a monkey on the railing, smiling like the Cheshire cat.

Mr. Humbert Fishy. Or that's how he introduced himself. Thin. Conceited. Wearing a long leather coat, black-red like old blood. I didn't ask what the coat was made from. Long oily hair. High white forehead. Pointed teeth. With his X-ray vision, he drew me from the inside out and knew my entire history. I couldn't hide anything from him. That was his power. A devil's.

"Little saint," he called me, laughing all the while.

In the pauses between his gales of laughter, he answered my questions. I didn't even need to ask them—he read my thoughts as easily as a fly eating shit.

Where do we come from, we the damned? Answer: from the same place as everything else, from God the Black Hole. Are we evil? No, why would we be? Living human beings kill more than we do. Can we escape our fate and die the true death? The stake, little saint, the stake or the daylight. Or perhaps starve to death from the wrong kind of food ha ha ha, little saint.

How can I transform them, then? That is, not kill them, but give them the Gift, as I'd gotten it? Not a chance, he said, only the very old and experienced ones can do that. Only those who had fed themselves the right food for hundreds of years.

He told me what I'd been suspecting all along. Only if I regularly drank human blood would I be able to develop into the "remarkable being" I was meant to be. The Crown of Creation, as he put it. He could not only read thoughts, he could fly and he could see entire cities at once, and he could zero in on prey with especially good blood; it was as if they glowed on a map. Yes, he said *prey* instead of *humans*. He was a gourmet, he said. Five hundred years had made him one.

Since not a shred of my soul or memory was hidden from him, he sniffed out my love for David right away. Oh, how he laughed!

"Now, my little mosquito," he said, "how do you think you could be close to him—a living boy? Don't you think he'd be scared out of his mind? And even more important, how could you resist biting him? You remember how you felt on the beach, right? His pulsing vein, your burning hunger? And you *ran away!* From such a wonderful piece of meat, from one who wanted to die anyway! You would have done him a *favor!*" Mr. Fishy laughed until he choked. And while he laughed, the whole boat shook, and a thousand pieces of broken ice applauded.

"*I* can be your friend," he said. "Absolutely! But only once you've become what you really are. Right now, you're nothing at all!"

He let the width and breadth of his damnation travel so deep into me I could feel my own nothingness and that nothing else existed. I felt crushed and laid on the boat like a whipped dog. Then I felt anger start to rise in me, at first just a spark. He noticed it, of course.

"Why are you mad at me, little flea? You're the one making it more difficult for yourself by trying to be something you're not. Focus on me all you want, but soon enough you'll realize the one you're fighting is yourself. Bye for now!" And he lifted up from the deck and fluttered like a stupid scarecrow before he shot into the air and flew away so fast I didn't see him disappear.

The strange thing was I felt more abandoned than ever. However horrible he was, I still wanted him to come back. But he didn't return. Still, I had many hundreds of years ahead of me to run into him again, right?

I was still mad. That small speck of anger grew and in my mind I heard his raw laughter—at my love and longing! I was going to prove him wrong. I would show him I could make it work—or be brave enough to try.

My wrath did not subside and neither did my longing. I decided to go on an outing to Hässelby strand. I was going to make myself as beautiful as possible. In an apartment, I found a lace dress; perhaps it was for a child, a flower girl at a wedding.

I'm so thin and tiny it fit. I wore perfume, and combed my hair, fastening flowers into it.

Then I headed to his house—David's house. I was so afraid I thought I might faint. I saw light in the window, I knew which room was his.

I was in luck: he was the only one in the house. It was about ten at night, but he hadn't shut the curtain. He was sitting on his bed playing guitar. He had just taken a shower and was wearing a black robe.

I couldn't stay outside. This was what I had been afraid of— that my longing would overpower me. I had not intended to go through the wall, but my longing forced me to, and there I was in his room.

At first things looked promising. He didn't seem afraid, only surprised. I don't know what I looked like in his eyes; perhaps I was nothing more than a breeze or a shadow, now that he'd decided to live. I wasn't a monster, at any rate. Perhaps a vague ghost, a feeling rather than an experience? He started paying attention, the way a cat focuses on something without us knowing why. I could actually read his thoughts: *There's something in the room. There's a ghost haunting this room.*

No, I wanted to scream, *it's me, Alma. The one who saved you; now you can save* me! *See me, embrace me!*

Then I noticed the photo on his nightstand. A stupid, cute, laughing, living human girl. A girl of the daylight, spoiled, sorrow-free. She'd used a gold marker to draw a heart around her childish face and the words *To David.*

What can I tell you? Jealousy, loneliness, unending pain— everything I mourned shot through me like a silent black explosion. I fell to pieces. Whatever had held back my hunger now dissipated and my true nature took over. In one jump I was on top of him. I'd turned into a demon, focused on his throat.

His blood—a dreamed-of nourishment, a drink more pleasant than anything I could imagine; I became whole, complete, at home in myself. He tried to defend himself, but it was all in vain.

But see, I didn't kill him. Don't look so frightened. He's still alive. Because I came to my senses when I heard Mr. Fishy's laugh echoing in my memory. I could stop myself because I realized I was doing just what, in his cynical and triumphant way, he'd predicted I'd do. So I stopped myself, I drew back, I pulled myself out through the wall. I disappeared down the street, out of the neighborhood, away to this wintery hill where I'm staying now. I'm ashamed, but I'm still proud I didn't kill him. I'm alone, in an eternal land of limbo, where my old dreams have no place. I can't dream of him. I can't dream of being human again. And obeying my own nature . . . no! Turning into that hideous phantom, stinking of cold blood, cynical and greedy, with no shame and no conscience.

So I'm staying here, and not just because it's closed for the winter, but also because I want to run into my mama who's still living in the apartment building across the way. I can read thoughts a bit, and I want to read hers to see if she misses me. If she ever loved me, even a little. David's blood has given me a shot of greater potential, so I can also read *your* thoughts. I know how much sympathy you have for me. Perhaps you have too much sympathy. You're writing down my winter tale even though you're freezing, with just this little space heater to warm you. This is the second long winter night you've spent secretly here with me, and soon dawn will break. Soon.

Still, before then, you're going to fill that little egg cup with blood for me. Yes, just enough of your heart's blood to fill that fine porcelain egg cup, and I promise not to want more later, not to demand more—don't come too close to me—I'll be content with just a little bit, it's not going to control me. Just a little cut on your hand—not your throat!—and then it will run down into that little cup and I'll drink it while it's still warm. As if it were hot chocolate. Put down your pen. I'll tell you more later. You need tales, just as I need blood. We're almost related. We're twins, you and me. You were sixteen once, weren't you? And you died from being sixteen and abandoned. Part of you died and from what remained you recreated yourself. You understand me. PUT THAT PEN DOWN NOW AND GIVE ME WHAT I WANT—THIS IS NOT A FAIRY TALE!

NORTHBOUND

BY LINA WOLFF

Saltsjöbaden

Translated by Caroline Åberg

Awhile back I decided to join a dating site and created a profile starting with the following description: *I'm thirty-six years old and I'm looking for a gentle, but not too gentle, man.*

Under "Interests" I wrote *none*, under "Favorite Writer" I also wrote *none*. As well as under "Favorite Food" and "Favorite Places." Under "Life Motto" I came up with: *Meeting the man mentioned above.* Then I thought about the word *motto*, that it's probably something else, a sentence or something you could use as your words of wisdom in certain situations. But I've never had a motto like that, so I didn't change it—even though that could say something about me, could reveal a nonverbal side that might repel some people. On the other hand, I wasn't looking for a verbal person.

After I'd written what I'd written, I posted a photo of myself. It's a picture a friend of mine took, where I'm lying on my stomach on his bed. My signs of aging don't show in the photo, because the only light comes from a few candles, and, like my friend says, most people look fairly decent in that kind of lighting.

A week passed before I logged onto the site again, and by then I'd gotten a flood of replies. Surprised, I went through them all, one by one. An older gentleman promised me an economically carefree existence in exchange for his sexual satisfaction three times a week. A twenty-year-old wondered if I could teach him everything I knew. I sat there with my cup of coffee and laughed, but at the same time I felt oddly moved; not so much by all this appreciation (the photo was really a fraud), but because it was clear to me that they all truly and strongly believed in love, and believed that I could give them what they were looking for.

Several more weeks passed before I went back onto the site. But once I did, I noticed that many of the men who had first contacted me had kept writing. Some had written almost every day for weeks. The twenty-year-old who thought I could teach him something almost seemed obsessed, and in one message he wrote: *I've always had girls who just talk and talk, they never seem to do anything but talk, but you feel so genuine, so free from words.* Genuine, so free from words. I liked the sound of that.

I wrote to him: *I guess you somehow send out the message that you like to talk. Try to send another message. Kind regards, M.*

Others had sent pictures of themselves, their cars and their sailboats. One had sent a photo of his organ, fully erect. They all said something nice about my photo, and at first I was flattered, and thought I might not be all that bad. Then I realized there was nothing to be flattered about. No, this was something else, something I couldn't quite put my finger on, that had nothing to do with me.

I replied to one of them: *Thank you for your words, but don't have any illusions about me. I am thirty-six years old, the photo is taken in a candlelit room . . . Here is a real picture.*

I attached a photo of me that I took then and there in regular daylight, the way I was: wearing panties and a bra (although I edited out my head). Without mentioning details I can only say that this picture was not as flattering as the last one, but still I managed to laugh a little at the cooling effect it would have on the man in question. But just a minute or so after I'd sent the photo came his response: *Besides the fact that your age implies that we could have many interesting conversations, and you most likely can cook a good meal (for which I would choose the wine), I'm convinced your body, which I guess has already been enjoyed by many, holds an abundance of possibilities. And your womb is surely a repository of dirty deeds that I wouldn't mind taking part in either.*

You fucker! I wrote back immediately.

But I remained by my computer. Frankly, I was curious about the man who had expressed himself like this. Curious about him, but also about masculinity itself, which I, the more I learn about, understand less and less, but despite this am still fascinated by it—conceptually, but also on a very concrete level. I seriously considered continuing my correspondence with this man. Maybe setting up a date. An adventure like this would have a strong antidepressive effect on me during the dark season we were about to enter.

So I wrote: *When can we meet?*

In three weeks, he replied.

What's your name and where do you live?

My name is Calisto and I live in Stockholm.

Calisto? I wrote.

My mom was Catholic, he replied, but I didn't see how that explained anything.

Your name reminds me of something, I wrote, but he didn't respond. *Okay, so I'll book a train ticket and a hotel*, I added.

You're welcome to stay at my place, he wrote, but I declined.

The weekend Calisto and I had set for my visit was in the middle of December. Two days before I was planning to leave

I heard there was a snowstorm on its way. It would be coming from the south, sweeping in over the country like a broom, covering everything in its way; trees would be falling over electric cables like pick-up sticks. People would be stuck in their cottages without electricity for days, maybe weeks. I compared my train's timetable with the weather report, and came to the conclusion that if I headed north directly after lunch, which was when my train was leaving, I should probably make it *before* the storm. And once it poured in over Stockholm, I would be sitting at some bar, with the wind howling outside, slightly tipsy, with Calisto. Yes, that's how I imagined it.

I took the train as planned. We left Malmö and kept going up through Skåne. Soon there were no more deciduous forests; instead we passed endless clusters of pine and fir trees, occasionally opening up to reveal dark lakes flanking the tracks. Everything was oddly still for hours, and I sat in my seat thinking about what things would be like once I reached my destination. What Calisto looked like, what he did for a living, if we were going to have sex. I fell asleep and woke up when we entered the tunnels south of Stockholm. My ears popped and right outside my window the rock face swept by at a tremendous speed.

Suddenly we were on the other side of the mountain, heading toward the city. The coach was silent and when I glanced around I saw that everyone was looking out the window. It was getting dark and the sky was tinged in orange and blue. We crossed bridges: water, rock faces, and beautiful houses with copper roofs surrounded us. The bodies of water were partly covered by ice and meandered this way and that; in the distance I caught a glimpse of the open sea. Everyone must be happy here, I thought. Healthy people, generations of ice-skating and swimming off the cliffs. They're probably sitting there behind their big windows with fine cups of coffee, looking out over mountains, water, and city with a view unimaginable to the rest of the world.

Once I stepped off the train I thought the people looked resolute and flawless, as if they were all clones from a movie. I instantly felt implacably imperfect. I longed for home, for Copenhagen where the spokes of the Tivoli Ferris wheel are always spinning just where the train comes in, and the smells of urine, smoke, and waffles hover over it all.

I had booked a hotel in the center of town. I checked in, and it turned out my room was in the basement, without any windows. Instead, there was a sauna in the hallway. I sat in it for a long time and then took a hot-and-cold shower before I returned to my room, crawled into bed, and fell asleep. When I woke up it was nine o'clock at night and the windowless room was pitch black. I got up and put my makeup on in the bathroom where the floor was still wet. Then I texted Calisto that I had arrived and was now rested and showered and ready to meet him.

We'll meet at Pharmarium, he texted back. *Sit at the bar and look like you're for sale and I'll find you.*

I asked at the reception desk what Pharmarium was and once I'd received directions I wrapped my scarf around my head and made my way out.

While I had been sleeping the storm had started brewing. The wind outside seemed to crawl along the ground before suddenly spiraling up into the air with gusts of powdery snow. I crossed a bridge and reached another island. The high brick buildings had beautiful copper roofs. Everything was grandiose and picturesque at the same time, and despite the cold and snow, there were a lot of people outside. I reached a square with a church. I circled it and spotted four bars; one of them was Pharmarium. It was located on a corner of the square and the entrance gave off a modest impression, but once I stuck my head inside I realized this was a place I could have chosen myself. The ceiling was low and it was warm. People were crowded together in small groups around low tables and colored fabric was hanging from the walls. As for the rest, it looked like an old pharmacy with wooden drawers that gave an alchemist's air to the place. *Sit at the bar and look like you're for sale and I'll find you.* That was what Calisto had written. I took my coat and scarf off and sat down at the bar. I ordered a drink, told the bartender I wanted his "best," and ended up with a smoky, sour piece of work that I drank fast. Ten minutes later a man approached me and introduced himself.

—Are you Miriam? he asked.

—Yes, I said.

—I'm Calisto.

—Hi, I said.

Calisto was overweight, had greasy hair, and was clearly intoxicated.

—Perhaps you didn't expect me to be this fat, he said a moment later.

—No, I said.

—Are you disappointed?

—Obesity has never been something that's bothered me, I replied.

—Good, Calisto said, and ordered a beer from the bartender. We sat in silence while he drank the beer.

—Will you come home with me now, was the next thing he said.

We walked silently through the narrow streets and eventually emerged on a wide street where Calisto hailed a cab. Then we rode for a long while—through the city, out onto a road that ran along the coast, eventually arriving in an area with large houses perched on cliffs overlooking the water.

—Wow, I said. Is this where you live? What's it called?

—Saltsjöbaden, Calisto replied curtly.

—Are you rich? I asked.

—Rich? he said, as if he didn't understand what the word meant.

—I mean it looks really swanky.

—Swanky? Calisto said, looking out the window. I don't think anyone uses that word anymore.

His voice was different, it sounded like his throat had tightened somehow. I peered out the window again: at the houses we passed, standing there grand and sort of obstinate, with their giant windows magnificently staring out over the water. Then the taxi turned onto a smaller road that continued into the woods. The taxi had slowed down, and we sat beside each other in the backseat in silence. I thought about what he had written before and that there had been confidence in his words, something I couldn't sense now. Had he just been acting? I glanced at the meter but Calisto didn't seem to care. When the cab stopped Calisto paid with his credit card. We exited the vehicle and he took a key out of his pocket and unlocked a large gate. Behind the gate was a wooden house. It was pitch black everywhere except for a dim light that shone from somewhere in the garden. A high, dark spruce forest surrounded the yard, and the sea suddenly felt far away even though it was probably just around the corner.

—Have you changed your mind? Calisto asked.

—No.

—And what if I'm a cold-blooded murderer? he said and laughed.

—The bartender saw us together.

—They see lots of people, he replied. If it really matters they don't remember a thing.

I grinned at him, because Calisto was the type of person who at first glance you'd assume wouldn't even hurt a fly. We got in, took our shoes off, and he showed me around. It was obviously difficult for him to move around with all those extra kilos. The house was sparsely furnished, the walls white. Every time we left a room he turned the light off after us. I wondered if he had a wife or if he had had one. Not that it mattered, and it shouldn't have been a hard question to ask, and still it was a question that seemed off limits with Calisto, as if he and his home exuded a loneliness that demanded respect and distance; as if this was his outlying land, and he was the only one who could find his way here. When we got to the living room he said it felt a bit cold, so he started a fire in the open fireplace. He pulled out a sheepskin rug and held out his hand, gesturing toward the rug.

—You can take your clothes off and wait for me there, he said.

—Excuse me?

—Take your clothes off and lay down on the rug. I'll be right back, Calisto said.

I laughed.

—You think I'm a whore?

—No, I don't. But we both know what's going to happen. And I'm not interested in lengthy foreplay, to say the least.

A gust of wind hit the window and we both turned to look at the same time. But the darkness was thick, and we only saw our own reflections. I couldn't keep from laughing.

—We look so small, I said.

—Yes. Will you take your clothes off now?

I took my clothes off and lay down on the rug. Calisto stood there watching me with his arms folded over his chest. I thought he would lie down beside me but instead he turned and walked out into the hallway. I heard him lock the bathroom door and for a long while listened to water rushing through the pipes. For a minute or so it was completely quiet. I laid there, staring at the ceiling. Suddenly I realized what was funny about his name. Calisto is the name of a Swedish popsicle. I laid there thinking about the popsicle, and about Calisto. I wondered how old he'd been when the popsicle had appeared on the market, and if people with a better memory for names would smile when he introduced himself. The heat from the fire made me drowsy and I must have fallen asleep for a second because when I opened my eyes again Calisto was standing naked in front of me. Like a huge mountain he stood there before me with all of his bodily mass, arms hanging at his sides.

—I have to tell you something, he said, staring straight at me. Maybe I should have told you right away when we started talking, but I was afraid you wouldn't give me a chance if you knew.

—What? I said.

—For the past several years I've only had sex I've paid for.

—What?

—It's been a long time since someone wanted to be with me out of her own free will. You know what I look like. It's not just the weight. It's everything.

He brushed his hand over his body, and at once he looked small, despite all the kilos. Small and, somehow, impotent.

—I've forgotten how to do it with someone who actually wants to be with me, he said, and gave me an apologetic look.

I wished he hadn't said anything about this. I didn't know him well enough to feel pity for him, and what we were about to do called for an easy mood that was impossible to achieve after this type of intimacy. But Calisto didn't seem to have a problem with these barriers, because now he was approaching the rug and lying down beside me. I could smell his scent. It was foreign, but I didn't dislike it.

—Can we just lie here, he said, and get used to the situation?

We laid there on our stomachs with our feet toward the fire. The heat licked my legs and crotch; it was a nice contrast to the hail that was now pelting the large windows. I asked him what he did for a living.

—I'm a literary critic, he said.

—Ah.

I had been hoping he wouldn't be too much of an intellectual. I don't like to talk about literature before having sex; that was not the experience I was looking for. I wanted to make that clear to him, but Calisto had already started telling me about something that had happened to him not long ago. Since he was young, he said, he had admired one author greatly. This author had been the driving force of almost everything Calisto had done, in his life as well as within the field. But now Calisto was over forty and had for some time felt like he was nearing the end of his relationship with this author. He wasn't discovering anything new, didn't feel anything anymore, didn't tread into any new dimensions. And Calisto wanted to discover new things; he was, he said, the kind of person who thinks life without evolvement is an unbearable stagnation. He wanted to *be young* in his discoveries, so to speak. Young, naïve.

—Get it? he said

—Yes.

He kept talking about this naivety; how someone who walked into a forest for the first time *saw* the pine trees, *felt* the air. He wanted, to make a long story short, a new author to look up to. He read lots of things but grew tired of everything after just a few pages. It all seemed so sloppy and stupid. Then he had been invited to an event a few weeks ago, and there, at this event, was the author. This was someone you rarely saw anywhere, and Calisto had never had the chance to get to know him personally. But there he was, in the middle of everything, with a glass in his hand, conversing lightly and openly, as if he was a well-adjusted person, and as if the knots and the darkness that were so evident in his books were all just fake. And suddenly, unexpectedly, the author had approached Calisto, put a hand on his shoulder, and said: *You're Calisto, right? I really admire the work you do. You, unlike many others, actually have something to say.* At the time, Calisto couldn't think of a single article he had written. All he could remember was this piece about burned-down buildings, and when he told me about this, he looked completely confused, as if he himself couldn't remember what burned-down houses had to do with anything, but this was the only thing he had been able to recall. Blushing and stuttering, Calisto had told the author about his admiration for him. The author stood there with his glass in his hand and looked at him compassionately. Five minutes later they were friends. Ten minutes later the author had told Calisto that he would greatly appreciate if Calisto would read a manuscript that he had just finished—a manuscript no one had yet read.

—Sometimes you end up in the middle of a mystery just by chance, Calisto said as we laid there on the rug. Sometimes everything just opens up.

—Have you read it? I asked.

—Half, he replied.

His voice quivered.

—I'll show you, he said. Come.

We stood up, Calisto lit a candle, and I walked behind him through the dark house until we got to his study. It was clean and tidy, just like the rest of the house. The desk stood in front of another open fireplace, and there was a strange sound coming from the chimney.

—It's the wind, said Calisto.

—Yes, I said.

On the near-empty desk there were two neat piles of paper.

—There it is, Calisto said.

He placed the candle on the desktop.

—I'm not sure I should keep reading, he said, and put his hand on one of the piles. I'm afraid the spell will go away. Sometimes, he continued while stroking the top sheet on one of the piles, I don't want to read because then I have to touch it with something so mundane as my hands.

—I see.

—There is only this one copy, he said. The author writes on a typewriter, and he hasn't made a copy.

—Why?

—Because it's too . . . valuable, Calisto said. If he had made a copy something mechanical would have impressed itself upon it.

—Mechanical how? I asked.

—I can't explain, Calisto said. But it's about respect.

—Respect for what?

—The inimitable.

I walked over to the desk and looked at the sheet of paper Calisto had under his hand and read: *Every afternoon he slept, and in his sleep he managed to let go of the reality that had become too tense, too worn out, that could only be released with a complete extinction of conscience.*

—This makes no sense, I said.

—No, Calisto replied, I understand every word.

We walked back to the living room. I was in front of Calisto and I knew he was watching me; that he was summoning up his courage for what was about to happen.

—With all due deference to the manuscript, I said once we were back by the fire, I'm not here to talk about literature.

—You are absolutely right, Calisto said, and laid down on his back on the rug. Now I want you to get on top of me.

I did as he said and Calisto pulled me toward him and tried to penetrate me, but I was tense and the situation with the manuscript hadn't exactly turned me on. It took time for him to enter me and it hurt. He put his hands over my hips and pulled me downward.

—Tell me you're my whore, he whispered. I need to hear it, tell me.

I shook my head. I didn't want to say I was his whore. I don't mind playing, but this was no game to Calisto. I leaned forward to kiss him and he stopped short. His lips were barely parted, but when I insisted with my tongue, his tongue started to find its way into my mouth as well. I could feel him grow bigger, harder, and then he started to touch me again, rougher than before. I sat up again and cried out when he pushed into me. They were shrill and rather silly shrieks, but it got him going, because soon he said he was almost there.

—First I want to ask you to do something, he said.

—What?

—Crawl across a mirror.

No one had ever asked me to crawl across a mirror before. I didn't know how to reply, but Calisto didn't wait for my response, and soon he looked ridiculous walking around with his erection bouncing up and down in front of him as he tried to decide which mirror was best for whatever it was we were going to do. Finally he found one that was long and rather narrow. He placed it on the rug.

—There, he said, crawl over it.

He stood beside me and grabbed his erection and started

masturbating. *What the hell?* I thought, and started making my way over the mirror on all fours, trying to distribute my weight evenly so the glass wouldn't break.

—I have to do you now, Calisto whispered. Stay there.

Then everything went fast—hard and raw. He grabbed me so my knees lifted from the mirror and my whole weight was on my hands. I heard the glass crack, and then I felt the pain in my palms. I screamed out, which only seemed to turn on Calisto even more, because he pushed into me violently and said a bunch of vulgar things that I don't feel like repeating. Eventually he yanked me back and forth a few times, and then let me go, dropping my body onto the glass.

I don't mind a slightly violent act. But when you start hurting each other for real it's sacrilege, because there really is something holy about giving yourself completely to one another that way. You can approach the line, but you need to know when you cross it, and you need to take responsibility. And maybe all this was something Calisto used to do, but this time, with me, he had crossed the line, because I'm not one to take things lightly. I rarely attack first, but if someone harms me, I make sure I respond immediately and forcefully, so I can get closure and move on without carrying around a bunch of old baggage. I had shards of glass in my hands and legs. My whole body ached and when I touched the inside of my thigh I could feel that there was blood there too.

—I didn't do anything against your will, did I? Calisto asked.

—Look, I said, and showed him my hands.

Calisto seemed scared when he saw the glass and blood.

—Shit, he said, then put his clothes on and hurried to the bathroom. Soon he came back with a toilet bag and took out a pair of tweezers. He started pulling the pieces of glass from my wounds, and then he disinfected them. I looked at him while he was working; his face was sweaty and puffy and red, and every once in a while he glanced up at me guiltily.

—You have to let me pay you for this, he said.

—You really think that's how it works?

Calisto let out a laugh.

—What I think is that I have forgotten how to do this, he said. I should probably see someone about it.

—You can pay my taxi back to town.

—That goes without saying. But you'll have to wait until they start driving again, until the roads are cleared.

A little while later we were sitting in front of the fire. Calisto had opened a bottle of red wine and made a salad, which we ate straight from the bowl. We had both showered and I had borrowed a pajama shirt that reached down to my feet.

Calisto soon fell asleep. His large body lay there, completely knocked out on the sheepskin rug. I imagined standing up and kicking him in the gut. A hard, strong kick. My foot with its cuts and wounds would disappear into Calisto's fat. Then he would open his eyes and I would lift my leg and plant my heel right in his face and at the same time I would scream with anger, loud and clear, the scream echoing between the white walls. I knew that if I didn't deal with my need to hurt him, it would remain inside me, sour and dark, and I wouldn't be able to get rid of it once I was home again.

Then I realized there was a much better way to hurt Calisto. I got up quietly so I wouldn't wake him and walked over to his study. I turned the light on: there it was, the manuscript. Lying there like the crown jewel of the house. Standing in Calisto's study with this author's manuscript in front of me was like standing in the middle of Calisto's heart, right before the blood supply, with a pair of tongs in my hand. I laughed quietly. I collected the two piles and carried the stack out into the living room. The fire had almost gone out and I had to blow on it to get it crackling again. Then I burned the pages. One after another I let them float down into the flames. I started at the back, in case Calisto woke up and tried to grab what was left. The fire got going again, as if its appetite had been awakened. I threw the sheets of paper on the fire until the manuscript was completely destroyed and there were only embers left, fully aglow among the ashes. Calisto was lying behind me, his belly up in the air like a mound, his mouth half open, saliva dripping down onto the floor. *Now we're even,* I thought. *Now everything is in balance and I can go back to my windowless hotel.*

I laid down beside Calisto and fell asleep almost immediately. A few hours later I felt him move and woke up. He sat up; then he laid down again behind me and pulled me in. I was sort of *enveloped* in Calisto. I smelled his scent and felt his warm breath on my neck.

—You wanted me without money, he whispered behind me. It's fucking unbelievable. And I hurt you. Can you forgive me?

—It's all in the past, I said.

I had never slept with anyone like I did with Calisto that night. I woke up now and then, heard the snow whip against the windows. The whole time he had his arm around me and breathed down my neck. Even when he was asleep his arm held me tightly.

At seven I woke from a new sound, snapping and reverberating; a hazy light filled the room.

—It's the ice breaking, Calisto whispered behind me.

Before my eyes I saw long, dark cracks that started out at sea and quickly ran through the ice to the shore. Here and there large pools of black water opened up. I put my hand over Calisto's and went back to sleep.

When I woke again it was ten o'clock and the pendulum

clock twanged throughout the house. Calisto stood before me—his face was as black as night.

—Where is the manuscript? he said through his teeth.

—What manuscript?

—I was going to the bathroom and saw that the light was on in the study. I went in and saw that it was gone. Now tell me where it is, do you hear me? You tell me where the author's manuscript is!

—I burned it, I said, as revenge for the glass.

Calisto stared at me. His eyes were bloodshot and the hair that hung down on his forehead looked wet.

—What did you just say? he asked, his voice sounding faint. You said you . . . ?

—Yes, I burned it. It's gone.

—You goddamn . . . Are you out of your mind?

I got up without meeting his gaze. He stood in front of me and breathed heavily.

—Calm down, I said. You could have a heart attack.

—You are completely fucking crazy. Completely . . .

I raised my hand.

—That's enough. I get it. I'm leaving.

Calisto slowly sat down on a chair and put his face in his hands.

—The author is going to hate me, he said.

—I really don't give a shit. And if you want to know my opinion, he wanted to get rid of it. Or else he wouldn't have given his only copy to a stranger. He might not see it that way now, but as time goes by he might come to this realization.

—But what about me? he said, resigned. My reading.

I didn't feel like standing there sharing my theories with Calisto, but I thought to myself that as far as his own reading went, I couldn't imagine there was as much at stake as he thought. If he had read the whole thing without being disappointed he would have just thought he understood something no one else understood. That would have given him a sense of superiority, which in time would have made him even lonelier than he already was. I know something about loneliness: it's not pretty. Calisto in this huge house; Calisto sitting in his tidy study reading manuscripts; Calisto who has to pay for sex; Calisto who laboriously moves his own weight around the house. Calisto being one of the only defective people in this cold, perfect city. And then me, in the middle of all this, just as lonely and defective as he was, but in a completely different way.

I got dressed. Calisto stood watching me the whole time, and when I went to the kitchen to have a glass of water he followed me. I put my shoes on, took my bag, realized I wouldn't be getting money for the cab, but didn't care; I was sure there would be bus stops, even in a place like this. I opened the door and walked out onto the front steps. The wind had subsided and the trees surrounding the house stood tall and straight. This is when he pushes me out and slams the door shut, I thought, but Calisto didn't.

KIM

BY TORBJÖRN ELENSKY

Gamla stan

Translated by Rika Lesser

The phone in my pocket was silent. Cold and dead. I sat on the Skeppsbron wharf while the summer night smiled at me with scorn. A cold, white twilight sun in a clear sky—scrubbed clean, as if to wipe out all traces of a crime that had been committed. I took the phone out of my pocket and flung it straight into the light, without once checking if a new message or missed call had come. I threw hard, right toward the sun, as if I were trying to hit it. With a miserable little splash, a disappointing plop, it fell into the water, while gulls circled and squawked with disappointment that it wasn't something edible.

You'd think that the warmth and the sun that shines almost all night in summer would make everything lighter, warmer, milder. But no. This cold summer night's light over Skeppsbron's old façades and down between the alleys in Old Town makes nothing better. It only makes the shadows denser and the secrets of the alleys deeper. It's probably meaningless to say, but I wanted to do a good deed. I wanted to help. Maybe I did? Maybe the truth is that there's no difference between good and evil, help and harm; in a cold cosmos it makes no difference what we do to one another. Against one another. Yet it does. Still. It must. Allow me, in peace and quiet, to tell you how I experienced it all from the beginning.

For me, Old Town is a part of the city which, with every passing year, loses a bit more of its magic. More and more Västerlånggatan is becoming a tourist trap that could just as well be some random street in Mallorca. The old shops, the musty bookstores, and the shabby little cafés have all been replaced by big clean places, where hardly any Stockholmers sit, not least because of the prices. But you can still manage to find alleyways where time has stood still, and the magic from earlier times lingers.

I'd been sitting up there at Tyska Brunnsplan, on a little isolated bench, reading and enjoying the last remnants of the atmosphere in Old Town, when my phone rang. Unknown number. I don't usually answer these since they're almost always sales calls. But this time, whether out of boredom, loneliness, or maybe hoping a friend would want to go out for a bite to eat, I picked up and answered anyway.

—Hello?

At first a long silence, then a weak voice; I couldn't decide if it belonged to an adult or a child, or of which sex.

—Hello? Who is this?

—Who are you trying to call?

—Don't know. You.

And with a tone that sounded weaker but simultaneously more piercing, more chilling than any I'd ever heard, the voice hissed: Help me! Please, you're my only chance.

—How can I help?

—I'm locked up. Only you can help me.

—You don't even know who I am.

—He said I should call you. Only you can help me.

—Who told you to call me? Where are you?

—Nearby. Here: in Old Town.

—Tell me where.

—I'm not allowed. You have to find me yourself.

—I don't have time for games like this.

—It's not a game. If you don't find me . . . He's coming. Answer the next time I call.

—But . . .

—Promise!

—Okay, okay. I'll answer.

I put the phone back in my pocket, anxious and irritated—not knowing if I should take this anonymous call seriously or not. People always allege that they can hear if a voice is telling the truth or a lie, just as they declare they're able to see if someone is good or evil, clever or stupid. But the truth is probably that in most cases wisdom comes only after the fact. Even old Nazis looked avuncular, and each time a genuine murderer is unmasked, a serial killer who's buried a dozen women in his garden, family and friends always say they had no idea, that he was so nice and polite, but maybe spent a little too much time by himself . . .

The book I'd been reading was no longer a temptation. I opened it, but my eyes couldn't focus on the pages. So I just sat there a little while in solitude and felt the phone in my hand, uncertain if I should leave or sit there waiting for more calls. Maybe this was all an elaborate joke being played on me, or maybe just a prank.

The phone rang again, so I took the call and listened without replying. Someone was breathing at the other end. And then a man's voice could be heard this time, utterly distinct: I know you're there.

—. . .

—I know that it called you. How did it get your number?

—Who *is* this?

—It doesn't matter. How did Kim get your number?

This was more an order than a question, and the tone provoked me more than a little.

—Damned if I know how that child got my number! Who the hell are you?

—Who I am is unimportant. Now it's your responsibility. That's all you need to know.

—Hello? What kind of . . . ?

Evidently the man had turned the phone over to the person he called Kim.

—Sorry . . . I heard the weak androgyne say, while s/he breathed heavily into the receiver.

There was something in the tone of voice and the wheezing that made me take it seriously. Yes, a helplessness, maybe outright pain, which I'd never heard so clearly, so distinctly in a voice, and I couldn't, as reason urged me, end the conversation.

—You have to find me.

—Where are you? I'll call the police!

—NO! If you call the cops he'll kill me.

—Who'll kill you?

—I don't know.

—What am I supposed to do? How can I help you? Don't you have any idea where you are?

—All I know is that you can help me. Maybe. You have to trust me. He says you must rely on me.

The voice sobbed with exceptional vehemence. Someone was subjecting Kim to something.

—What does he do to you?

—You have to do it.

—Do what?

—What he does. It's the only way.

—No. I don't want to. What does he do?

—He owns me. Buy my freedom. That's the only way you can help.

—Have you been kidnapped?

—You don't understand. Wait.

The man snatched the receiver again. His voice was firm and determined.

—Do you want to own it?

—*It?*

—This worthless slave.

—Kim?

—Are you simpleminded? Do you want it?

—No.

—Then it will die tonight.

—Then yes! I want it!

—Then you'll be able to handle it?

—Yes, yes! Just tell me what to do!

—Instructions will come. Keep your phone turned on and the line open.

There was a click on the other end and the conversation was over.

My whole body was shaking. This was like nothing I'd ever been involved in before. It felt like a secret I didn't want to keep had been thrust upon me. And now there was something that connected me with this Kim, and with the man who evidently held her captive. When I looked up and observed the solitary wanderers in Old Town, the tourists with their maps and the natives who knew which side streets to take so they could be alone, I saw them all together from the outside, as if through some kind of thin glass, as if they and I no longer lived in the same world.

Where could Kim be hidden? What was it that had happened? And why was *I* selected to be the one capable of freeing her? It distressed me deeply that the man on the phone had called Kim *it*. It? Like a slave? Though I probably should have been grateful that he didn't say *that thing*.

Should I go home now and wait for the call? Stay in Old Town? The two conversations had forced me to assume a responsibility that burst my frames of reference and created an uncertainty within me that intensified the feeling of solitude that even earlier on this tediously beautiful summer afternoon threatened to eat into my soul. An emptiness that was deep inside of me, and when my desire for solitude had been so completely satisfied I wanted nothing more than for someone to contact me, meet, get a bite to eat, talk, have a beer with me in peace and quiet. Now I'd been given an opportunity that seemed to preclude all others until further notice.

I toyed with the idea of going to the police. They could certainly trace the call and solve this whole riddle without my involvement. But what would I say to them? Even if they took me seriously they'd scarcely begin to make a move before it was too late. I felt in my bones that it could already be too late. It was serious, I was convinced of that. Both the male voice's firm matter-of-factness and Kim's pitiful despair, the entreaty in her tone when s/he said that I alone could free her, were clear and distinct proof, all the proof I needed, that this was serious.

The bench was hard. It chafed and I was sore; I took a little walk through the nearest alleys. Round and round, making little turns. How small Old Town still is. It felt as if I were moving in a little labyrinth, a simple path with no way out, but also with no end, as if the inner space were greater than the outer, with infinite possibilities. Old Town was like a brain, the city's brain, and I was a lone obsession, a song stuck on replay in the head, going around, up and down and back and forth between the small squares and alleys, searching for some way either to get out of this damned part of the city or really get into it.

Evening came, the long, light summer evening, and the sidewalk restaurants filled up with tourists drinking beer and wine and gorging themselves while they believed they were experiencing Stockholm, the Venice of the North. Bitterly I thought that they knew nothing. They saw nothing of ordinary city life, but only this Skansen, this outdoor museum-city re-designed for tourists, which slowly grew out of Old Town and little by little conquered the neighborhoods close by, the area around the King's Garden, known as Kungsträdgården, north-ern Södermalm, places which once had been shabby, dark, with nothing of interest but isolated ice-cream kiosks and dank cafés, now resplendent with green magnificence, well-raked footpaths, special paths with views along the cliff side of Sö-dermalm, Italian-style cafés, and everyone pretending that this was the natural, the normal, the real Stockholm which, in some peculiar way, I'd been reminded of by Kim's conversation. I knew that beneath this smiling city lay a scornful, hateful city deformed by drink, like a cirrhosis of the liver, with its outcasts, prostitutes, drug addicts, all that which must be swept aside at any price so that the illusion of the shiny-clean city could be maintained for all the tourists and, for that matter, all the hicks who'd moved in, who wanted Stockholm only as backdrop for their lifestyle choices.

Who could it be? Had I ever met Kim or the man? Had they called me at random? Fear and anxiety coexisted in my breast with a feeling, not entirely unpleasant, of being chosen. And as the hours passed, the evening became as dark as it could; some-time around midnight, without having received another call, I reluctantly decided to set off homeward and retire for the night. On the one hand, of course I was worried about Kim, whom I thought was my responsibility to save, to take care of. But on the other, I worried that my chance to be somewhat important wouldn't come.

I settled myself in bed. Unfortunately I no longer lived in Old Town, it had become too expensive. Years before I had sublet an apartment, a little studio, on Norra Dryckesgränd, but now I lived way off in western Kungsholmen—a part of town that wasn't exactly thought of as the city but was on its way up to luxury. Gentrification, I suppose. But the process was not so far advanced, and there was still the occasional drunken bum found sleeping in the nearby parks.

Although my body lay in bed, my consciousness was still in Old Town. My disappointment slowly increased, so much so that I played with the idea of saying to hell with all these odd conversations—pretending that I'd never heard of Kim, turning my face to the peach-colored wallpaper from the eighties, and falling asleep—when the plink of a text message sounded from my phone. Instantly I was wide awake and completely present, in the now again, and I read the message hoping to find a new clue. But it was only a text from Krister, who wondered where I'd been. We'd planned to meet up and have a beer with his colleagues in their office which was also in Old Town. Funnily, as long as I'd wandered around there I'd never once walked by their office on Baggensgatan.

Now I was awake and far too uneasy, my body far too restless to return to sleep. So I sat up in bed with my laptop over the covers on my lap and surfed the Internet, just to pass the time until I got tired enough to drop off to sleep again. Everyone knows that you can't sleep if you're sitting with a computer in bed at night, and it was already close to two o'clock in the morning, the sun rising again, so in every way it was a stupid choice. But truly, I had no desire to sleep.

I'd received ten e-mails from an address I didn't recognize.

But I instantly understood where they came from. The address was yourslavekim@xxx.com, so there wasn't any doubt as to what they were about. All the e-mails had large attachments. I was cold throughout my body, alone in the universe, full of remorse for having felt so important earlier, and again I thought of going to the police with all of it.

None of the attachments had names, just long combinations of numbers and letters. I opened the first one, which was a zipped file with twenty photos. No, I didn't want to see them, my forearms were heavy as lead and I really didn't want to look. And yet I looked. A naked body lay on its stomach on something I couldn't identify. Its arms and legs were stretched out and tied up. My telephone number was written on its back. Seeing this image was like having a dagger plunged into my chest. As if I were guilty. Although I didn't yet know of what. Nobody seemed to be harmed, and in any case games like this aren't illegal.

The body looked extremely young. A girlish boy or a boyish girl. I tried to find something by which I could recognize it. Medium-length blond hair. No body hair. Maybe I'd get to see more in the next picture if I looked. I opened the file. Same body position. A rather large man, between forty and fifty, wearing a dark suit and shoes polished to a high shine, dragging Kim—for I assumed that the naked body could belong to nobody else—by the hair so that its head was bent backward. I sensed resistance in the body, which my own reacted to with the uncontrollable tensing of my muscles. The pictures continued with little variation. The body was tied up, the man in the suit drew it taut, pulled it by the hair, pressed his polished shoes against it. And on the body was my telephone number. It was as if I were there. I felt the body's pains in my own, like a weak reverberation. But uglier than that, despite the fact that

I pushed the thought away, I also felt, yes, I actually identified with the corporal grip of the man in the suit, the feeling of the cloth against the naked body, my own hand striking the body while I wore leather gloves.

The next e-mail contained a GIF. It depicted Kim's completely hairless backside, with an anal plug stuck in its asshole. The genitals were carefully covered with something that made it impossible to identify the gender. The body writhed in discomfort and resistance and I quickly closed the file. I then opened the remaining e-mails to verify that they too contained attachments of various sizes, but I didn't want to see them. I shut down the computer and lay down on my bed. First I pulled up the covers, then I kicked them off, now it was too cold, now too warm. It wasn't that I was aroused. I don't get aroused by BDSM or violent porn. But at this point I really had to get some sleep, so I jerked off mechanically in bed, while trying not to think of anything, even though the pictures floated before my mind's eye the whole time. After coming, I turned to the wall and, eventually, drifted off.

After a few hours of uneasy sleep I was awakened by the telephone ringing. I didn't reach it in time and the ringing stopped. Three missed calls. I'd barely slept at all; I'd floated feverishly within different dream scenarios, all of which circled around Kim in myriad ways, somehow not being woken up by the repeated phone calls.

Suddenly I found myself sitting on the edge of the bed. I felt sweaty, filthy, needed a shower before going out. But the restlessness in my body put me on autopilot; I pulled on my jeans and the same, no, a new T-shirt at least, and I went out into the cool Swedish summer-dawn light and began to walk toward Old Town again. The sense that I could be important and must be at hand was so strong that my legs automatically took me all the way back there, along Norr Mälarstrand, the tourist buses to city hall, past the hideous traffic interchange between city hall and the central train station, and over the Vasabron, past the old seats of power—Parliament, the Royal Palace, the House of the Nobility, and the Bonde Palace.

In need of caffeine, I entered Café Tabac, sat down at the bar, and downed a cup of ordinary brewed coffee while I leafed through *Dagens Nyheter*, the morning paper, seeing neither the pictures nor the headlines. The images of Kim being sexually abused somewhere near here, maybe in a cellar just under the café where I sat, had burned themselves permanently into my retina so that they lay like a film over everything I saw.

Something to eat? No. I had no appetite, even though my stomach was completely empty. I put a few sugar cubes into my coffee instead, took the phone out of my pocket, and looked at it, as if I should be able to conjure up a conversation telepathically. And then it actually rang. Quickly, fumbling, I put the phone to my ear, only to hear about a new electric company. I hung up without even saying anything nasty. When I lowered the phone again I saw that a text message had come in at the same time that the salesman delivered his spiel.

Did you look? was the text.

I tried to answer immediately with a simple *Yes*, but my phone wouldn't send it.

Another message came at once: *Do you want to?* What? Rescue Kim? Participate in Kim's torture? It was maddening, being made a party to a conversation in which I couldn't respond.

There's nothing you have to do, but if there's something you want, you must come now. Come where? Once again I felt it would be best if I abandoned the whole business, forgot about Kim, pretended that I'd seen nothing, knew nothing. But how could I obliterate the memory of a body that was forced to assume a grotesque backbend while its anus was opened wide with a speculum and its mouth gagged, plugged with a ball to keep it shut. And there was my telephone number, written on the victim's back.

Like a sleepwalker I wandered back uphill toward Tyska Brunnsplan. The streams of tourists were now more intense on Västerlånggatan even though it was still early in the morning. I sat down on the same bench I'd sat on the previous afternoon. The phone burned hot in my hand. My head was entirely empty, and all my attention was directed at—nothing. Then it finally rang.

This time it was Kim's voice on the other end. It still sounded androgynous and awfully young, but now there was a new tone of despair, as after many hours of crying. And it seemed to lack focus. I wondered whether Kim was drugged, or just groggy from being subjected to sexual torture all night long, without respite. I shoved these thoughts aside, but I couldn't keep fantasies about Kim's treatment from surfacing in my own dazed consciousness, I couldn't defend myself against them, they touched something, a cord inside me. I told myself it was my opportunity to save this creature who so affected me. Yes, this was my chance to be something of significance to another human being.

—Where are you?

—Don't you know?

—Why aren't you here yet?

—I don't know where *you* are . . .

—He says that . . . A scream of pain interrupted Kim in the middle of the sentence.

—What? What's that? What's he saying?

The connection was still there, but it was quiet on the other end. I listened hard for sounds. I could hear weak sobbing, something like a long whimper. It was awful, but it was more appalling to admit that the sound gave rise to a warmth that spread through my chest, as if the blood inside me were rushing violently.

A reflex went through me, quick as lightning, when a window across the square was shut with a bang. Quickly I looked up and tried to get a glimpse of where it came from. Which window had been closed.

—Hello? Hello? I shouted into phone while simultaneously scouting around the façades of the buildings, unable to determine where the window had been slammed shut.

—If you want to free it, you have to own it. To own it you have to deserve it.

—What kind of filthy swine are you? What kind of fucking game is this?

I was stupid enough to be shouting. A young Asian couple with backpacks and an open map looked at me in terror and speed-walked away from Tyska Brunnsplan, down into the alleys.

—Don't play dumb. I know you like it.

—Do I know you?

—I know you, that's sufficient.

—How do you know me?

—Through Kim.

—Do I know Kim?

—You know who Kim is.

—Have I met Kim?

During the whole conversation I continued to scan the façades around the square, trying to catch a glimpse of someone in a window, or some sign of activity that could lead me in the right direction. I understood that they could see me, but I still didn't know who Kim was, had no clue.

—What are you prepared to do?

—What must I do?

—Care enough to want to inflict harm.

—I don't want to hurt anyone!

—Talk with Kim yourself.

For a while there was no sound on the other end of the phone. Then Kim's voice was audible once again.

—Are you there?

—Yes.

—Will you be able to handle it?

—What do you mean? I'll help you. You'll be free, I promise.

—Then come!

This was the most frustrating thing I'd ever experienced. The call was terminated, and I couldn't decide if this was the result of poor reception or if Kim or her tormentor had broken off the conversation. I sat down on the bench, heavily. Not despairing, only resigned, sensing that, yes, the whole thing was merely a game, that they were toying with me. Maybe they were filming me from one of the windows, maybe there was a hidden camera, or maybe this was a trap, an attempt to snare me and then blackmail me by putting me in a liaison with this Kim, or whatever it was they were doing now.

It rang again.

—Why did you hang up?

—We were cut off.

—Okay.

It was quiet for a long time again, and I caught sight of a row of windows in one of the most attractive houses on the square. They were covered with black draperies. As if the apartment inside them was darkened. My stomach was in a knot.

—Are you there? I think I know where you are.

—Then come. Though I don't think you can manage it.

—Manage what?

—You won't manage me. You're too timid.

—Don't be afraid. I'll free you.

There was a new element to Kim's whisper . . . something scornful, challenging . . . which I didn't exactly understand, and since I didn't understand I didn't readily perceive it. Until afterward.

I made my way swiftly, purposefully, to the gate of the house with the covered windows, and tried to open the gate. Simultaneously there was a long, protracted, painful moan over the phone, then we were cut off again. I rang doorbells at random, hoping that someone would buzz me in. But no one answered. In vain I pulled the handle a bit harder, as if I hoped I could force the locked gate open. How would I get in? The veiled windows were on the third floor.

There was a buzzing in one of the speakers, but no one said anything. Neither did I. Then the lock on the gate clicked. I pushed it open and walked in, my whole body cold and concentrated—driven by a determination beyond my experience. Taking two steps at a time, I climbed the old uneven stone stairs until I stood in front of the door to the apartment with the veiled windows. It was unlocked. I held my breath as I slowly entered the apartment. It was empty. Newly renovated, it smelled preposterously fresh in relation to the old building. In two adjacent rooms facing the square, the windows were covered with black cloth. In the middle of one was a massage table covered with a bloody sheet. There were plastic straps fastened to metal rods, which had presumably been used to hold something or someone in place. But the apartment was lifeless.

Blood rushed to my gut. For the hundredth time I cursed myself: certainly I should have called the police at the beginning instead of play-acting detective myself. What was it that had tempted me to try and solve this riddle, decode this nightmare, whatever it should be called? I gingerly touched the table with my hand. It was still damp with sweat, blood, saliva, and several substances I didn't want to think about. My heart raced. They must be somewhere nearby. I wanted to leave, I wanted to stay, I wanted to search for tracks but didn't know where to begin. I wished the phone would ring.

And it did.

—Well done. That wasn't so hard, was it?

He was mocking me.

—Where's Kim? What have you done with . . .

—It?

—Him.

—The slave is waiting. In the cellar. Can you find your way down?

I ran out of the apartment, stumbled down the stairs, down, down, with every step I took there only seemed to be more flights, and I was overcome with a nauseating impression that the stairwell was growing impossibly long, down, down, and very suddenly I came to a heavy iron door, which with great difficulty I managed to push slightly open, so that I was able to squeeze through, coming upon a new landing, which led to additional uneven stairs, and in turn more stairs, down another flight, down, down, farther down in the building, several floors beneath the building itself, all the way down into the cold underworld. Every blind footfall felt like a headlong dive over a precipice. In the end I knew in my soul I was down as deep as it was possible to go.

The ceiling was low. I sucked at the thin musty air, damp from being closed in, with a tinge of mold and an extra tang, likely an ancient sewer pipe leaking inside the walls. I pushed farther into darkness. It enveloped me completely. I was forced to squat so as not to bang my head, the medieval brick vault was so low. I attempted to light my way with my phone, but still scarcely saw anything, nothing more than rusty brown and my own fingers that held the phone before me, as if it were a weapon.

With aching slowness I groped forward, running a hand along the rough walls, until suddenly I detected breathing that was not my own, weak, panting, flickering like a flame in a draft, without strength, nearly extinguished. I reached out, straight into the black. Warm, living skin brushed my fingertips, and I recoiled.

—Is it you? I managed.

—Who are you?

—Is it Kim?

—Who is Kim?

—What's your name?

—I have no name.

—Stop it. Answer.

—It's Kim.

The voice of the man on the phone came from somewhere behind me.

—But you'll be helping *me*.

I spun around and tried to catch a glimpse of him in the light of my phone, but he ducked away from me and receded. From somewhere in the distance I heard the iron door to the cellar close and lock.

Adrenaline was now the only thing that kept me standing.

—What have you done?

—What have *you* done?

—Let me see you!

—Let me see *you*!

At that moment a naked ceiling lamp was lit, and the young

androgyne sat before me, as naked and white as the lightbulb.

—Do you know what you want? s/he asked me with a small, faint smile.

—I want to get out of here. Now.

—Don't you want to rescue me anymore? Don't you want to own me?

—I don't want to be part of this game.

The man in the dark suit, whose face was concealed by a piece of black cloth, now appeared behind the androgye. He placed his hands around its neck.

—If you want to have me, you must take me. Show that you're a worthy owner.

The man pressed harder, and I could hear Kim's breathing stop. Her face turned blue.

—Stop! Stop! I'll do it.

—What? the man asked without releasing any pressure.

—Show you I'm worthy!

He quickly let go and Kim sputtered for oxygen. Now I saw that s/he was sitting, lashed to the old office chair with cable ties.

—I knew you wanted it, Kim said weakly.

—I don't want anything, but I'll do what I have to, I answered.

—Then do it, said the man, and took a step to the side.

For a moment I played with the idea of overpowering him, freeing Kim . . . but he was too big, too menacing. Instinctively, I stepped toward Kim and tried to look dangerous, wanting her to cringe and shrink from me. S/he tittered, and I slapped her, which made her laugh out loud.

—What was that?

—Shut up!

—Can't you do it?

The man stood in the background with his arms crossed over his chest and remained silent. I looked at him, but he just nodded at me.

—Again! s/he challenged me.

I struck another blow, harder now, with an open hand.

—Make a fist, you fucking faggot! Kim hissed at me, as if s/he were the one who was making a threat.

I clenched my hand into a fist, gave him a good solid shot in the face, which knocked her head backward. S/he quickly recovered, stuck her tongue out at me through a bloody nose.

The man standing by looked more and more exhilarated. *Perverted scumbag,* I thought, and punched the androgyne in the stomach so that s/he gave a fast hard expulsion of air.

—Is that enough?

—You'll learn to tame me. You'll own me.

—I'll set you free!

—Don't you understand anything? He's the one you'll set free.

I prepared myself. Struck again. Gave in to some sort of primitive, violent desire I didn't know I had. The androgyne's challenges spurred me on. I'm ashamed to describe in detail all the things I did, but a torturer serving in Pinochet's military police force would have been proud of my effort. This continued for a protracted period of time that I was incapable of measuring, for I was sucked out of time itself, out of myself, into some sort of vehemently malicious personality that welled up out of my depths, beyond language, beyond emotion, beyond civilization and judgment, and finally beyond me, although it came from my truest self, from my deepest interior, like magma within a volcano, with the same indifference to life and death.

In the end s/he went silent, and I gently removed the plastic straps, stroked around the wounds, held Kim close to me, while tears, wholly foreign to my experience, trickled from the corners of my burning eyes. This, and a strange, deep satisfaction, made me forever a stranger to myself. The androgyne comforted me all the while, petting the nape of my neck.

—Can I go? asked the man who'd been quietly watching the whole time.

—Yes. He'll pass.

Then I lost consciousness.

I woke up on Skeppsbron to the creeping light of a summer dawn. I was born anew. A void, empty.

The phone was cold and dead . . . I threw it into the sea, as if to liberate myself from the fever dream of the past twenty-four hours. Though I didn't for a moment imagine I'd be spared more conversations in the future. I understood that I'd taken the man's place. And worst of all, what I tried hardest to defend myself against, with the pathetic gesture of hurling the phone away . . . was the knowledge that I'd enjoyed it. Already, I anticipated Kim's next call with the most sublime pleasure.

BLACK ICE

BY INGER FRIMANSSON
Södertälje

Translated by Laura A. Wideburg

J ust a feeling, the impression that she was not alone in the house. The grandfather clock chimed twenty past eleven. She intended to go to bed.

Just as she was entering the bathroom, a short, loud bang came from the basement. Maj Lindberg knew her home, she'd lived in it her entire adult life. She was intimately familiar with all the creaks, groans, and sighs of her old house built of wood and brick.

But this was entirely different.

She switched on the hallway light and walked to the stairs leading to the bottom floor.

"Hello?" she called out. "Is anyone down there?"

Of course there was no reply. Her fingers gripped the railing tightly as she started to make her way down. Step by step. Once she reached the bottom, she turned on the light. The laundry room, the guest room, the hallway—all appeared normal. She lifted her head and sniffed the air like an animal, flaring her nostrils. Was someone there? A scent? Something or someone that didn't belong?

The front door downstairs was locked. There was another door at the other end of the hall leading to the garage. It was ajar. Strange. She was sure she'd closed it. Every morning she checked the boiler. She knew she'd done so that morning. She switched on the garage light. Empty. The boiler banged away as usual in its corner. The Volvo, the apple of Hasse's eye, was parked in its normal place. She looked inside the windows. The key was in the ignition. Last week she'd driven to the superstore to shop for groceries.

Nobody was inside the car. Nobody hiding in the backseat.

She hadn't expected anyone there, really. But what was that noise? Did she imagine it? Anneli had been saying lately: "You're starting to get forgetful, little Mama. Soon you'll be forgetting your own name."

Maj shook herself, closed the door leading to the garage securely, and walked back upstairs to her bedroom. She hadn't felt frightened while she went on her reconnaissance mission, more bewildered. Now fear swept through her like a wave. She was gripped by a longing to clutch her cats. She wanted them to follow her into the bedroom and jump on the bed, to curl up next to her and warm her.

The cats never joined her on the bed.

She knew they were inside, as she'd enticed them indoors with sardines. They'd slid onto the porch like two thin shadows and crouched in the darkness. She wanted them to stay inside all the time these days. People said cats were being stolen for dog-fighting bait. Just the thought made her dizzy. One evening, she'd tried sealing the cat door shut with masking tape, but they'd gone crazy. The tape hung in bloody strips the next morning and the cats were outside.

For days after that incident, the cats acted in an odd manner. They slid along the walls and refused to be touched. They jumped whenever she stood up and dashed under the sofa. Even Kitten. Kitten was now a grown cat, but she was used to calling her Kitten, so she didn't bother calling her anything else. How old was Kitten now? Maj tried to remember. It had been after Hasse's death. A mother cat and a kitten. Somebody had found them on a balcony in Fornhöjden. Three other kittens had died. The owner of the apartment had been away in Thailand for a number of months, abandoning them, or so Maj had been told.

Lovisa had brought the cats in a cardboard box. There was the sound of scratching and mewing. "Here, Grandma, they're for you! Now you won't be so lonely!"

Her granddaughter was a true gift from God.

She closed her eyes and tried to fall asleep. It didn't work. Her entire body was tense. Perhaps she should call Anneli. No, that would make both Anneli and Johnny even more eager to move her into a retirement home.

"You'll have your own apartment and you'll get all your meals served. You won't be so lonely."

I'm not lonely, she thought. *I have the cats. And this is my home.*

Johnny usually sat down next to her and laid his heavy arm, pale as death, around her shoulders. "Anneli and I will help you, of course. Little Maj, you understand we're here for you. We'll sell the house for you. We'll fix it up and make sure it's presentable. We'll make sure your move goes smoothly. You won't have to think about anything. You can relax in your new armchair and watch your favorite TV shows, *Bingolotto* and *Så ska det låta*. Just enjoy yourself and take it easy."

Just wait for death, she thought.

She tried to force herself to yawn. Sometimes she could encourage sleep that way. She'd yawn and get a lungful of air. She'd curl her tongue into a bow and let the air be drawn over it.

Then she heard it again. Noise downstairs. Rustling, like shuffled papers and footsteps.

She was suddenly angry. Who dared come into her house and disturb her in the middle of the night? Get the hell out! Now! She flung her bedcover aside and leaped out of bed. Blood rushed hotly to her temples. She grabbed her umbrella with its sharp pointy tip. She started down the stairs, but then the fear caught up with her. How would she, a lone woman, attack a burglar? What if there were more than one?

She heard Johnny's rant inside her head: "Fucking Turks. They hate us. They think we have it so good . . . as if we got everything for free. As if we didn't work our asses off. They want everything for free! Soon they'll take over the whole town!"

It was true that Södertälje had taken in a great number of immigrants from Iraq, from Lebanon, from Syria. More than the United States and Canada combined.

She protested: people in a free and peaceful country like Sweden should open their doors and welcome these despairing human beings fleeing poverty and war. She remembered the images she'd seen on TV: mothers with dark circles under their eyes; children filled with sorrow.

Johnny would stare at her, eyes so filled with disgust that it quieted her.

"Yeah, yeah, just fling our doors wide open and let them move in. You could fit a whole herd of them into this big house. So why don't you?"

His words made her speechless.

There was no one inside her house. Of course not. Her mind was playing tricks on her. She'd searched every nook and cranny, even the space behind the boiler until her nightgown was covered in soot.

She decided to sit up for a while. Perhaps doze in her new armchair. It was a wonderful chair: soft and wide. She'd gotten it as a birthday present last year. She walked past the kitchen and picked up a few pieces of candy from the bowl. Peppermints. Anneli had brought them the other day. They seemed like a bribe. She'd seen through the pretense right away. It didn't take long before Anneli turned to the subject of the house.

"For my sake, if not for yours!" Anneli leaned forward, grasped her hand, giving it a squeeze, and then with a small smile, she continued, "I'm worried about you, Mama! Don't you see? Anything can happen."

Maj had gotten angry. "Listen to me! This is my home. Try to understand that I feel just fine right here. I want to stay."

"But Mama, it's so big. It's hard to manage. You can't count on me and Johnny coming by to help you cut the lawn and fix things up!"

"And I haven't asked either of you to do so, have I?" she replied. It was true. She'd been handling the lawn, garden, and house all on her own.

Her home with Hasse—all their lives, they'd lived here. The house was built on a slope. The main floor opened to a wonderful view. The basement level was open to the outside, with a large garage door and a second entrance. Counting the huge attic space, it was three floors, really. And although they had to fight gravity to do the gardening, the view was incredible.

Maj had always loved the house. Anneli was right that a few small problems would become big problems given enough time. But not just yet.

The house was at the top of a hill, and it had been harder for her to get outside these days, especially in the early winter when the snow had been plowed from the road and left on the sidewalk. Or in late winter, when melting snow on the road iced over—black ice, people called it. You thought it was wet asphalt, but it was frozen. At her age, if she fell and broke something, it could all be over.

Maj walked into the living room. As she was sitting down, she spied the keys—the standard one for the front door and the long one for the garage. They were centered on the flower-patterned tablecloth. She stood and stared at them for a moment. She would never toss keys on a table. Never! Leaving keys on a table brings bad luck—everybody knew that.

Her heart beat like tiny, quick feet. Had Lovisa been here? Had her granddaughter borrowed the keys for some reason? No, not for a while. Had Anneli used them? No, not for days. Her hand trembled as she reached for them. They belonged in her purse. She'd recently gotten a large purse, which could be slung on her back like a miniature backpack, and it had a pocket for keys. She always put her keys back into her purse after she'd used them.

She felt a dizzying sense of anxiety as she walked over to the window. She could see the lights from the AstraZeneca building on the other side of the canal. She liked the way they glittered on the water, making her think of Manhattan. Farther up the hill, she could see the apartment buildings in Ronna. They were part of the "million homes" scheme. These days very few people spoke Swedish as their native tongue, and Ronna was a known immigrant area and as infamous as Rosengård in Malmö—neighborhoods with a greater percentage of criminal activity, including shootings and murder. The name sounded harsh to her ears, even though she knew the original meaning was pleasant. Ronna meant *running water.*

A rhythmic throb made her turn her head—a boat, one of those large container ships, heading between Lake Mälaren and the Baltic Sea. The lantern at the prow seemed to her a sharp, glowing eye. The tower of its bridge passed by a bit later. She had a childish desire to wave and call out: *Here I am! Can you see me? Hello!*

When Lovisa was small, Maj had often taken her in her baby carriage and walked along the side of the canal on the way to the locks. She'd pick up Lovisa and show her to the men in their orange overalls. They'd wave and make faces at her. *Boat* was one of the first words Maj had taught her. Yes, in fact, *boat* had been her very first word.

The vessel passed and the water was now as smooth as a pool. Maj felt exhaustion wash over her. She moved away from the window and into the bedroom, turning off the lights as she went. The stairs to the basement level were a huge, gaping maw of black.

Once she'd returned to her bedroom, she realized she'd forgotten to brush her teeth.

"Don't care," she muttered to herself, a flutter of defiance in her chest. She took off her dirty nightgown and found a new one. She stood and stared at her naked body in the mirror with a sense of resignation. Thin limbs, a stomach poking out, and breasts that no longer did. Her pubic hair had almost disappeared. She grunted and shut her eyes.

The bed creaked as she settled into it. She pulled her nightgown over her feet to warm them. Her body finally began to feel heavy. She took a few deep breaths and was just about to drift off to sleep when the noise returned. A bang and then scraping sounds, as if someone were moving around the house. She heard it clearly coming from the basement hallway. She opened her eyes and lay fully awake. Anxious. Empty.

Could it be the cats? No. The cats were always silent. Mama and Kitten. The thought rose as a scream, desperate and silent, inside her mind: *Mama, Kitten, come here and be with me!*

A dog could defend itself. Defend her too. Cats lacked that kind of loyalty.

She hesitated before turning on her bedside lamp.

Had she forgotten to lock the front door after all? She had checked, hadn't she? Or had she just thought she'd checked? The papers were filled with reports of burglaries in Södertälje. People were supposed to stay alert.

"Hello?" she called out. "Anyone there? Come and show yourself!"

For a moment, she thought it might be Hasse. She slipped back in time and Hasse was returning home after a night out with the guys: a night that lasted into the wee hours of the morning. They'd meet in someone's garage and work on their cars together. She could see him standing on the hallway rug, wearing his grubby, oil-stained overalls, his large hands hanging at his sides.

After his death, she'd seen him a number of times. Not imagined him—she'd *seen* him. Once he was sitting on the side of the bed with his face, filled with love for her, turned in her direction. She hadn't been the least afraid. Another time, he was on the stairs to the basement. He'd stood and watched her without saying a word.

"Hans? Hasse?" she'd whispered, and it felt as if all the blood had drained from her head so quickly that she became dizzy. "Hans? Is it really you? Are you here?"

She'd grabbed the railing and begun to walk down. "Wait for me! I'm coming!" Then a bolt of lightning had seemed to go through her skull—sharp, fire-red flames. She didn't dare mention the visions to anyone. One day, she read about the phenomenon in a magazine. It was called *änkesyn*—widow's vision—and it was fairly common. Nothing to worry about.

Her feet felt like blocks of ice. Where were her slippers? She usually put them beneath the chair where she hung her clothes. She couldn't find them. Strange. She always put them there, side by side, beneath the chair. In bare feet, she snuck into the hallway. The floor had loose gravel on it, small grains that pressed into the soles of her feet.

"Kitties? Mama Cat? Kitten?" her voice cawed like a crow.

She almost reached the bottom of the stairs.

"You're imagining things!" she said aloud to herself. "Pull yourself together! Otherwise you'll find yourself in a home whether you like it or not!"

She walked back up to the main level for the third time that night. *At least I'm getting my exercise!*

As soon as she reentered her bedroom, she understood something was wrong. Hasse's bed. She always kept his bed made. His cover was thrown back as if he'd just gotten up to pee. She caught her breath and then let out a dry, rattling cough. She was truly frightened now. Her entire body was shaking.

Is Hasse here? Is my dead husband here in the house? She moaned and her hand went to her throat. *What does he want? Does he want to hurt me?*

I have to call someone, she thought. *Anneli, I have to call Anneli.*

She stared at Hasse's bedcover as she headed to her nightstand. Her red cell phone had extra-large buttons so she could easily make out the numbers. Anneli had gotten it for her. Normal phones were too difficult to use.

She picked it up, but her shaky hand dropped it immediately. It hit the wooden floor with a bang.

She knelt down to look for it, quickly realizing it was unusable as it had broken into two pieces. She pushed the two halves together and put it back on the nightstand. Tomorrow she would see about getting a new one.

For now, she had to pull herself together. She glanced over at Hasse's bed. There had to be a logical explanation. There always was. Perhaps she had moved the bedcover herself without noticing it. She might have gone into Hasse's bed instead of her own. She missed him, she was freezing, she longed to be with him. It must be that simple.

She moved his pillow to her bed and propped it up behind her back. In this half-sitting position, she eventually fell into a fretful, dreamless slumber.

Maj woke up at dawn. By the subdued gray light, she judged it to be about six. She got up, dressed in her long pants and the thick sweater she'd knitted many years earlier, before her arthritis had gotten too bad. She brewed some coffee and opened a can of cat food.

"Kitties!" she called out. In spite of having sardines yesterday evening, they should be hungry by now. Still, entire days could pass without them eating anything. Perhaps they found food somewhere else. Once she'd discovered a half-eaten rat foot outside the front door. It had flesh-colored toes with tiny toenails. She'd felt nauseous as she swept it up and dumped it in the garbage can.

She touched the lid of the bread bin, but decided against it. She had no appetite. She stood in front of the window as she sipped her coffee. The light outside grew brighter. She heard the sounds of a motor—the newspaper deliveryman's yellow car, slipping and sliding along the asphalt. She adjusted her glasses and took a look at the outside thermometer—it hovered around freezing.

Finally day broke. She began systematically searching each room of her house. If someone had been inside, she would detect it and then she would contact the police. The kitchen seemed undisturbed. So did the living rooms. The pillows on the sofa were in their proper places. The potted plants were drooping—she had to remember to water them more.

She walked to the top of the stairs that led to the basement. She listened and imagined Hasse downstairs. He was busy with the boiler. He'd soon walk up, scratching his cheek as he always did when he was unhappy about something. The scratchy sound stubble made.

"Something's wrong with the boiler! I can't get the heat going!" he'd call up to her.

She'd sigh. "So what should we do? It's starting to get cold. There was frost last night for the first time."

"I know," he'd reply angrily. She'd hear the decisiveness in his voice. He wouldn't give up.

Maj headed to the bottom level. The hallway was dark; it seemed the lightbulb had burned out. Dumb. She'd have to ask Anneli to come and change it for her. It was too high for her to reach, and Anneli had a good sense of balance and could stand on a chair. Perhaps Johnny could come. He was good at fixing things. Still, she didn't like to ask him for anything.

I'll be fine, she told herself. *It's only a small thing. It can wait.*

Maybe Lovisa could come by? When was the last time Lovisa was here? Of course, she was busy with school. She was in her senior year and would graduate in the spring. Her dear grandchild. Johnny had children from his first marriage too, a pair of sinewy, silent boys. Twins. She would offer them cookies, but they'd always refuse, shaking their heads and saying nothing.

"All children love cookies!" she said out loud, and then was surprised at the sound of her own voice.

She caught sight of something down there—she couldn't make out what it was. She returned upstairs to get her flashlight. She found it in her junk drawer in the kitchen, but the battery was nearly dead. Still, it was enough to shine a weak beam down the stairs. She swept the beam back and forth and spied something on the third step from the bottom. One of her slippers! One of her own slippers that she'd carefully set beneath the chair in her bedroom when she'd gotten undressed last night. A percolating effervescence filled her skull. Had she been wearing her slippers when she'd gone downstairs last night? No, she remembered she was barefoot. How had it ended up here? And where was the other one?

The cats, she thought. *Strange, but it must have been the cats.*

She picked up the slipper and pressed it against her chest. She aimed the flashlight at the ceiling, where the old pipes ran like rough intestines. Everything seemed to be in order. She inhaled air through her nostrils, making a weak, whistling noise. She pushed down the handle on the door leading to the garage and the smell of oil hit her. She turned an ancient knob and the garage was filled with blinding fluorescent light. It shone over the car. She slid into the driver's seat, shifted gears, and turned on the ignition. The motor started immediately. It had always been dependable. Hasse's old cap was in its place as always, as if he'd just set it there, as if he'd just parked the car and was heading up to the kitchen for a cup of coffee.

A short scream resounded within her eardrums. It took a few seconds before she realized it came from herself.

"What am I doing?" she said out loud. She straightened up and heard her spine creak and pop.

She'd just turned off the motor when she heard footsteps above her on the main level. Her heart began to pound. She spied the axe in the corner. Nobody had used it after Hasse had passed away. She got out of the car, picked it up, and snuck back through the laundry room.

Yes, someone was upstairs, all right. She saw a pair of muddy shoes. She could taste iron in her mouth.

"Hello? Anyone up there?" she managed to croak.

"Mama!"

Relief spread through her like a warm wave. "Anneli? Is that you?"

Her daughter's face was red and glowing. "What are you doing, Mama? Cutting wood?"

"No, well . . ."

"Why didn't you pick up the phone? I've been calling over and over. I started to worry. You have to pick up the phone, Mama! You have to pick up when people call you!"

"I dropped it on the floor and it broke in half," she said, suddenly remembering what had happened.

Anneli raised her shoulders. She was tense and stressed, standing in the middle of the hallway floor. "How could it break in half?"

"Go see for yourself." She gestured toward the bedroom, but Anneli shook her head.

"I believe you. But now how am I supposed to reach you?"

"I'll just have to buy a new phone."

Anneli shook back her dry, henna-dyed hair. "No, I'll take care of it. But I don't have time this week."

Maj stepped closer to her daughter to give her a hug. Just to show she loved her. They were still mother and daughter. They would always be mother and daughter. Until the end of time. But something in Anneli's rigid stance made her draw back.

"I've got to get going." Anneli glanced at the clock in the kitchen. "Is that the right time?"

Maj nodded.

"Mama, have you thought about it some more? You know . . ."

Maj's stomach clenched. "About what?"

"Really, Mama, it would be so much easier for me if I knew you were all right. If I knew there was someone who could look in on you, someone who made you meals, and all the rest of it. You have to try to understand my side, Mama. I can't just pick up and leave work when you don't answer the phone. Things are difficult right now. There might be more layoffs."

"Sweetie, you don't have to worry about me, I'm doing just fine—"

"But for how long, Mama? How long? You have to think about the future too."

"We'll cross that bridge when we come to it."

Anneli grimaced. She looked tired and worn. Her jacket had frayed along the bottom edge.

"Wait a moment," Maj said. She went into her bedroom and opened her linen cabinet. She moved a heap of pillows aside and took out a few hundred kronor from their hiding place. "Here. Take this and buy something nice for yourself. Spoil yourself a little."

Anneli turned her face away and mumbled something Maj couldn't hear.

Maj stuffed the bills into Anneli's jacket pocket. "Go on, so your boss doesn't get angry at you. I'll be fine. I promise."

Maj stayed inside all day. The cats too. They came out to sniff at their food bowls, but she never saw them eat. She wasn't hungry either.

Anneli worked at Scania. She was one of the ones able to keep her job after the layoffs a few years back. Still, Anneli had had to take a wage cut. Johnny had also worked at Scania, which was where they'd met. He'd been one of the ones who lost his job.

"You should find someone else," she'd grumbled to Anneli. "My daughter deserves a better man."

Maj decided to lie down and rest for a while. A strange despair came over her and tears welled up in her eyes. She hardly ever cried. Not even when Hasse was in the hospital and they moved him to a hospice room, and she'd realized what that meant. Not even then!

Their black-and-white wedding photo hung on the wall in the bedroom. They looked so incomprehensibly young! Shy and expectant. Where had all the years gone?

She pulled her blanket over her and shut her eyes. Perhaps she slept. Yes, she must have fallen asleep in the mix of wool and warmth. When she opened them again, it was dark. At first, she didn't know where she was. She tried to sit up, but her tailbone was aching and she felt a stab of pain that made her cry out. This happened sometimes. It must be age.

What time was it? As if it had read her thoughts, the grand-father clock began to strike. She counted the strokes—it was nine. Nine at night? Must be. It was dark outside. Had she really slept the day away?

She was thirsty. She walked into the kitchen and switched on the light. She was just about to turn on the faucet when she saw what was on the counter. Her wedding picture. She and Hasse on their wedding day. Fear shook her shoulders. She swallowed hard and stared at the bouquet of roses in the young girl's hand—the hand that had been her own a very long time ago.

At that moment, she heard a loud bang on the stairs. Terror struck her with great force. She saw the cats had crept beneath the table and pressed against each other. Their eyes were wide and filled with fear.

"You heard it too, didn't you, kitties?" she whispered.

Kitten got up and his tail hit the floor hard a few times. He crept toward her on his silent paws and wound around her legs.

Mama Cat had also gotten up and moved toward the kitchen door. She raised her back and all her fur stood on end. She hissed. Her brushy tail swished. Her ears flattened.

"What is it?" Maj asked. Her voice was shriller than she realized.

The cat bared its teeth. Maj saw its canines, its fierce predator stare. She could hear the pleading in her own voice. She tried to calm down and speak quietly.

"You're not in danger, kitties. You don't have to be frightened. I'm here to watch over you."

She tried to turn on the light in the hallway and remembered the bulb was out. Where was her flashlight? It was no longer in her junk drawer. She found a paraffin candle and some matches. *This is the way people lived in the olden days,* she thought. *People survived without electricity. They were fine.*

Her hand gripped the candle as she started to walk downstairs. The flame flickered and she noticed her own shadow grow. She was in stocking feet. She felt dampness on her foot and lowered her candle to see. It looked like blood.

Something is seriously wrong, she thought. Someone was there. Someone was trying to scare her on purpose. Someone wished her ill. And this person, whoever it was, was here inside her house.

She hurried back upstairs and grabbed her purse. She glanced inside, saw her keys and money. She added a few cans of cat food. She put on her coat and her heavy outdoor shoes.

"Come, kitties, come with me," she called them. To her relief, they followed her. "We're going on a car ride." They had to flee. She decided to leave through the upstairs front door.

Of course, the police, she thought. *I have to go to the police. They can come and search the house and find the intruder. They'll arrest him for sure!*

With difficulty, she managed to raise the garage door from outside. Hasse's Volvo was right there, waiting for her. She opened the back door and the cats jumped in. They settled intertwined on top of Hasse's cap.

She got into the driver's seat, pressed down the clutch, shifted into reverse, and hit the gas.

The door slammed. Anneli leapt up from her chair and stumbled into the hallway.

"Johnny?"

He was pale and traces of blood had spread beneath his nose.

She wanted to cry.

She watched him take off his sneakers and head right for the kitchen. He opened the cupboard door, took out the vodka bottle, and poured himself a drink.

"Want some?"

She nodded.

Johnny sank down by the kitchen table. He pushed aside the newspaper and took a swig. "Damn, it's slippery outside. Sirens were going off constantly out there."

"They announced the dangerous conditions on the radio."

He pointed at his nose. "But I didn't slip on the sidewalk. I fell on her goddamn outside stairs. This hurts like hell!"

"Poor thing," she said. She took a sip of vodka. It both warmed and burned her throat. "What about . . . ?"

He gave her a wry smile. "My nose kept bleeding all the way to her door. I had to rummage around inside the house to find something to stop it."

"Did she notice you inside?"

"She kept getting up and looking around, just like last night. Up and down the stairs like a yo-yo. But she never saw me."

Anneli covered her eyes with her hands. "I hate this. I hate all of this."

His glass slammed down on the table. Drops of vodka flew out. "Don't think for a moment I don't hate it too!"

"I know . . ." she whined.

"We both agreed to this. So don't start saying it was all my idea."

She shook her head heavily.

"It's for her own good!" he yelled.

A short sob escaped her throat. "Yes."

"And we need the money. We need it now! Not two years from now. Not a decade from now. Right now! With that view, we can get four to five million."

"I know."

"If only she hadn't been so stubborn We had to do it. She forced us into it."

"Yes."

He lowered his voice but still did not look at her. "She'll be fine, Anneli."

She pulled a paper towel off the roll and blew her nose. "Yes," she said again.

The doorbell rang. A sharp, demanding sound. They stared at each other. She saw fear in his eyes.

Don't open it, he mouthed.

But she'd already gotten up and was looking out the peephole. Two people were standing outside. One man and one woman. She opened the door.

The two people pulled out their police identification.

"Are you Anneli?" the policewoman asked.

She nodded.

"May we come in?"

She stepped aside to let them past. Something had happened. Something worse than she'd imagined. She turned around, glared at Johnny.

"I'm afraid I have some bad news," the policewoman said. She had short, almost stubbly blond hair. "It's your mother, Maj Lindberg."

A white blaze lit her skull. With a wail, she began to pound Johnny with her fists like hammers.

"You bastard! What the hell did you do to her?"

He did not defend himself. He shrank; became soft and small.

She felt the policewoman grab her shoulder. She quieted down.

"Let's sit down for a minute, shall we?" the policeman said. "Let's all be calm."

Anneli pulled out a cigarette. Her hands shook as she lit it. She inhaled deeply and kept staring at Johnny. He looked at the floor. Blood had begun to drip from his nose.

"What did you just say?" asked the policewoman. "What are you talking about?"

Anneli shook her head.

The policewoman remained silent for a moment and stared at her. "Well," she finally said, "again, I'm sorry to be the bearer of bad news. For some reason, your mother was driving—"

"My mother never drives. Never! Not at night."

The policewoman gave her a look that managed to be both sharp and sympathetic. "I'm afraid she was driving tonight. Do you have any idea why she would leave home on a night like this?"

Anneli took a deep ragged drag, wanted to scream.

The policewoman's voice came from far away, as if it were a mournful chant: "She must have had some reason. She had two cats with her in the car. None of them . . . well, it's extremely slippery outside, black ice, you know. It comes every year, but still takes us by surprise. So your mother, well . . . she lost control of the car and drove off the road by the bridge . . . Must have been an hour ago . . . and I'm sorry to inform you . . ."

PART III

The Brutality of Beasts

THE WAHLBERG DISEASE

BY CARL JOHAN DE GEER

Drottninggatan

Translated by Laura A. Wideburg

Those nights on Drottninggatan! The building was an island in a sea of ruins; soon they'd be erecting Celsing's bombastic Culture House, including an artificial pond with a huge phallic sculpture made of glass, surrounded by spraying water. Though at that time, there was nothing but a huge hole left by demolition, noisy by day and gloomy by night.

Drottninggatan 37 is in the center of Stockholm, now mostly known for a shoe store called Jerns. The original building was from the eighteenth century, but it had been rebuilt many times. In 1964, I had access to rooms there on the top floor, previously an old photography studio once used by the legendary photographer Arne Wahlberg. An enormous sloped glass roof over the main room let in plenty of light. Several smaller rooms had been used as storage space and an office.

I wasn't actually renting the rooms. I'd run across an old friend and colleague, a fashion photographer, who'd rented the place with what in those days was called a "demolition contract." He'd just moved out, relocating his studio to a more permanent address. We were having a beer at Löwenbräu, at the time still located on Jakobsgatan, just a block from Drottninggatan.

"Take them," he said, tossing a key ring onto the table. "The building is completely abandoned. They'll start tearing it down pretty soon. You can hang out there for now. The light is good. You'll have to figure out the keys on your own."

The building had been designated as a historical landmark by the Stockholm City Museum, which gave it some protection—at least, as far as the façade went. When I walked in, the abandoned shoe store seemed spooky. I had to go through it to get to the stairs. Shards of glass and unswept gravel covered the floor. In the evenings, the atmosphere was desolate and the crunching noise my shoes made echoed in a creepy way.

If you want to see what it was like, you can go to the library and look at page 49 in my photography book *The Camera as Consolation: Part One* (published in 1980). In Wahlberg's former studio, my closest friends and I set up a ping-pong table. We met every Thursday at three o'clock in the afternoon. Håkan, Pierre, Staffan, Jackie, and me. We'd have little tournaments, and Staffan always won. When he was a teenager, he'd played for the team Engelbrektspojkarna. We should have realized that it was a bad omen: that our previous meeting place for ping-pong, the Co-op Union's abandoned slaughterhouse and sausage factory, had burned to the ground one year before. The flames had eaten up our ping-pong table, complete with its net, paddles, and balls. We had no way of knowing that the same thing would happen again.

So I ended up spending lots of my time at Drottninggatan 37, high up on the sixth floor, working on my barely existent photography career during an extremely unhappy period in my life. I often had to stay in the building overnight. It wasn't always easy. I realized right away that candles would be too much of a fire hazard. And flashlight batteries were expensive. Sometimes I'd have to choose between a Spartan dinner or a working flashlight at night. Earlier in the fall, things were more or less fine, since there was still running water and electricity, but as winter approached, the utilities were cut off. Soon I'd have to abandon the place.

As I said, it really wasn't easy sleeping there. I would lie down on a lump of old clothes that smelled bad. I heard strange sounds in the supposedly empty building. I knew some homeless men lived here and they were restless at night. They had it rougher than I did; they slept right on the broken glass and trash. It was a real hell. They'd light fires in old tin cans, which made me nervous. They also snored. The most alarming sounds, however, were the determined footsteps coming up the stairs—and the knocking on my door. Then I'd grab my bag containing my ten-year-old Hasselblad 1000F. I'd gotten it cheap when Hasselblad released the 500C and all the professional photographers dumped their old 1000Fs—their shutters were loud and unreliable.

The sound is easy to imitate: *cla-DUM-hiss*. If that last hiss did not come, the shutter had frozen, which meant the shoot was over. I also had two magazines for 120 film, a Linhof tripod, and a Lunasix light meter. My camera bag was always packed so I could take off whenever I wanted. My only other possessions were a thermos and the clothes on my back.

The neighborhood around my building, with all its condemned and half-demolished buildings, did not invite strolls at night. I'd read that slums incited people to crime—a belief the psychologists and doctors of Sweden had held for a long time. According to them, this is how it worked: in these slum quarters, children and young people ran around without control, they'd shoplift, fight, and vandalize. A certain doctor by the name of Beijerot kept trumpeting this on television debates and in newspaper articles. Slums are vectors of criminality, he believed. The obvious cure was to tear them all down. I think he confused cause and effect; a rather common problem then, just like today.

Then a new concept came along to replace the old one: modernity. The city politicians, listening to the doctors, got caught up in the spirit of the times. Old buildings needed to be torn down because they were in the way. Highways were to be built through the city, opening it up to light and fresh air.

One night, smoke came in from under my door. I have never woken so fast in my life. I rushed down the stairs to locate the source. Broken furniture and heaps of old newspapers were burning in the stairwells of the fourth and fifth floors. I grabbed some fire buckets filled with sand (complete with small spades), part of the obligatory equipment of any office in those days. It was possible to put out small fires with them, which is what I did. I was coughing and sweating, my face and arms covered in soot, my clothes torn ragged by the time I got back up to the sixth floor. I opened all the windows I could and stood there for a long time, breathing in the city's cool night air. I still had hot water left in my thermos, so I went to make coffee in another room. I used freeze-dried coffee, which I liked a lot back then. I also wanted to appear to be modern.

In those days, the old patriarchal society was falling apart. Changes in trade and manufacturing during the end of the fifties meant that many men (and it was mostly men who worked outside the home then) were losing their jobs. They comforted themselves with alcohol and, in their frustration, sometimes they beat their wives and kids. However, a new social structure was coming into being. Women started to demand, and get, divorces. If there were children, the women had the right to keep the apartment, so their former spouses were out on the street. Some of those became alcoholics with no other place to live but the street and they often met an early death. Perhaps it was a just punishment for treating their wives and kids so brutally.

When I was young, I loved cars. I had a Ford Prefect, one of the worst vehicles ever made, which was a somewhat larger version of the Ford Anglia, also just as bad. The Prefect was a four-door and I'd bought it one day when I'd managed to scrape together eighty kronor. It didn't last long. It wasn't Mr. Frost's fault. This homeless guy had chosen to sleep in its backseat one chilly night. This car was so tall and narrow it had gotten the nickname "Hot Dog Stand." The reason Mr. Frost (yes, that was really his name) could sleep there at all was because he was constantly exhausted. Whenever I'd go on an errand, he would be there in the backseat.

We didn't talk much. I'd try to give him food, sandwiches, but he'd refuse them. He would just vomit up all real food. His alcoholism was so far advanced that the only calories he got were from sweet strong wine. He found it himself. I did not want to go to the State Liquor Store and get it for him. I looked young, so I had trouble buying alcohol. The cashiers mistakenly believed I was just sixteen with a fake driver's license. I was, in fact, ten years older. Anyway. Once I was driving up the Western Bridge heading south when Mr. Frost got scared and started screaming. Smoke had begun to fill the inside of the vehicle, and I quickly opened the retractable front windshield, a feature not found on later models. (This one was from 1953.) Air streamed in but it made no difference. Cutting off the engine while still going up the bridge would be a mistake, I thought, but as soon as we crested the top, I let the car roll down to the Långholmen exit. Thanks to the fact that we still drove on the left in those days, I was able to pull off immediately and I parked the still smoking car on a piece of lawn. (Right-hand traffic was introduced three years later, even though a large majority of the Swedish population had voted against it.) When I opened the hood, I saw that a bit of rusty metal had fallen on the battery and shorted it out.

I abandoned the car where it was, and Mr. Frost and I hoofed it, somewhat unsteadily, through the city (images of destruction beneath white powdered snow) back to Drottninggatan 37. I let him in, and he disappeared immediately into the office of the former shoe store. Afterward, I stopped locking the front door. I was never sure how many individuals this saved from freezing to death on the streets; at least they could have a roof over their heads.

In the forties, Arne Wahlberg started getting migraines whenever he had to focus his camera. When I found that out, I began to call it the Wahlberg Disease. There was just one way to focus a camera in those days: you had to slowly turn the lens. On larger cameras, you'd expand or contract the bellows using a rack-and-pinion system until the image appeared in focus on the ground-glass screen.

As a photographer myself, with the same tendency to get migraines, this wasn't surprising. Straining the eye to focus the camera could set them off. You never get used to migraines. My siblings had them and so did my mother. Still, you got used to one thing: the nervous anticipation that, all of a sudden, it could go *bang* inside your brain. So I felt fine with the idea that the man who'd been here before me had suffered from the same illness. In the end, Wahlberg's migraines forced him to give up photography. I hoped I would not be stricken by the same fate.

I slept so uneasily on Drottninggatan, I would wake to make nightly rounds. I soon became familiar with each and every corner of the building so that darkness was never a problem. The shoe store and its offices on the ground floor. The import firm on the second floor. The former lawyer's offices on the third floor. The strange firm on the fourth floor—I never figured out what it had been. And "mine" on the sixth floor. All of it a laby-rinth. Each room had its own smell.

Everywhere, except on my floor, were sleeping men. The rumor of an unlocked building spread and so the number of homeless men was growing. Bundles of men wrapped in blan-kets and rags. Some of them talked nervously in their sleep. Others seemed to plunge straight into unconsciousness. Mr. Frost was one of the latter. I felt I was being a good person. By leaving the front door unlocked, these individuals were saved from sleeping outdoors. One night, I even counted them: there were thirty-seven.

My own living arrangements were a bit marginal for some time. I had moved from one temporary address to another. It's funny how memory can trip you up when it comes to years gone by. I remember 1964 to 1967 as three years of loneliness, filled with paranoia and masturbation. But if I check the facts, I was actually married during those years—in fact, I got mar-ried twice. And I remember relationships on the side as well. I remember one woman, also married, who would sneak off from her job as an office manager to meet me at number 37. Per-haps you're wondering why I wasn't living with my wife if I was, indeed, married. But I couldn't live with her, even though we were friends, because she, too, was homeless. In those days she was living temporarily at the apartment of a writer on Väster-långgatan in Old Town.

By the age of twenty-six, I was riding a career roller coaster. I was part of the cultural life of the capital city. The marriage, if you're still wondering about that, was not exactly burning brightly. Although we weren't living together, my wife and I, we'd get together for work. She was in the theater and was an excellent fashion model. The fashion house Mah-Jong bought our photographs. We hadn't gotten around to getting a divorce, because in the late sixties people didn't bother with empty conventions like that.

I had built a somewhat precarious living as a photographer by visiting the editorial offices of all the magazines in Stockholm, showing them my photos. And on those occasions, I would make an effort to seem like a congenial coworker. Some editors gave me small assignments; they would test me and then try someone else. In those days, everyday transactions were done on a cash basis. Whenever I'd been given a job and delivered my pictures, I'd go to the cashier and pick up an envelope with bills. I usually thought the amount was too small. My ability to use a camera was greater than my ability to fit in with the job and its jargon.

This jargon had no words for the ideas I turned over in my mind—for example, the words to seriously define the problems with/of photography. The most important of these was the one most often ignored: the psychic energy needed for each photograph. They say when photography was invented, around 1840, many people refused to be photographed as they believed the camera would steal their living souls and leave them as empty shells. In a way, that is true. But it's not the subject who becomes an empty shell, it's the photographer. Every exposure demands concentration. I did not use a flash (my technique was based on natural light and the steadiness of the tripod), but the inside of my own head flashed each time I hit the cable release. Migraines lie in wait for every photographer.

Another issue in photography: the subject is flattened and always smaller than reality. Larger prints don't help; the real landscape or cityscape is at all times larger than the print.

Theoretically, a portrait could be different. August Strindberg, when he contemplated opening a portrait studio in Berlin, had the theory that the human soul could be captured only if the negative was the same size as the subject's face. He had written a short story he would read while the picture was being taken. The person sitting for the photograph had to remain perfectly still while the photographer (in this case, also the writer) would remove the cap from the lens and then put it back on it after the last line was read. The story, therefore, became a timer replacing the mechanical one. The story lasted twenty-five seconds. Strindberg's homemade lens was as slow as the glass plates of the 1880s. The negative format was probably 24 x 36 cm and the glass plates had to be specially made. Not impossible, this required painting light-sensitive emulsion onto glass plates in a darkroom. On the other hand, he could never get his homemade camera—with a simple lens from a kerosene lamp—to work. You can have many plans—but not all of them will be realized. Just ask me.

Capturing the range of exposure is another problematic factor. Think of a room right before twilight—outside the window a street is lit by the setting sun. For the person inside, it is easy to differentiate both the light outside and the darkness inside, thanks to the human eye's exceptional optical range. Now think of a photograph. It's necessary to choose an exact exposure. If the outside is clear, the inside is black. If the room is clear, the outside is completely white, or *washed out* as we professionals say.

But I had my subjects—not portraits of people, as I was much too inhibited for that. Strindberg's excellent ideas about a portrait studio were not possible for me considering my own level of expertise. But cityscapes, where people appeared at a distance, that was my specialty. I saw them, but they didn't see me. I liked to study their movements in an almost scientific way.

The movements of people. Yes. Very interesting. Perhaps you remember the old theory that cars about to turn didn't really need their turn signals? The beginning of the turn, that subtle initial indication, the slight deflection of the front wheels as they turn to the left or to the right, should be enough for other drivers to know what would happen. People's walking movements can be interpreted in the same way. That man there will soon turn—or stop; that woman with him—or not—are they walking beside each other because they are friends or colleagues, or are they strangers who just happened to be walking near each other at the same moment and will soon head in different directions? All of this is endlessly fascinating. You could draw them as figures on a graph.

One November day, the snow-covered but sunny Drottninggatan outside my window felt like the right choice as my photographic subject. An f-stop of 16 and five hundredths of a second. In spite of the strong light, mysterious figures seemed to sneak about trying not to be seen. I wanted to capture them, list them, make it clear to myself what was about to happen. But in the photographs, they were always turned away. Then I decided to take pictures of the room instead. The window became a rectangle without detail. The floor covered in glass shards and dirt. The furniture smashed. Artistic pictures, perhaps, but to what end?

The spirit of the times: the realization that injustice was exploding in countries all over the world demanded that stenciled pamphlets must be written and distributed. The subjects included Vietnam being bombed by the United States and France, with an independence movement in the North. Spain, Greece, and Portugal—dictatorships all, with Portugal fighting a gruesome war against the independence movement in their colony of Angola. Latin America, where many regimes relied on torture. South Africa, with its unsustainable apartheid system. Just a few examples. We young people were outraged by all the neglect and oppression going on in the world. Perhaps we were less observant when it came to the disparity on our own streets.

During the evening, I would observe the movements of the people outside my window and develop my own theories. On the other side of Drottninggatan, all the buildings had already been torn down. A large construction site was extending in all directions around a gaping pit in the center to form a so-called super-ellipse. The remaining residents had to use temporary stairs and wooden walkways. These were rebuilt every week and were not easy to navigate.

The patterns that people made, evening after evening, interested me very much. Three men were different from all the others. They seemed together and yet were not. They moved stealthily as if they did not want to be seen. They spied and wrote down secret things in their black notebooks. I would sketch them and their movements. My sketchbook was filled with page after page of identical labyrinths. I called them the Three Wise Men. Agent Caspar, Agent Melchior, and Agent Balthazar. The patterns they made would form the letter Z or the number 8. What did they want? Sometimes a fourth person would appear, a woman in a brown dress and a small hat. She seemed to be their boss. In my notes, I called her Maria. She'd use slight tilts of her head to indicate to the other three where they should go.

The late fifties and early sixties were an odd time in the history of Stockholm. Huge swaths of downtown were demolished. It was the largest rearrangement of an inner city in Europe, especially for a country that had not been bombed during the war. That area we now call "city" looked so much like a war zone then that my pal from art school, Håkan Alexandersson, and I made a short war film there in 1960. In those days, every household in Sweden had received a brochure called *If the War Comes* about the dangers of falling atomic bombs. We titled our film *Until the Fire Is Out* due to the ridiculous advice in that brochure which in our minds minimized the danger. *If your clothes start to burn, roll on the ground until the fire is out.*

One afternoon, I had a desire to search for any of Wahlberg's leftover negatives and—with the help of a crowbar—I broke open a Masonite wall to find a closet-sized space of about two square meters. Both walls had cracks. The space itself was empty. Of course, it felt only natural to test one of the cracks with my crowbar. A layer of broken bits fell to the floor. Dust flew up and I couldn't see much for a moment, but when it settled, I found a very old door. *Crack!* The crowbar did its work; the door fell toward me and I jumped out of the way. The dust had to settle once more before I realized I'd found an old passage to the building next door, Drottninggatan 35.

There were a number of conspiracy theories in those days. One of the basic theories speculated that the owners of Stockholm's old buildings let them decay until tearing them down would become inevitable. Repairs and renovations were held off until it was too late to do anything. Over eight hundred buildings were torn down in Stockholm from the midfifties to the midseventies. Most of these had been constructed in the eighteenth and nineteenth centuries. Very few were considered part of our cultural inheritance. One exception was my building, Drottninggatan 37, which, of course, was irritating for the developers. All they saw was space to exploit with a protected building in their way. That they would go so far as to set fires to the buildings themselves—that was a theory that even I, a diehard Communist, found hard to believe.

All that time, I had to force myself to believe that there had to be a reason for the social heartlessness in Sweden, the architectural helplessness in Stockholm, and my own situation.

Actually, I have to say that my paranoia was proven justified, because I came to be interrogated by two policemen who wanted me to confess that foreign powers had employed me to bring anarchy to the streets. They had three possible employers in mind: Albania, Cuba, or China. I was brought to the police station on Kungsholmen and I would probably have laughed in their faces about the absurdity of the accusation (these poverty-stricken countries couldn't afford anything like this) if the policemen hadn't been so intimidating. They placed me on a small chair in the middle of the room—well, I've described this matter in detail before. It had to do with an art installation I'd had at Galleri Karlsson, a little space near Odenplan. And I was declared guilty by the judge, but not for spying, as the police had hoped. Just for desecration of a state symbol and for agitation. The latter stemmed from a lithography where I'd written, *Betray your country, don't be nationalistic.*

I was prepared to be followed after I left the police station. I kept my eye out for agents, peering from a window on the second floor, a window in the same abandoned office where I'd met my married friend. Agents in American films have black suits, ties, and dark sunglasses. Not in Sweden. Here they sport what we call *leisure wear* in English. Light gray jackets, brown pants, black shoes with rubber soles. Perhaps a water-repellant hunter's cap with a small brim—you know, those hats you can fold up and put in your pocket in case you need to slightly change your appearance. For the same reason, the jackets could be worn inside out. Their clumsy shoes, for larger-than-average feet, always gave away who they were. At Galleri Karlsson, we had called them "Säpo's Art Club."

At first they didn't scare me. But one evening at twilight, as I went through the floors of my building, I found about ten kerosene cans behind a stack of empty cardboard boxes. I'd lived in other places that had kerosene heat, but kerosene was not used in Drottninggatan 37. This very building, where I stood with my flashlight, had no kerosene furnaces. It had had water circulating in a central heating system before it was all cut off. No utilities in the building were functional. I had a moment of clarity. The Three Wise Men! The increase of arson! That's how the final destruction of historic buildings would be handled.

A bad night. I tossed and turned constantly. My broken sleep was then interrupted by a thundering sound. I got up, fully dressed as always because of the chill. Smoke was seeping into Wahlberg's studio, the second time this week. Definitely not a coincidence. I was coughing as I ran to my emergency exit—the door I'd found hidden in the closet, the one leading to the building next door. I could hear screaming from the floors below. I stumbled in the darkness, tripping over all kinds of garbage. I found myself in the decaying attic of Drottninggatan 35 before I had any time to think. I'd left my camera case behind. My Hasselblad, the ping-pong table—all gone. Like the paddles and ping-pong balls. Just like before.

Perhaps those skulking men committed murder. Perhaps not. In extreme situations, certain emotions, like empathy and indignation, disappear. Those screams from below, they came back to me afterward, much later, as an extra-horrible detail in my memory. I should have acted differently. I should have opened the door to the stairway and found the others, shown them the way out. Mr. Frost, with his weatherworn face and his silence, comes to me sometimes at night. I'd heard his screams before, in my car. Did I hear them then? A few minutes have been erased from my memory. In a smoking world, a person can become a robot on autopilot.

The building was later rebuilt with a poured-cement façade

to imitate its original wooden one. Behind this façade, there's a modern office building. On the ground floor, there's an elegant shoe store.

I still feel, even after such a long time, that nobody takes me seriously.

NINETEEN PIECES

CARL-MICHAEL EDENBORG
Slakthusområdet

Translated by Caroline Åberg

19

—No more now, miss. That's enough.

My swollen face in the mirror stares back at me. My mouth speaks without intention. My pupils are pistol muzzles, my forehead beaded with sweat, jaws working. There are furrows in my brow that go so deep the ice-cold restroom lighting doesn't reach the bottom of them.

My dry lips part again.

—Just a little more.

I shake my head, take the wallet from my purse; with trembling hands I manage to open the zipper, take out the stamp-sized paper envelope, stick my finger in it, lick off the bitter, putrid powder, rub the last of it into my gums.

—Keep it together, Bengtsson!

I clench my teeth. My lips pucker. A denture sends a sharp pain into my jaw. I clear my throat, put the wallet back in my purse, and leave the restroom. My half-finished beer is there on the counter. Branco looks at me with lazy eyes as I swallow the last of it, washing away the acrid with the bitter.

—What do I owe you?

It's a running joke of ours. He snorts. A few free beers is a good price for a friend at the CID.

—News?

—Someone sent me a piece of flesh at work yesterday.

—Human?

—I hope not. Would make a nice Sunday roast. Three kilos.

—Three kilos. Big roast. Bring it here and I'll give it to the chef.

I button my coat and use my cop voice, joking in yet another familiar way

—What's going on here?

—Nothing much, Branco laughs, his fat head rolling on top of his shoulders.

I leave Tucken and step out onto Götgatan, get in my Ford, and head off, through the rain, to work. My jaws are tense. I pop a couple pieces of chewing gum in my mouth. The alcohol warms me up from the inside; the speed cools me down from the outside.

A thick, low blanket of clouds has been pushing down on the city for weeks. The light never makes it through. I pull out a cigarette and open the window, but change my mind as the raw air slaps me in the face; I roll it up and keep going through the fog.

18

Holmén meets me in the hallway outside my office, his face even more red than usual, one of the many drunks on force.

—You're late, he says.

—I've been on a stakeout.

—There's another package.

—For me?

—Pretty disgusting.

—Define disgusting.

—Intestines, a liver, kidneys. It's all been sent down to Linköping.

I close my eyes and shake my head slightly.

—What kind of sick bastard is this?

—Maybe you should find out.

—Of course.

I open my eyes and stare at the tall, thin man.

—I'll do it for the meat. I want to know where he gets meat so cheap he gives it away.

Lame joke.

Lame laughter from Holmén.

17

The news reaches me around three in the afternoon the next day. I'm close to solving the crossword puzzle in *Expressen* when I hear shouting in the hallway. I finish my bathroom business and go out to see what it's all about.

Holmén, redder than usual, babbles.

—Linköping says human, no doubt about it.

Two older men yawn, a younger talent opens his eyes wide:

—Dismemberment!

Holmén continues:

—And the murderer sends it all to Inspector Bengtsson! The third package contains parts of the back muscles and the left arm.

I march over to them. My boot heels click on the dull linoleum floor. Holmén cackles:

—Who do you think's been murdered, Bengtsson? And who's the murderer?

—Your mom. Both of them.

The two pale ones giggle with a hissing sound. Holmén turns even redder, lowers his voice:

—The boss wants to talk to you.

—I've heard that one before.

* * *

When I enter Superintendent Gunnarsson's office he's looking fresh in a black suit and tie, with his bare feet up on the desk and a pained look on his blurred face. I close the door behind me.

—Your feet hurt, darling?

—You can't imagine, Aggan. Sit down.

He lowers his feet, straightens up in his chair, turns his computer so I can see the screen. On it there are photos of the three packages, my name clearly visible in print, and as a colorful detail: their insides—red, white, and grayish.

—Why you?

—I guess I have a secret admirer.

—My feet hurt like hell.

—You question some poor runt again?

—Those where the days.

—Always the feet.

He stands up and paces around the room a couple of times. It looks like he's trying to rub the soles of his feet against the carpet.

—Some bastard killed another bastard and sends the leftovers to you. At any moment now *Expressen* will be calling. Can we try and solve this shit right away?

I shrug.

—Want a nip?

I say nothing.

He pulls out the bottom drawer of his desk and removes a bottle and two glasses. We clink our glasses and empty them.

—That felt good.

—Roof?

—If you have some.

He puts the bottle and glasses back, stuffs his feet in a pair of rubber boots that are too big, then we take the fire escape to the roof. I give him a cigarette from my pack of red Prince, he coughs after his first drag, spits something inhuman onto the tar paper between his feet, and puffs on:

—They're complaining about me drinking at work.

—People have always been drinking at work. How else would you stand it?

—I can count on you, Aggan.

—You can count on me, Gunnarsson.

We look out over Kungsholmen—it's hazy and raw and cold, the city hall tower is lost in the fog; I'm not wearing a coat over my sweater, and I'm shivering.

—Who the hell would want to send you pieces of human flesh?

—Who wouldn't?

The superintendent pats me on the ass and laughs. I laugh too. We finish our cigarettes in silence. When we are on our way down again he mutters:

—Try and fix this, will you?

16

My cell phone rings. The display shows *The ex.* I hesitate but answer. The old man snorts on the other end. I hiss at him to calm down.

—It's Peter.

—Yes, I figured that out.

—He ran off again.

—That's what you usually say. But he's not a minor anymore.

—He hasn't been doing well lately.

—What do you want me to do about it?

—Look around? Maybe he's back with the druggies. He's your son too.

—I'll see what I can do.

—He's your son too.

—I heard you the first time. But honestly, I don't give a shit about him, the same way he doesn't give a shit about me.

—The two of you should talk.

I'm about to say something nasty, but realize it could be the speed that's making me irritable and so I clench my jaws. After a while I hear a sigh.

—Why are you so curt, Aggan? Why don't you come over for a coffee or dinner? I have wine.

—I'll get back to you.

I kill the image of his sheepish face on the display with the push of a button. I finish my beer. Branco offers to fill it again; I place my hand on top of the glass.

—Never more than two glasses when I'm driving.

—How's your family?

I shake my head and take out a cigarette. The bar owner continues:

—And the flesh packages? All over the news this morning.

—There's probably one waiting for me right now.

—How come you're so popular?

—No idea. But you have some friends from back when. Maybe you can check and see if they know anything?

—Not many left. Most of them have moved back home.

—But you know people. You can ask.

—I'll ask.

15

—Times like these make you miss the old post office. We've tracked the four packages; they were all mailed from various tobacco and grocery stores in Stockholm suburbs, no obvious patterns, and no one who was caught on camera, except possibly this anonymous person you can see here on this beautiful Hollywood-style footage.

Superintendent Gunnarsson fiddles with his computer; the projector comes to life and shows a grainy black-and-white surveillance video from a small corner shop, to judge by the looks of it. A person draped in a large coat, with a baggy, knitted hood pulled up over the head, and large sunglasses leaves a package, pays cash, and exits. The whole time the person's head is carefully turned away from the camera.

—What does the salesperson say?

—She doesn't remember anything. *Package not so heavy is what can remember,* is about all the inspectors got out of her.

Gunnarsson pronounces the testimony with a heavy immigrant accent, which makes some of our colleagues in the room laugh and other sigh irritably. No one has anything to say until Holmén raises his hand.

—Sex? Age?

—Nothing.

—Maybe it's a queer, Holmén says jokingly, so nervous his voice almost cracks.

I'm the only one who laughs. I don't understand why the embarrassing fuck doesn't give up. Same thing every time: I'm the only one who laughs.

14

When the sixth package arrives the whole headquarters takes on a half-heated, half-exhilarated atmosphere. And I'm at the center of it. I don't like it. Wherever I go to get some peace and quiet, I am assaulted, everyone from Kling and Klang to little gay investigators from the sex division who want the dirt on the investigation. I almost avoid powdering my nose or having a beer altogether since all eyes seem to be on me.

I can't get away either. Gunnarsson calls me into his office from time to time to ask me this or that, urges me to solve the case, looking for company over his gloomy bottle, wanting to share a cigarette on the roof. Holmén bustles about, trying to get the investigation's sluggish, unruly team to cooperate.

No one has a clue what they're doing.

There is surveillance on all post offices in the county. It's expensive as hell. But the sixth package, which contains a big fat piece of a right leg, from the toes all the way up to a few centimeters over the knee, is delivered by hand. The interrogations with the delivery guy don't amount to anything either.

They establish that each package weighs exactly 3.2 kilos. The murderer, if it is a murderer, is careful about the weight. I was the one who opened the first brown box in my office. It was wrapped in ordinary brown paper, with a hemp string tied around it. Inside the package there was a plastic grocery bag from Lidl, sealed with silver tape. Within that bag there was another clear plastic bag, containing the meat. There was hardly any blood; the body must have been thoroughly drained before it was dismembered.

The rest have looked the same. The ladies down at the post office are scared out of their minds. The most recent packages haven't been opened here, they've been sent directly to Linköping.

This case could be an opportunity for me to show my colleagues that I'm not as useless as they often imply. It could give me a little shine before my retirement; not many years left. I can see the headlines: *She Solved the Case of the Three-Kilo Murderer: Aftonbladet Has Het With Inspector Agneta Bengtsson.*

I adjust my stockings, fiddle with the butt of my pistol in its holster, and leave my office, headed back to Tucken to see if Branco has found anything.

13

—Let's see what we've got.

The man from internal investigations is small and thin and clean-shaven. He is dressed in a tight navy suit and a light blue shirt without a tie. His colleague is a younger woman, blond with a ponytail, navy wool sweater, pearl earrings.

I despise her instantly. As if the hatred I feel for all of her partners isn't enough: those petty, sly police officers that go after their own, leave the rough stuff on the streets, and think of themselves so goddamn highly, shining knights of morale and equality.

Besides, the bitch just glows Upper Östermalm snobbism. I give her the evil eye; her neatly plastered face doesn't flinch.

—As Inspector Bengtsson is the addressee for all seven packages, we have started an internal investigation.

—What am I under suspicion of, officer?

They look at each other briefly. He clears his throat and continues:

—All day yesterday and most of today we have been going through your files—all documentation, your jobs, and so on. And, well . . .

He turns his head and looks at his colleague. She can't help smiling, the spoiled bitch. He remains serious and keeps going:

—We haven't found any serious incidents or complaints from the people you've investigated and interrogated. On that point you seem to be doing a good job. A very fine job, even. You haven't been accused of violence or other violations more than a time or two, which is uncommon. Most other colleagues on the force tend to have some clients who find themselves treated badly during their early years. But you've made it through without incident.

—Is that bad?

—We're looking for people from your past who might be holding a grudge, who might want revenge. But no matter where we look, we can't find any obvious enemies. In fact . . .

He turns to his colleague again. She puts her hand over her mouth to cover up her smile. But her eyes are pearly with laughter. Those two have something going on. The hatred shoots up through my body. The man looks at me again.

—Like I said, the fact is, we haven't found much at all. We can't seem to find that you've achieved much of anything worth mentioning during your twenty-eight years on the force.

I clench my fist so tightly my nails dig deep into my palm.

—You've been part of a great deal of investigations, but we haven't found anything that indicates you were instrumentally involved in any of them. You've solved a few cases, but they've been remarkably simple. It's beyond both of us how you ever became an inspector, how you advanced from patrol lieutenant at all.

I clench my jaws so tight I can feel a tooth chip in the lower right side of my mouth. It feels like it cracks straight through to my jawbone. The pain shoots out from my forehead all the way down to my cunt and it's so sharp I want to scream, but I don't let out a sound. The man doesn't seem to notice my reaction.

—So obviously we're wondering if you yourself might have any clues that you could help us out with.

I manage to utter:

—I'll think about it.

I get up so quickly my chair falls onto the floor with a loud bang. The two civilians jump up; the man makes a quick note. I march out into the hall, straight to the restroom, lock the door, and take out my wallet. My heart is racing, I'm so furious I almost don't manage to get the zipper and the little bag open. But once I can taste the bitter powder that smells like detergent on my tongue, I say to myself: *You've got to get through*

this, Bengtsson, you've got to get through this. But first: the dentist.
Fucking lousy teeth.

12

New day, new flesh. Eight packages now. Many pounds of flesh for the Jew.

I'm called to the superintendent's office again. He's barefoot this time as well, rubbing his soles against the carpet like a cat with dirty paws. We share a drink, he pats me on the butt; I have no idea why he does this.

—Tell me again what we know, Aggan.

—Man. Dead a week or so. Dismembered and packaged in pieces of 3.2 kilos each. So far there are eight packages, all addressed to me for some goddamn reason. No tattoos, distinctive birth marks, or scars. Dismembered with a sabre saw, according to Linköping. Hardly a professional tool: laciniated edges, torn-up veins and nerves, unraveled muscle fibers, splintery bones. No doctor or hunter, I'd say.

—No. So not a real pro, that is. Or maybe it's a real pro who wants to hide it. I just wish we could smoke in here.

—Roof?

It's raining. Those brownish-gray clouds are heavier than ever; the November air is hardly breathable, it's too heavy and packed with darkness.

—They're complaining, you know.

—The internals?

—A lot of talk. You're a good lady, Aggan. Never disappointed me.

—What do they want?

—Yeah, well. I've asked myself that question many times. What do the internal investigators want?

—They have nothing on me.

—That's the thing.

—You know I've worked hard all these years.

—Of course, Aggan.

—I can do this.

Superintendent Gunnarsson's eyes usually look like two oysters rotting in their shells. But now they tremble and reveal something that could resemble life.

—You can do this?

—Trust me.

He takes a deep drag and waves his cigarette in front of my face. The bastard even smiles.

—I knew it!

A heavy drop of rain lands right on the ember and puts out the half-smoked cigarette with a quick fizz. Gunnarsson curses and laboriously lights it again.

—How did the dentist appointment go?

—He yanked it out. All junk. Glad to be rid of it.

—Hasn't that happened before?

—Third tooth. He says it seems like I'm chewing.

—Chewing what?

—Chewing myself.

Gunnarsson shakes his head with a worried look.

—It's a tough job, sweetheart.

—I guess so.

—You need to take care of yourself.

—Sure do.

Gunnarsson has one last drag.

—You have to take it easy.

—I will.

11

The ninth package arrives by taxi. The driver walks into the

204 // Stockholm Noir

police station with it tucked under his arm. Within ten seconds he's surrounded by police officers and searched.

There's not much to say about the one who handed the package to the driver. The person was dressed in heavy clothing, the head wrapped in a large knitted scarf, big dark glasses. A couple of officers drag the taxi driver into an interrogation room, scold him, scare him to death, and let him go.

In the package there is a thigh.

10

I'm on a stakeout. Sitting in my Ford, smoking and sipping on a Pripps beer while watching the house across the street. Svante Witha P lives on the top floor; an old-time gangster in a dirty little pad used by anyone and everyone for crashing, drug use, and mail fraud. There are ten names on the door.

No one opened when I knocked half an hour ago. I'm about to give it another try. I have my expandable baton with me when I go panting up the stairs. I pound on the door and hear steps.

—Hell is it? someone mutters on the other side.

When the door opens I grab the knob and yank it toward me in one violent move. Svante Witha P falls out into the stairwell and tumbles against the wall on the other side. I grab his neck and yank him back into the apartment and slam the door shut. He seems to be home alone.

Svante Witha P is not in good shape. He's a withered skeleton with skin hardened by alcohol. Nothing else. Everything about him trembles and quivers and chatters. He only has three teeth left, all of them in his bottom jaw. I'm guessing Parkinson's, Alzheimer's, and the rest of those old farts all pounced him at once.

—Remember me?

—Shit, leave me alone.

—Inspector Bengtsson. Remember me? You don't look too good, Svante.

—Leave me alone.

I've pushed his skinny body onto a brownish-orange couch covered with the black traces of cigarette butts.

—How come they call you Svante Witha P?

—Leave me alone.

—Is your real name Pante?

—Stop it.

—You hang out in all the right crowds, Svante.

—Leave me alone.

—And you hear things. Maybe you've heard something about the cut-up body.

The old man's face is completely motionless with its countless wrinkles, but the trembling and the scratchy record that seems to be spinning inside his chest let me know he is still alive.

—Leave me alone.

—Someone has been cut up with a sabre saw and the pieces are sent to the cops, three kilos at a time. Whaddya say, Svante! You have a lot of good friends: I'm sure someone knows something.

—Leave me alone.

I write *Dismemberment, Bengtsson,* and my phone number on a piece of paper and throw it onto the coffee table. The old man watches me as I leave the apartment.

In the car I fold down the shade and look at myself in the mirror. *Jesus Christ, what a joke. You're so incredibly fucking useless. Now take some more, get your head going, come on!*

The bitterness in my gums starts a shiver that makes the hairs on my arms and legs stand straight up. I swig some more Pripps and get going.

9

—I might have something for you, Inspector," Branco says, and pouts his lips while scratching his bare head.

—You have something for me? Are you coming on to me, you goddamn thug?

I teasingly lift my glass and throw back some beer. The ice-cold liquid cools my whistle, in a moment my tremor will calm down, I wish I had benzos, more speed, anything. The bartender mutters and shakes his head.

—Something about the meat.

—What?

—I got a postcard.

—What are you jabbering about?

He crouches down and gets something from under the bar and hands it over to me. I turn it over. The postcard has a picture of Globen and the new arena on it. It's addressed to *Branco at Brother Tuck*. The only message is written in block letters: *19 PIECES. SLAUGHTERHOUSE AREA.*

—What the fuck does this mean?

—You'll have to answer that yourself.

—Someone must have heard you asking around.

—That's possible.

I stick the postcard in my purse and take a few more sips. Branco turns around and counts the cash in the register. The coins trickle out from between his fat fingers while he counts out loud in Serbian. Those fingers have carried many beer kegs, frying pans, pieces of meat, and, considering the shape of the knuckles, they have done some fighting. Maybe killing?

—Maybe not a great lead, he says after counting the coins. I smile.

—Better than nothing. Let me know if you hear anything else.

—Are you going to show your colleagues?

—No way. I'm solving this alone.

He shrugs. I grab a cigarette from my purse, go back to the Ford, make a U-turn on Götgatan, and head toward Slakthu-området, the Slaughterhouse area.

8

The twelfth package is sent with a drunk. He slipped a few times in the rain on the way to the precinct, so the wrapping paper is soaked in gray water. The receptionists sounded the alarm as soon as they see him walk through the door with the package in his arms.

After he was forced to the floor with two officers on top of him, one knee pressed up against his neck, they found a relatively new bottle of Kron in his coat pocket. They sent it to be analyzed. The old man got so scared he pissed his pants.

Once I get there the whole scene is played out. The corridor is empty again other than a janitor mopping the floor. I get the whole story from the receptionists while offering them a cigarette out on the front steps.

—The old man got the whole floor wet. With the officers on top of him.

I start laughing. The girls stare at me.

—It's gross!

I shrug.

—Yeah, you can't help wondering why you do this job sometimes.

—Only druggies and psychos and idiots.

Like the people who work here, I think to myself, and put the cigarette out.

7

—Linköping analyzed the vodka bottle. No prints, no hairs,

no skin samples have been found. But when the content was analyzed there was organic waste with DNA that didn't match the courier's. It seems our murderer couldn't actually keep from taking a sip. And when he or she did, there was apparently a little saliva or piece of skin from the lip that ended up inside the bottle. Not a huge amount, but the lab is still analyzing the DNA.

—I wouldn't mind a small one myself, I whisper to Gunnarsson who giggles.

—Must have been a hell of a thirsty murderer. That was the first mistake, the superintendent whispers back, and rolls his eyes at me.

—Who can blame the asshole? Thirst is thirst.

He lets out a muffled laugh; the sound reminds me of a cat getting ready to fight. But this cat stopped fighting a long time ago.

Holmén continues up on the platform:

—And as many of you have heard, the thirteenth package arrived today by taxi. Despite all our measures the deliveries make it through every time. This time the bag contained a couple of . . . hrm . . . buttocks. A couple of hairy, I mean heavily hairy buttocks, if that can be of any help.

Everyone in the room howls with laughter. Unfortunately, Holmén wasn't trying to be funny this time.

I squirm in my seat. I can't wait to get to the restroom.

6

I go back out to the Slaughterhouse area. Last time I didn't see anything of interest. Why would the murderer be here? Because he's cutting up meat? Far-fetched. But I don't have any better clues than the postcard.

I park my Ford outside a lunch restaurant for slaughterhouse workers. Their white coats are stained in a range of colors, from bright red to brownish black.

I go in and order a hamburger with fries and a local beer. I sit down next to three slaughterers of various ages eating away. I nod at them, they nod back.

—A real beer would've been nice, I mutter mostly to myself.

—That'd be a hell of a treat, the oldest of the slaughterers adds, and smiles like crazy.

When I reach over the table to grab the ketchup I catch the same slaughterer staring at my breasts. The adrenaline hits my bloodstream like a firecracker; the speed has shaved off my impulse control.

—What the hell you looking at? I hiss. Don't you have a wife at home?

—W-wife? he stutters, confused.

—Get your eyes the hell away from my boobs, you goddamn buffoon.

—I wasn't . . .

The two other slaughterers don't know what to say. They stare at their plates with embarrassed looks on their faces and keep eating. I'm sweating nearly as much as when I was going through menopause; I'm completely soaked. Sweat, paranoia, it's all because of the speed.

—I wasn't looking at your breasts, the guy manages to say.

Suddenly I get it. I laugh.

—Sorry. Police. Don't worry.

—Oh, Jesus fuck.

He's so relieved he almost screams.

—I thought you were a thief.

Everyone at the table laughs; I show my holster and the badge. The youngest of the slaughterers, he can hardly be more than twenty, straight out of some agricultural high school, looks at me with a pensive glance.

—I think I know you, but I don't know from where.

—I've been on TV a few times lately.

—Yeah, maybe. I've seen you somewhere. I'm pretty sure.

The oldest one:

—How come you been on TV?

—The dismemberment case.

Everyone around the table starts babbling at once. I interrupt them:

—I got a tip that has to do with the Slaughterhouse area. If you hear of anything, call.

They promise to do so. When I'm about to get up the youngest one asks:

—Can't be much left now?

—Left of what?

—Of the body.

—Maybe not.

—He'll save the head for last, right?

—Who the hell knows? And why would you think it's a he? Why not a she? Or a whole gang of them?

I speak with authority. The youngest one shrinks, impressed, but still asks:

—What do you think will happen when all the pieces are sent? I shrug.

—Hopefully nothing.

—Are you sure we haven't met somewhere? You look so familiar.

—Are you hitting on me, punk?

5

—They said they would fire you if they could, that you've been wasting resources for years that should have been used for pre-venting crime.

The memory of the blonde with the ponytail and pearl necklace causes me to jerk. I'm afraid I'll bite through another crown, so I relax my jaw and take a deep breath.

—I don't give a shit. What's your take?

—You're a good girl, Aggan. I like it when your lips are slightly parted like that. It's sexy.

—You're twenty years late, asshole.

Gunnarsson cackles and rubs the soles of his feet against the carpet. He circles the room before he sits back down. He's just about to bend down to open the bottom drawer when the door is flung open and he sits back up. One of the secretaries is standing there looking at me.

—There's an important message for you.

—Again?

—It's your ex-husband. He's trying to reach you.

—No news there.

—He wanted me to let you know that your son still hasn't come home.

—That's very nice of you, sweetheart.

I glance at Gunnarsson; he rolls his eyes. The secretary leaves, the bottle is brought out.

—What was today's Christmas present?

—Most of the left arm. No tattoos or visible scars. I can't see why it's so hard to find out who the victim is.

—I suppose he's not that greatly missed. Any news con-cerning the DNA from the bottle?

Gunnarsson nods while pouring the glasses.

—Sure, it's almost complete. But no hits.

I slip my flannel nightgown over my head, swallow three

Imovane with some cheap scotch blend, and get into bed. Suddenly my cell phone buzzes with an unknown caller.

—Bengtsson. Who the hell is calling this late?

—It's Svante.

—Svante who?

—Svante Witha P.

—The hell do you want?

—I got a postcard. I think it's for you.

I sit up with a start. I'm dizzy.

—There's a picture of Globen on it.

—I don't care what the fucking picture is. What does it say?

—It says, *Kylhusgatan 19 pieces basement.*

—*Kylhusgatan 19 pieces basement?*

—That's what it says. And it's addressed to you.

—I'll pick it up tomorrow.

I end the call and put the phone down. Finally a concrete tip. I check the address: the Slaughterhouse area. It'll be next day's outing.

The pills shut my head down; I drift off to sleep. If you can call it sleep. I wake up a hundred times during the night and toss and turn, uneasy images and dreams.

In the morning my nightgown is bunched in my armpits, and I find my sheet on the floor, twined like a rope, soaked in sweat.

4

There's something unhealthy about the atmosphere when I force open the basement door at Kylhusgatan 19. I have strengthened my nerves with some nose candy and a few mouthfuls of whiskey, but my bowels keep rumbling and my heart beats a never-ending drumroll. The Slaughterhouse area is submerged in a brownish fog; each breath I take is like a little trickle of rain in my pipe.

The few slaughterhouse workers I see are hurrying past to get inside. But around this house, which appears to be an abandoned old redbrick slaughterhouse with a broken sign on the façade spelling, MEAT SAUSAGE PATÉ, there's no one.

The lock is rusty, but finally I manage to get it open. Behind the green door there's a concrete corridor; I turn the switch and one of the four fluorescent lamps in the ceiling flickers and starts glowing unevenly. I pull out my gun. I realize I've never pulled it out before while on duty, except a few times on the shooting range in the beginning of my career, but that doesn't really count. At home I've done it a number of times, drunk, in front of the mirror, or while I've been watching a suspenseful action movie, pointing it at the bad guys on the screen.

Now I can feel its weight in my hand. I cock and load it. I avoid putting my finger on the trigger; don't want to shoot myself in the leg. I'm trembling like a motherfucker.

It smells of old blood and rotten organic waste. At the far end of the dirty corridor there's a steel door, it looks like an entrance to one of the old shelters from the Cold War. I unbolt the door and push the heavy thing open. It squeaks its way into the darkness.

I avoid turning on the light, I don't want anyone to see that there's someone behind the dusty old cellar windows. I take out my penlight and turn it on. The beam slides over the interior of the room. In the middle there is a slaughtering block with legs of steel and a thick oak top. In the ceiling there are hooks. The once white tile floor is covered in black gore. It stinks. I gag a couple of times before I walk on in.

I reach the table. There is a big scale on top of it. Alongside the longer wall there are a few refrigerators and freezers. I start walking toward them.

Suddenly there's a sound, a scraping as if someone is sneaking around. Between the rows of refrigerators and freezers there's a doorway. I squint and glimpse someone coming toward me. I can't make out any details, but it is a person without a doubt, and I'm sure it's carrying a large butcher knife. I raise my gun and point it at the person's legs. I'm trembling. The figure keeps bobbing and swaying before my eyes.

—Stop. I'll shoot. Lower your weapon.

The person keeps walking toward me. It raises the hand carrying the knife. I am sweating so heavily I can hardly see, the stinging salty drops gather in my eyes. I put my finger on the trigger.

—One more step and I'll shoot.

The person keeps walking and I fire. It bangs like hell. My ears are ringing. It's the first time ever I've fired my gun on duty and it feels good, real good. I want to do it again.

I take a few more steps toward the doorway but so does the other one. I shoot again, this time I'm aiming for the stomach. The figure keeps heading my way. I fire three more shots before I lower my gun. I wait; I can smell the gunpowder, mixed with blood. It's completely silent except the ringing in my ears.

I shine my flashlight but the beam finds no body on the floor. I take a few steps toward the doorway and realize there is no doorway.

It's the chromate freezer. There are five black holes in the steel. My face is there too; my eyes don't look so well. I yank the door open.

Peter stares back at me. It's been a long time since I've seen my son. Now I've found him all right. One of the bullets has gone through and entered his forehead. But there is no blood. His detached head had been emptied of blood long ago.

—I had to, I tell him.

He laughs. I laugh too.

—That's what happens to snitches—you know it and I know it, dear son. You said I was a bad mother and you were going to set me up. Even though I said I was sorry.

I smile and shove my gun back into the holster before I walk over to the other side of the room. I take my coat off and put on the big plastic apron. I plug in the sabre saw and test-drive it for a while. The ten-centimeter blade glides speedily back and forth.

I'm just about to put it on the slaughtering block and get the last few pieces of my son when the door is bashed in, a sharp light fills the room, and someone shouts, I'm sure I recognize the voice, it's the bitch with the ponytail:

—Agneta, you're surrounded. Drop your weapon. Don't worry, it's all going to be fine. Just drop your weapon!

I turn toward the cops. Their lights are so bright I can't see them, but I'm guessing there are a bunch of them making their way into the room, my sanctuary.

—Agneta, listen, take it easy now. Put your weapon down and we can talk about it.

—This isn't a weapon.

—I can see that you're carrying a weapon, Agneta. Now put it on the table slowly and we can talk later.

—This isn't a weapon. This is my Savior.

I push the button again and start the saw. I lift my arm in a smooth arc and push the saw into my own throat. Dying doesn't hurt. I get down on my knees, as if I'm praying, with blood whirling over my head like a halo.

DEATH STAR

BY Unni Drougge

Hammarbyhamnen

Translated by Rika Lesser

Back then, gentrification hadn't yet managed to destroy the aggregate of small-scale industries, warehouses, workshops, hovels, and shacks which characterized the area along the polluted Hammarby Canal. Nonetheless, a doomsday atmosphere pervaded the district, partly because the city was ready to level it to the ground, partly because executions regularly took place there. It was easy to dump bodies in the algae-green stream.

It wasn't the thought of bloated corpses amidst scrap iron and timber down at the swampy bottom that lured Berit Hård to take her daily walk along the water at dusk. Rather, it was a diffuse yet deep sense of solidarity with South Hammarby Harbor's maladjusted elements. She found a certain beauty in this dilapidated marginal area that was teeming with life, where rats scurried through chemical spills, where she had to zigzag between mossy stacks of boards and rust-eaten machine parts, where filthy old men sat under moldy tarps and burned garbage, over which they would warm themselves or grill sausages.

The smoke didn't bother Berit; she was a smoker too and could easily find black-market cigarettes in the stalls near the approach to the main road. She could even get cheap bootleg liquor there.

Her great love for these doomed surroundings, despite everything, had roots in a love of a more carnal sort: Rafel. The first time she'd seen him standing and welding sheet metal in a building that resembled a hangar, where the canal widened into a pool, her heart skipped a beat. When he took off the mask, his intense gaze hit her like sparks from the welding gun. Every late afternoon when Berit found her way to this place, she relished the opportunity to look into the mystical depth of Rafel's eyes.

She moved constantly in the daydream called "hope for the future," for she was only twenty years old and had seen more life than death.

But that evening in October, Hammarby Harbor's silhouettes rose up above the fog banks like ghastly skeletons. Or maybe this was only how she remembered things afterward. For this was when she saw a young person lose her life.

She'd witnessed this from a distance just as she was nearing a decommissioned lightbulb factory. The building's functional architecture appeared like a cluster of wooden blocks, one of which stood on its end, crowned with something that resembled a glass booth on columns. As Berit examines the smashed windowpanes, a body came floating down from a high ledge and disappeared behind a clump of trees. Berit expected to hear something when the body hit the ground, but there wasn't a sound. She rushed up the grassy embankment, layers of thick fog drifting in front of her as she desperately searched for the body. The mangled form on the ground wasn't visible until she reached the building.

A slender girl with dark hair, scarcely older than eighteen, lay racked on a big chunk of concrete with protruding iron rods. Her eyes, framed with kohl, were open and her lips, painted black, vaguely stirred. Berit walked toward her and bent down over her body.

—Cos . . . the girl panted. Cos . . . mo . . .

—Cosmos? Berit repeated, as a nasty rattle came from the girl's throat and she went silent.

The girl's pulse faded away under Berit's thumb. Berit set off for the road just behind the factory. After staggering breathlessly for a few seconds, she pulled up her tight skirt above her hips, and once she reached the road, she tried to flag down the first oncoming car. When it emerged from the fog and slowed down, Rafel sat behind the steering wheel in a small olive-green Renault with a disproportionately big rear end he'd built himself, presumably to make room for all the junk he liked to tinker with. Rafel stopped the car and asked Berit what happened. She told him what she'd just witnessed.

—Is she alive? Rafel asked in his deep bass while Berit plunked down into the seat beside him.

—No, she died as I got there.

—Did you see anything else? Rafel grumbled, as he crossed over toward a gas station near the bigger intersection, a frown on his face. His voice sounded harsh and hollow, as if he spoke through a pipe. And despite the seriousness of the moment, Berit felt a shockwave of desire when he turned his dark, inscrutable gaze toward her. Only then did she realize how obscene she must look with her skirt rolled up, revealing her lace panties and garter belt. She clumsily pulled her skirt down while she answered that she couldn't see so clearly in the fog, but she repeated the word the girl's lips had tried to utter: *Cosmos*.

Rafel turned into the gas station and dropped her off. He'd been forbidden to drive and didn't want the cops to find out, he explained sullenly before clattering away.

Fifteen minutes later, in the din of shrieking sirens and the crackling of a police radio, Berit gave her minimal testimony at the gas station. A cop asked how she felt, would she need "crisis counseling"? But Berit was content to be dropped off on a side street that led down to a group of protected houses where she rented a room. It was a paradoxical idyll, wedged between the water and a forested hill, just below the constant stream of traffic on a nearby road that connected the southern part of the city and the many suburbs along the subway's southbound Green Line. It was green too in Brovattnet—a lush garden of fruit trees and berry bushes, all well-maintained and yielding huge harvests.

To forget the sight of the young woman whose eyes were numb with pain as rebar pierced her body was, however, impossible. Being impaled must have been excruciating. After a couple of hours in a cold sweat, making fruitless attempts at falling asleep, Berit got out of bed and carefully walked down the creaky stairs. She didn't want to wake Thea. Thea was a writer and so easily disturbed that she really shouldn't have had tenants. Thus Berit and Thea scarcely talked to each other, which was fine with Berit; she was a recluse herself. In any event, the blinking blue lights from the bridge abutment must have troubled Thea's sacred nocturnal slumber, for there was light coming from the kitchen.

As Berit stood in the kitchen doorway she heard a gruff voice. A moment later she met his piercing gaze. She couldn't stop the feeling throbbing through her genitals nor the glow that rushed up, making her face flush. She suffered a "little death" and had to hold onto the doorframe. Rafel stared straight into her innermost self. Berit excused herself and poured a glass of water before shamefacedly padding back up to her room in her nightgown. Maybe it wasn't so strange that Rafel sat in Thea's kitchen. He and Thea had been childhood friends in the red-hot seventies, she'd mentioned it once when he'd come by to borrow some tools from the shed. But running into him twice that day still seemed odd.

The dying girl's gaze and Rafel's expression in Thea's kitchen revolved over and over in her mind, and for some peculiar reason she felt guilty, though it was unclear of what. Certainly it was irritating that Rafel brought her to orgasm simply with his eyes, but he probably hadn't noticed anything.

She didn't manage to fall asleep until after the early-morning trains had started rumbling over the nearby bridge, and only slept for a short time. She woke abruptly to the shrill sound of a crow cawing while it peered through her window. The day was cloudy, fog still thick over the little yard outside the house. Rafel's car was nowhere to be seen.

The walls of the room seemed to be closing in on her, as if wanting to push her out. After a quick shower, she got dressed, hoping that the hectic pace of her job at the hospital would make her feel normal again.

On the way to work she kept looking over her shoulder. She felt persecuted, which in a way she was, persecuted by the images in her brain. The obsessive thought of putting herself in the impaled girl's place wouldn't leave her. Had it been deliberate? Had the girl seen the iron rods hidden in the fog? If she'd chosen to die, wouldn't there have been easier ways? Berit stopped on Skanstull Bridge and scouted the accident scene. Dying should be simple, like walking over a bridge. Dying ought to be a slip out of the material world, not something to get stuck in, not being racked by rusty iron spikes, as if life and matter wanted to leave a last reminder of their harshness.

That evening, when Berit came home to Brovattnet, Thea was so sociable that Berit almost suspected something was up. She had intended to go to bed right away and reclaim her lost night of sleep but was instead treated to roast beef and potatoes au gratin and a full-bodied red wine. Thea held forth on the hardships of being a writer and the necessity to sometimes sweep all this aside and to eat and drink well. Despite her youth, Berit knew that effusive cordiality almost always disguised ulterior motives. But the food was delicious, and it definitely beat what she might otherwise grab from a sausage stand. Not until cheese was served and a second bottle of wine uncorked did Thea's real purpose emerge.

—Why, yes, she said, and pushed back her oat-blond, shoulder-length hair. As a writer I have a well-trained sense for the unsaid, almost as if I possess a sort of X-ray vision sometimes. Somehow I can hear what others are thinking.

Then I hope that you hear what I'm thinking, Berit reflected, *namely that your opinion of yourself is way off.*

—Exactly, Thea laughed, sensing Berit's skepticism in her silence. You think I'm up on my high horse, and I understand. Nobody is particularly thrilled when someone comes along and says she has the ability to read their mind. But to the point: you're pining for Rafel.

Berit stopped chewing; she felt as if she'd just swallowed an ox.

—No harm done, Thea continued, and moreover you're not the only one. That's where I was heading. I don't know if you know about Cozmo LSD.

Berit remembered what the dying girl had rattled out: *Cosmos.* Or was it only *Cosmo?*

—It's spelled with a *z*, Thea said, and it is—or was—Rafel's professional pseudonym. So you didn't know; there's scarcely anyone else who does. He was always made up to be unrecognizable when he was onstage. I took care of all communication with his record company. He was quite successful, on the top of the charts awhile too.

—What did the music sound like? Berit asked.

Thea went into the living room and came back steeped in echoing gloomy harmonies sung in Swedish in a serene and plaintive voice. But without a doubt Rafel's voice. A shudder went through Berit.

—You look perplexed, said Thea. I can understand. That's not the immediate picture of Rafel when you see him, am I right? But don't we all have dual personalities in some regard? Thea turned off the music and refilled the wine glasses, then continued: Cozmo LSD later changed his name to Cozmo Limited under pressure from the record company. But Cozmo's cult status grew along with the piles of fan letters, which I also took care of. Rafel never appeared onstage as himself, he avoided publicity, and for every performance that the record company demanded of him, he grew increasingly afraid of being recognized as *just another mortal*, so to speak. But his status grew alongside his shyness, and at one concert some girls climbed up on the stage, Rafel fled, and the throngs of fans followed the girls' example; in the ensuing panic, several fans were badly trampled and had to be taken to the hospital. A sixteen-year-old girl died of injuries. Afterward Rafel decided to back out and kill Cozmo Limited. Through me he sent out a press release and then more or less went underground.

Thea lay her hand on Berit's and her voice spoke softly.

—I saw your face when you caught sight of Rafel last night. But you must give up your dreams of winning him. You have to stop persecuting him.

—*Persecuting?* Berit inhaled, now more furious than ashamed. With flushed cheeks she stared down at the table and grabbed a corner of the red-checkered tablecloth. Wanting to jerk it away so that everything fell to the floor.

—Sorry if I've upset you; you must honestly be shocked by what you witnessed last night, Thea continued with her insufferable insight. Surely you wonder if Rafel has asked me to convey this to you, but first you need to understand the background. As you know, Rafel and I have been friends since we were very young and lived in a collective. He can seem sullen and tough but he's a sensitive soul—which naturally is an attractive combination to everyone but himself. Through music he found an outlet for his vulnerability, but after the death at his last public performance he was terribly shocked. He feared his own power of attraction, thought that it was cursed. All the yearning fan mail from ragged kids didn't help either—many of the letters had suicidal undertones and I didn't know if I should forward them along to the police.

Now Berit understood why Rafel appeared so troubled after the incident. Thea said that the young woman who'd died at the old factory was really a stalker who'd harassed Rafel for years, drowned him with letters, and finally succeeded in ferreting out where he lived. Afterward she'd snuck around the area, on the lookout for her idol. Berit wondered why Rafel hadn't reported the girl to the police, but then Thea explained that Rafel saw himself as a citizen of the world and loathed the authorities' surveillance of people. To report a person to the police went against his strongest convictions; but now the cops were going through all of Hammarby with a fine-tooth comb, directing their abuse at those who'd chosen to live outside the system, which is why Rafel had asked Thea to give the voluminous fan mail from the dead girl to the police.

—So perhaps you understand, Thea concluded, that Rafel is terribly shaken by what's happened. He needs to be alone and he can't deal with any followers right now.

—You can tell him that he shouldn't worry, Berit said brusquely, and got up. Besides, I never thought he was all that special.

Thea offered a maternal smile that lingered as Berit grimaced at her reflection in a nearby mirror. Her embarrassment was written all over her face.

The next day the suicide howled from the headlines, as the papers caught the scent of a "pop star." While there was no commentary from the pop star himself, there were plenty of photos in the archives to run. Moreover, selections from the dead girl's fan mail had been leaked to the media and were there in print, so every Tom, Dick, and Harry, as well as noted experts, could expatiate on this dangerous idol worship.

The following day the media machinery around Rafel and Cozmo Limited went into even higher gear. Hack journalists had uncovered another suicide that had taken place some years before, which could also be linked to Cozmo Limited. One of his songs was titled "Death Is a Friend," and parallels were being drawn between it and the Werther effect. Rafel was no longer a "pop star," now he was a "death star." The two suicides were swept together with the accidental death at the concert. There was also a glut of new details about the earlier suicide. The girl had fallen from Skansbron, a drawbridge she'd clung to when it was raised, then lowered herself down into the narrow lock where she'd drowned. Both suicides had occurred in Rafel's neighborhood, and both girls had written numerous fan letters to him. Both of them were outcasts and came from dysfunctional families with absent fathers and maladjusted mothers. They could have been Berit.

In the hunt for scapegoats, no culpability fell on either heredity or environment, rather on the death cult that was allegedly being marketed by Cozmo Limited. This caused various public figures to warn against the media's anti-intellectual orientation and simplified reasoning which could establish breeding grounds for artistic censorship. Indeed, all the hullabaloo about the "death star's" victims seemed to end with the question of artistic freedom. When no sexual infractions could be connected to the deaths, despite all the hype, the story lost its steam. Nevertheless, the record company was delighted when Cozmo Limited started climbing up the charts.

But Rafel consistently kept clear of publicity. It was Berit who sensed his presence—on the way home from work his car would glide alongside her for a stretch before he stepped on the gas and drove away; in the garden he snuck around like a fox. If Berit went strolling along the water below the stretch of woodland, he would unexpectedly step out of the little shipyard in his oilcloth coat and stop to watch her, as if *she* were a wild animal. And at night he wandered around in her dreams.

But then he disappeared, as if he were suddenly swallowed up by the earth, and only remained in the echo chamber of her mind.

One hazy Sunday afternoon Berit decided to resume her promenades on the wild side. She wrapped her long leather coat around her—the weather was unusually mild for this time of year, even though the deciduous trees' naked shapes told of winter's approach. She walked by the thermal power station, moved along the canal with swift steps, trembled a little when passing the shuttered lightbulb factory—she hadn't set foot there since she'd seen the young woman pierced by the rusty iron bars. When she reached the flat slab of concrete she saw that it was covered with flowers, lanterns, stuffed animals, photos, sketches, and other expressions of love. A poster hung on one of the iron rods. A poem painted in graceful handwriting hung from it. Berit read:

Who were you?
A guest a thief
or the missing wing?
You came like light,
like fire, like a rush,
and said you were no one.
Now you're the blues.
Now you're dead.
Now you're only an angel,
but my angel is death.
Death is my friend.

Bullshit, Berit thought as she marched toward the ghetto of small workshops—the place she'd first seen Rafel. The ground between the shacks was muddy, a clucking hen ambled around, farther away a mongrel was barking, and here and there came the clattering of tools and machines. Berit inhaled the peculiar mixture of smells—oil, gasoline, earth, marshy ground, garbage, and smoke. This was the way her father smelled when he'd surprised her outside school, before he'd disappeared for good. *The only thing I can teach you is this: Always be on guard. Believe only what you see with your own eyes.* That's how he'd spoken, and Berit had tried to follow his advice. But he hadn't explained anything about love or carnal knowledge. She tramped on, her pulse quickening.

Guitar notes pressed through the cacophony of welding irons, grinders, and sledgehammers. Berit was drawn toward the music—she wove her way along the oil drums, the tarps hanging on their lines, the sheet-metal hangars, and the barracks, until through the darkness and fog she caught sight of a brightly colored trailer beside a clump of trees. Lanterns shone softly from branches around the trailer. It was idyllic, like a fairy tale. The sound of the guitar was stronger now; a voice began to sing, a voice that was powerful and yet as soft as a caress. And there was Rafel sitting on a stepladder, singing to the red-violet trailer with bright green decorations that looked like snakes or plants with twining tendrils. Berit stopped ten meters away and listened.

They were the same words she'd read on the poster at the scene of the accident. But when Rafel sang it with his sensual and full-bodied voice, it didn't sound banal at all. His voice wound itself around Berit and made her stand up straight, as if rooted to the spot.

When Rafel let the last chord fade away, he got up and went into the trailer, quickly returning without the guitar. He walked straight toward her, his long wavy hair flowing over his broad shoulders, his oilcloth coat open, his hips swinging freely.

Rafel said nothing at all when he stood half a meter from her, nothing when he bent forward with parted lips and beautiful, half-open eyes.

Never had Berit been kissed in this way. It wasn't only the sugar cube that dissolved between their tongues and made the kiss sweet. Never had a tongue been so soft and rubbed so easily against hers. No lips had so encircled hers and been as easy to meet as his. And somewhere down in his throat lived a singing voice that could take her to the end of the earth.

Rafel led her to the cliff that dropped down into the black water. Behind them rose a group of high-rises on the fringes of this no-man's-land run wild. From there, occupants could look out over streams and bays and the entrance to the harbor. There the inhabitants of this Venice of the North could huddle up in their houses, gaze out wistfully through their windows, and dream of the far-off summer when they could sail away to the archipelago's flower baskets.

Rafel and Berit stood on the edge of the cliff. They saw the cars' headlights creep along the highway like glowworms, saw the glitter from the floating pleasure palaces on their way east, and the gossamer shimmer from the buildings of the city center. It was an amazing view. A wide cloud of mist covered Stockholm like a blanket of whipped cream, and above it the spires of various churches stuck up like candles on a cake.

Berit thought she saw everything as it was. The sky sparkled with a warm fluorescent sheen, and beneath her feet purple and green brooks billowed below the precipice to join the pitch-black canal in a beautiful paisley pattern. It was exactly the same pattern as her father's scarf. The paisley scarf was one thing he'd cherished, it was always around his neck, even after he'd begun his life as a homeless wanderer.

Rafel walked back a few steps.

—Do you want to be my friend? My personal angel? he asked in a rasping yet sonorous voice, as if singing the phrase.

—Angel? Berit repeated, and imagined she saw the thick white fog spread a pair of wings.

—Death's angel. Death alone is our friend.

The words flew away and dissolved before she'd caught their meaning. Instead, other words rose within her. *Always be on guard. Believe only what you see with your own eyes.* She turned around right as the tall figure came rushing toward her, and quickly threw herself to the side. The thick blanket of fog seemed illuminated from within, the light so white that she was blinded. And there—in stark contrast to the fog—was the sharp outline of a big black bat that immediately vanished. Only contours remained, like a piece removed from a completed jigsaw puzzle. She caught the fleeting impression of a hard wind blowing through the hole until the fog closed around it, erased it.

Berit was still sitting on the cliff. The cars' yellow eyes swept forth below on the main road, but with growing distance until everything went dark. She realized that she was freezing, got up, pulled her coat more tightly around her, and slowly walked one last time through the motley, messy neighborhood where she could once dream herself away from ostentatious civilization. The lights from the shacks and workshops were off, the fires no longer burned. One solitary man with a halting gait walked forward in the rubbish, occasionally bending his neck toward the ground, like a pecking bird. A murder of crows flew from the spot where Berit had first seen a young person die. The poster with Rafel's lyrics was still there. The first line went right through her: *Who were you?*

Now she knew.

But death wasn't a friend. And Berit was no angel.

Over the next few days Berit scrutinized the newspapers, but there was nothing about a man who'd dropped from a great height and lost his life. She neither saw nor heard anything about Rafel anymore. And she never learned if Thea had been trying to protect her. She packed her bag and turned her back on the past. This was how Berit lived, in order to stay alive. She could have gone to the police, but they probably would have believed that it was all in her imagination, and maybe it was. That a couple of scruffy young things, under the influence of LSD, took their idol's word that they could fly—this would soon be trumped by police work of considerably higher priority, namely the hunt for the man who'd murdered the country's prime minister. And the tide of time, which is often called progress, swept away the cluster of sheet-iron hovels and illegal workshops in South Hammarby Harbor, for the location proved attractive to a new population. The toxic ground was cleaned up and then came social engineering. Renovated houses with magnificent views went up over the canal, built at a frenzied pace for a growing and socioeconomically homogeneous group of careerists within the burgeoning industries, for which the political and technological new order paved the way. Schools, day care centers, cafés, restaurants, and finely calibrated establishments for the elderly and disabled were built for the resourceful inhabitants. Freedom got a new meaning; its battle cry was, *Bet on yourself!* The shuttered lightbulb factory was lit up by a TV production company that delivered advertising-financed entertainment to the masses and generous profits to the owners. Being rich was no longer judged harshly, and those who didn't grow rich only had themselves to blame. Those who now had to blame themselves were housed in the far-off suburbs' symmetrical storage closets, a safe distance from the exclusive environs along the Hammarby Canal. That a sanctuary for the maladjusted had once been situated there was unimaginable.

Sometimes this tidy enclave is still haunted. You know it by a shiver in the hazy air at the hour of the wolf, when the long winter is on its way; it can come rumbling from the soul of a PR consultant who, despite Bikram Yoga and Celexa, feels encumbered by his own success. Through the big picture window with a "seaside view," the silhouette of a large bat quickly appears and evokes the yearning to be out and away. Far, far away.

As if death were a friend.

10/09/03

BY NATHAN LARSON

Kungsträdgården

08/09/03

C rap coffee bar, doing my best to hail the Swedish girl behind the counter, the blonde with the ponytail over by the cash register picking at her nails . . . But this dirty Iraqi or Pakistani or whatever she is won't get out of my way.

Her saying, "Another Americano?"

For a moment I think she's asking if I'm an American, and I nearly smack her filthy fucking face. Yes, her Swedish is street garbage, but it's more that I'm not accustomed to these new names for a fucking cup of coffee.

"Yes. *Tusen tack*," I say to her, and smile big . . . though I would love to pretend to not understand her suburban accent.

However. Last thing I want is to be remembered, so the modus is—keep it cordial, and bland.

I'm working today.

Now. Generally speaking, when it comes to an everyday kinda political hit like this one, usually in some asshole or armpit like Bratislava or any of the former Yugoslav territories (take your pick) . . . generally, I couldn't be fucking bothered.

Farm it out locally, or if that's not viable, fly down some disposable thug, and be done with it. You could say my job is more administrative than anything else. But in this instance, it's different.

232 // Stockholm Noir

I want to see *this particular bitch* die.

Indeed—I plan on relishing it, giving it special attention. She's a piggy, soft-handed and pink like a female Goran. And after all: this is on my home court, quite rare in this business.

The Iranian or Libyan or Afghan interloper bangs that scoop-like device they use to make this dago coffee on a railing, knocking the packed grounds out in a puck. These machines, these hyperactive faux-retro contraptions, always with Italian logotypes, Fabrizio, etc., it's all bullshit, likely constructed in China.

This coffee joint, which really is a piece of shit and to which I hope to never return, does have the advantage of being smack in the middle of Norrmalmstorg, with plenty of glass through which to observe the goings-on.

I tap out a blend. I ask you: what in God's name was wrong with the coffee of my youth, the coffee of the Konditori, that lovely poison that only seemed to get better the longer it cooked on its burner? The stuff of the farmer, the factory worker, the Swede. That is, was, and forever will be Swedish coffee.

This fantasy dago coffee trend. It will pass, like so many other trends before it.

Yes. This current job is personal. And very local.

Fire up the cigarette, despite the General Snus parked under my lip. I like to double up.

They just banned smoking in *bars* in New York City if you can imagine that, a horrible trendy pandemic that no doubt the faggots in our parliament will line up in enthusiastic favor of . . . so we'd better smoke while we fucking can, living as we are in not just a nanny state, but a nanny world.

Trans fats. Sodium. All the components of a traditional diet. They're trying to legislate, to politicize our diet. Herald loud the death of traditional Swedish food.

Toll the bells for Swedish tradition, period.

Making this current job all the more pressing, all the more *essential.*

Stockholm. Sure, it's been a cesspool as long as I can recall, but today? Hardly recognize it. Dark skin everywhere you turn. Dark eyes. I saw the blackest imaginable African and a full-blooded Swede, as white as purest snow, traipsing down fucking Kungsgatan, hand in fucking hand like it was the most natural thing in the world and *we are supposed to simply accept the fact of them.* It was all I could do to not vomit.

Sushi and Korean "BBQ"—in the same fucking joint.

All the expected American fast-food garbage.

Fucking *mosques!*

"*So varsågod . . .*" The immigrant materializes again.

I've worn a Hugo Boss suit I bought at the airport in Frankfurt, faintly patterned white shirt, prissy Germanic metal-framed glasses—the northern European business uniform that makes you absolutely impossible to describe to the cops. *He had a blue suit . . . loafers . . . a checked shirt . . .* You see? Useless.

The darkie girl drifts away. I glance toward the blonde, who is watching a wall-mounted TV, arms folded. Fucking hell, at least she could pay attention, I'm nearly the only motherfucker in this place.

"And I'll go ahead and settle up, please." I don't know if anyone hears me.

Here's the situation.

The target is a female, middle-aged.

The target is with a friend, a female civilian, also middle-aged and quite well off.

They're having a lovely day, two cows getting older, shopping, Fika, etc.

234 // STOCKHOLM NOIR

Over the last several months we have observed three other such jaunts, and they generally follow the same pattern—the ladies meet up, work their way to Stureplan by taxi or car, and if the hour is right they lunch at the Oyster Bar.

After this the pair tends to stroll down Biblioteksgatan to Norrmalmstorg (where I am currently situated), where they will visit the Acne, Marimekko, Filippa K, and the Noa Noa stores before proceeding east down Hamngatan to the NK.

And this is where we will take her.

The hope is that they will not go to the outsized Åhlens, which they have been noted to do on one occasion, as the operation would prove much more difficult in that environment. Too many people, very close quarters, less space to work.

The significance of the date, September 10 . . . it's the most ridiculous thing, but if you can believe it, the client is convinced this will somehow act as a misdirect and point toward Islamists. Incredibly sophomoric, like an unimaginative spy novel, but nonetheless. The client gets what the client wants, within reason, and any day is as good as the next.

More to the point is that this evening, apparently, there is some sort of debate regarding the adoption of the euro, which the bitch supports of course, so eager to join the "Union" is she that all other concerns are swept aside.

Not a political animal, no way. But Swedish money should stay in Sweden. Not to support these fucking aliens (another matter entirely) with their babushkas and hordes of filthy children, but just on principle.

The Norwegians have the right idea with all that oil money. Keep it close. Spend it to make your country great. How can anyone refute this logic?

The client: politician too. Boringly. Perhaps the most unengaging, least charismatic man one can imagine. From our one brief, furtive meeting I can recall his stale breath, his dandruff, cheap suit, his compulsive jiggling of the knee. His stiff, high-pitched speech. Just useless. Muttering about deniability, this being most important did I understand that there must be no direct communication, that discretion is paramount, that he knows no details, droning on and on, as if this were my first rodeo. I had to bite my tongue. The very fucking nerve. Talking to me like I'm new to this.

Somehow this man, I'll call him Johan, believes he is the true successor to the throne. Old friend of fat-fuck Goran. Been waiting in the wings for a decade and figures it's his turn, and the only barrier between prime ministership and yet more years on the periphery is this bitch who has inexplicably and rather swiftly positioned herself as the next choice for the goddamn Social Democrats . . . It's become, apparently, an obsession. His drug problem certainly hasn't helped him think straight. And his taste for underage hookers (which I am not ashamed to say I helped provide, it's sort of something we do on the side, so many eager boys and girls from Latvia, Estonia . . . what they'll do for a passport and the promise of a shit job, say, in this shit café I now find myself in, who am I to deny them this life?), well, this information gives me leverage and a bit of control, and the client knows it.

The rub, and I chuckle now thinking about it as I grind out my smoke, the upshot though . . . there's not a chance in hell the client could win *any* election. Not a chance in hell. He's like a flat cardboard cutout, stiff, awkward, and barely there. He doesn't have the stuff.

If he had the stuff, he'd do it himself. I'd walk him through it. Throttle the bitch on the floor of Parliament.

But his lack of political future is beautiful. Cos it opens up the field for the true Swedes, friends in the Christian Democrats and the Farmers Party . . . citizens with the correct ideas, those who will carry us into the future and away from the failure that is Europe. The dirge that has been the Social Democrat era, seemingly endless, will come to an abrupt (and most welcome) halt. The time is now, you can smell it, you can taste it, ripe fruit.

Enough politics. I've got a focused pain behind my eye, no doubt brought on by all this political tripe . . . I take three Alvedon, down the capsules with the last sip of coffee, now cold.

Waiting on the word from Carl-Erik via the radio in my ear. The client wants it nasty. Fair enough . . . I can accommodate such requests.

"You're on. No escort," says Carl-Erik in my earpiece. Meaning the ladies are headed my direction.

And without protection. Naturally.

These arrogant, smug, stupid fucking "civil servants." One would have thought after Palme it would be a given that SAPO would step it up, but no, that lesson has been completely lost on these fools. They just wander about like drooling geriatrics. The arrogance. That's what it is, arrogance. Inflexibility. Safe little Sweden.

I rotate slightly on the raised chair. Your usual Saturday crowd, maybe a bit less foot traffic than usual. Get a visual on the ladies easily. The matching glasses, squat little things. They come to a stop before the Filippa K window, consult each other, then wander inside.

Consider next moves. "Get someone in there," I murmur into my lapel. It'd be ridiculous to lose her.

The decoy is positioned at the southernmost edge of the square on Hamngatan, and will ultimately drift up to NK should they wind up there. He's not on radio but knows what to do if I indicate I have lost visual.

I need to get out there.

Did I not ask this sand nigger for my check? Don't want to be ducking out on the bill, they'd remember that.

Of course she's disappeared, the Kurd, and the blonde remains immersed in the television, an American rap "artist" hopping around like a crazed monkey.

As gently as possible, I try to flag her. For Christ's sake, the place is empty.

"Miss?"

Takes her sweet time looking my way. Giving me suburban sass. A proper Swede, physically, if a bit too much makeup. The suburban influence. A tragedy.

"Might I pay?"

"What did you have?" she asks as if unbearably put upon, stepping to the register.

"Two coffees. Two, what, Americanos."

Her fingers are poised over the keyboard, tickling the air. "A coffee or an Americano?"

"I'm sorry?"

"Was it a regular coffee or an Americano?"

Jesus fuck. I can't help it, I throw a glance back toward Filippa K . . . I don't like that I can't see directly into the store, and in order to speak to this pure-blooded yet stupid cooze I have my back to the shop.

Gentle now.

"Two *Americanos*. I was told you didn't have regular coffee."

The blonde raises her eyebrows, taps twice on the keyboard. "Forty-eight kronor."

Just a moment. A hot flash of red momentarily obscures my vision, and fuck, I can't help it, I find myself saying, God I can't stop it, "Well for fu . . . How much is a cup of regular, just regular coffee?"

"Oh, twelve kronor."

Steady now. I hear myself say, "But that's what I asked for in the first place. That's what I wanted to begin with. I didn't ask . . ."

The blonde believes that I do not see her roll her eyes, but I see it. I have to be careful here. I cast a furtive glance back out the window.

"Sahrish," she calls.

No credit cards on an op, not ever. I'm fumbling with cash. Coins, bills . . . gotta get out of this fucking place.

"It's, ah, quite all right, I'll just pay for the—" In my ear: *"They're moving. They're moving."*

"Sahrish," she calls again.

The gypsy pokes her head out of the kitchen. I should walk out of here but I must not be memorable to these gashes.

"Did the gentleman have two Americanos or regular drip?"

Sahrish or whatever the fuck her name is indicates a coffee machine with long red glitter nails, hooker nails. The machine is wrapped in its power card.

"S'broken. Still."

"Oh, right," says the blonde. "So yeah, forty-eight."

I can't help it, I slam a fifty-kronor note on the counter. Both girls jump. I try to counterbalance this action, saying reasonably, "Yes, thank you. Keep the change. Keep the change. Thank you." And I'm up and through the door before I fuck up this whole job by gutting these two irrelevant cunts.

Striding across the square diagonally, my back to the shop and the target . . .

"To you," says Carl-Erik.

"Where they headed?" I ask, not turning around.

"Subject attempted to buy jacket—"

"Fuck the details, please . . ."

". . . *salesgirl directed her to NK outlet as they didn't have her size at the store. Seems to be destination as expected. Getting in the van with our friend.*"

So all as planned.

Our friend being the "crazy" Serb . . . who is about to be one busy little Slav.

09/09/03

Connect with "crazy" Serb kid at the Kungsträdgården tube.

Kid has been out of the institution for about five days. We've got him stashed in one of our flats and thus far he's just been shuffling around, not seeming to take an interest in anything. Except for *Grand Theft Auto* and the DVD player, which we have stocked with nothing but his favorites: *Mission Impossible I*, *Mission Impossible II*, and a compilation of our target's greatest hits, especially her comments with respect to support for the military action in Bosnia, etc., etc.

As promised, the boy is about to meet Tom Cruise, the man who sprung him—and be given his mission orders.

Yes, we've been given the intel that this boy has some sort of illusion that Tom Cruise is communicating with him. All we're doing really is indulging his fantasy. How can there be harm in that?

Down in the dank tube station . . . watching him at a good distance for about fifteen minutes, concerned for a bit as he seems to get crafty, skulking around the station trying perhaps to figure out where I might be . . . After all, how thrilling to be meeting with Tom Cruise himself.

I can sense his twitchy nervousness from across the station, me thinking, *Fuck, we're gonna have to reassess.*

But now here he is, seated on the number 11, as instructed,

which is being cleaned before it reverses course and heads back in the direction of Akalla.

I enter the empty train to his back, slide into the seat behind him in a black hooded sweatshirt. Saying, "Obviously don't turn around or I fucking kill you. Your apartment satisfactory?"

Kid stiffens, then nods. I speak Serbian, with what I hope is an American accent.

"You ready to do this?"

Kid nods eagerly.

"Have you got the weapon?"

Kid nods again. Simple fuck.

Me saying, "Make it bloody. Make it ugly. This is yours. Gut her. Do it like she's a dirty fucking Croat. She might as well be. Do it street style."

Another head-wag.

"You won't see me, kid, but I'll be there, so no fucking around. I won't step in and bail you out should you fuck up. Others will direct you to her. Wear that stupid hat you've got on, and a shirt with a recognizable logo."

"I have a Nike sweatsh—"

"That's fine. Listen to me. When you've finished, walk directly out. Ditch your hat and switch jackets, you'll be handed a fresh one."

"What about the—"

"Shut the fuck up. You don't speak until I say it's okay. The weapon you drop with your clothing. Do you understand?"

"I can't believe . . ." He trails off.

Jesus. I can't have an actual conversation with this mouth-breather. Even from behind I can tell the kid is smiling.

"I want to turn around."

"To look into my eyes is to die, kid. You know that. I'll destroy you with my mind."

"Yeah. Yeah, it's just . . . I can't believe I'm talking to Tom Cruise," he mumbles, dreamy. "You're fucking wicked, man. You're like a genius. You can speak *Serbian*, that's fucking wicked, man."

"That's right. I do this using Scientologist technology. Now when the police take you, because they will, what do you say?"

"Deny it, deny it."

"They show you the video. They smack you around. Looking bad for you, kid. What then, genius?"

"Confess."

"To what, now?"

"To . . . to the crime. Shit, am I saying the wrong things?"

"No. But speak properly. Don't stutter. You say nothing of Leijonborg. Nor that he brought in Tom Cruise. Nothing of this, nothing of the Impossible Missions Force. Nothing of *your* mission. Yes?"

"Yes. Yes."

"You confess as a lone actor. We're watching your mother. Do you understand?"

Nods, laughing. Kid thinks it's a gas.

"On behalf of the IMF I deputize you, Mijailo Mijailovic, for a period of forty-eight hours. *Boom.*"

"Fucking wicked . . ." says the kid, dazed.

"The IMF will admit no involvement. We have agents everywhere."

". . . best day of my life," breathes the greasy Slav.

Eyeroll. In English I say, "I don't doubt it. You have your orders."

And I'm gone the way I came in.

Carl-Erik and I, in the lobby at Berns ten minutes later. He reads *Expressen* and drinks a mineral water.

"What's your assessment?" he says, not looking up as I sit to his right.

I open up *Aftonbladet*. My eye stumbles on something about fucking *Estonia* and the EU, Jesus wept, just why not let everybody in, you fools?

"Don't fucking know, do I? He's nearly retarded, huh? Or maybe that's how they all behave now, these kids."

"Nah, certainly not retarded. It's an act, a defense posture. He's not all there but he's well aware of what he's doing. Kid was abused . . ."

Boring. I get up, look around the room. Feel a hot rush of anger, perhaps unwarranted. Plop the newspaper where my ass just was.

"So why ask me my assessment? You just gave me yours and you seem to be the more informed of the two of us. Wasting time . . ."

"Oh come on," says Carl-Erik nervously. It won't do to attract attention obviously.

In my peripheral vision I note he almost looks at me. I'll be docking him for that. But he's good, Carl-Erik. He's meticulous, careful.

"Tomorrow is a go," I say, eyes to the door, now heading toward it.

10/09/03

Moving across the square diagonally toward Hamngatan. I'll stay in front of the target.

"Nordiska," I say into my lapel.

Several things will happen now. At a bus stop down the street near the Central Station, the "goth" Nazi will commence defacing the SD poster of the target, in his ridiculous gray trench coat. He will do this as loudly as possible, and we will of course make sure it's all very well documented. The van will pull up at the side entrance on Regeringsgatan. Carl-Erik and the crazy Serb will remain inside and will move only on my say-so.

Three untraceable phone calls will be placed directly to Stockholm police, the first regarding a fight in progress in the cafeteria at the Kulturhuset. The second regarding a suspicious package in an abandoned taxi at Bromma Airport. The third with respect to an armed man at Djurparken. In the children's area.

Two bomb threats will be called in, one to the Vasa Museum, and one to the Stockholm Stock Exchange Building.

Just scatter the pigs a bit, not that I'm the least concerned. Useless as they are.

"Plans for the companion?" inquires Carl-Erik.

"Who?" I say.

"Subject's friend."

"Not unless there's interference. But he should be prepared."

"Right," says Carl-Erik.

I'm passing the Nordea Bank on my right, some asshole on his cell phone shoulders me. Without a word of apology.

And immediately I'm nearly run down by a flock of terrifying-looking women, all with double-wide prams, bearing down at great speed, blocking the entirety of the sidewalk with smug entitlement. I am forced to press myself against the wall lest I be flattened.

Fucking Stockholm. Fucking women having mongrel half-breed children by the dozen, all on state support, so we might enable their shopping habits. God forbid they should have to work to support their spawn.

"Stand by. Subject has entered Zara."

I wonder what the fuck Zara is. "Where?"

"Adjacent to the McDonald's."

Realize that's behind me. I pause near a bank of cash machines. There's an Arab female in front of me, in (I kid you not) a full burka, digging through what could only be described as a beaded coin-purse. Yet another pram, decorated with voodoo black-magic totems, Islamic symbols.

Her ugly child, a little girl, tilts her face up to mine, spits out the Bamse binkie for which she is far too old.

Am I in Libya? Am in a North African medina?

God help us. God help us. This is not Sweden. I stare at the child, willing it sterile. *May your womb be dry and barren, child.* Her mother turns, and I offer the discolored creature the gift of my smile.

She looks away quickly, returns to her purse, puts her back to me.

No, I can't stand it. Focus on work. Continue walking . . .

"Have the twin moved into place."

Carl-Erik says something in Serbian.

Moving swiftly a half-block, closer now to the entrance to NK, I watch the double enter through the front, baseball hat, grayish Nike sweatshirt, tan work pants. The cameras will have duly noted this for posterity.

Good, good.

"Subject has exited Zara, to you . . ."

Good, good.

Elsewhere the goth Nazi is defacing yet another poster, at yet another bus station. I wonder idly how useful this will be, but figure the more elements the better, provided they're contained.

I turn back toward Norrmalmstorg, already feeling that deflated sensation one gets with the completion of a job. Even as I see the pair of tants toddling up the street, might as well be sisters with their stocky lesbian bearing, hardly women at all . . .

even at this moment I'm thinking about my laundry, thinking about what I'll be doing tomorrow.

Shake this off. Still much to be enjoyed.

Something occurs to me, as the ladies draw nearer, laughing about something. I pause near the column at the department store's grand entry. A beautiful building, really, completed in 1915 and reflective of early art nouveau architecture, built and designed by *Swedes,* with good *Swedish* steel . . . All this bullshit could be cut short if I just shot the bitch myself, right here and now.

It could be good fun. Sure, a bit whimsical, a touch ad hoc, some improvisation, a little stressful . . . but think of it: precisely like kiddie-fucker Palme. SAPO would shit themselves. What a glorious scandal.

Allow myself to touch the Sig Sauer near my heart, under my suit jacket. Feel the dense Braille of the grip.

I'm not seriously considering doing it, although nothing would be simpler. Merely daydreaming.

The ladies are almost upon me. Frumps, the both of them. Sexless frumps.

No, nothing so simple as a shot to the head. What we have planned will be so very, very much more entertaining, more colorful.

I can't help it, I have to tweak it a bit.

I spin and pull open the door to NK, as if I'm rushing through my day, make as if I happen to notice the approaching duo, and then, with maximum gallantry, stand aside and hold the door for them. Again with the wide smile.

As they trudge past me, the target's eyes flicker across my face, flit away. Her arm brushes my open suit jacket, centimeters from the handgun. I'm pushing it.

As the ladies pass, though, do they *thank* me? Do they so much as acknowledge my chivalry?

No, they do not.

Because this is Sweden. The cunts have trained themselves out of such behaviors. The men are no longer men, they are lactating, self-hating slaves, forever prepared to flog themselves raw over the sins of their grandfathers.

There goes the back of her head, up the short staircase. Once again, I could simply . . . but no.

Now that the bitch is inside, it's just a question of following procedure and, naturally, remaining flexible.

The two security guards who are in our employ will track the cattle from here. I don't have much left to do but witness events unfold.

Find myself in the makeup section, overly lit.

"Transferring eyes to local law," I say, "All parties go."

The Serb and Carl-Erik will be entering the building from the side street . . .

I'm making my way casually toward the escalator. Take note of a blond salesgirl who, catching me looking at her, makes like she's wiping off a bit of glass. Then glances at me again.

As I say: I make a note.

The bitches certainly take their time dawdling, but once they descend to the second floor (having started from the top), I see the designated area for the first time since I scoped the whole thing about two weeks back—and realize again why it makes sense.

The Serb is nearby, almost at my heel, doing a very good approximation I must say of the casual tail.

Shame to do it like this, really, but it seems to me that there's more of an opportunity to really fillet her if there's some coverage.

Within a store, open plan as they are, he'll be able to pull her behind a clothing rack, or display case, or something, buying an additional five or ten seconds, which will be invaluable and will make the difference between a maiming and an actual, definitive kill.

Momentarily distressed to see they've shifted things around, moved the displays . . . but it hardly matters.

The shopgirl within is engaged with another customer at the register, who seems to be attempting a complex return of some kind. The girl on the floor has gone in the back for the moment, likely to look for a size for the bitch, who stands there squawking with her friend.

"Okay. Do it now," I say into the radio.

Carl-Erik walks past quickly and brushes against the Slav—this is the signal.

MM takes it, and moves forward with intention. With swagger.

Good boy. The knife is out, he holds it close to his thigh.

I turn on my heel, begin walking rapidly as if I'm headed past the shop . . . Manage to see the first two solid stabs: one directly in the chest, *thunk*, surreal the silence that precedes the realization that this is now happening, the bitch is being cut . . . A second blow, as her arm comes up in a defensive move, *thunk*, in the meat of her armpit.

She begins speaking to him, attempting it seems to make this thing rational. She wears a half-smile. She believes, even now, that this is something she can talk her way out of.

For a moment there is, strangely, no blood whatsoever. And all at once, there's blood everywhere, spraying a rack of white blouses like a Jackson Pollock.

Then more sound: her friend shrieks, the target seems to actually be continuing to *talk reasonably* to MM, I think, not realizing the inevitability of her situation . . . another *thwack*, heavy and wet. I'm wondering how much longer the bitch can keep yammering.

She's hit again and makes a barnyard noise in her throat as she loses her balance and goes down, at last . . . There's the flowering puddle of liquid across the hardwood floor, and the Serb moves in to continue . . .

And that's unfortunately as much as I can stick around for, as I'm now moving down the escalator . . . Much hubbub to my rear, though far less than one would imagine. Still no alarm . . . our guys in house are seeing to that delay.

Plenty of people, however. Just hovering there. Mouths making little Os. Doing nothing.

Shame I couldn't really get a long look, shame I can't take the time to *enjoy* . . . but then again, there will be the video, to which I greatly look forward.

Within a minute, MM slams past me, taking the steps two at a time. I smell sweat and something intestinal. Good, he split her open.

MM is free and clear. Turning, I see no one in pursuit. This surprises even me. Nobody? Nobody at all?

I watch the Serb as he hits the ground floor, and moves out of my line of vision, presumably out the door, folks stumbling from his path. Free and clear.

Bon voyage, Slav. If you follow your instructions, the DNA on your discarded clothing will be sufficient to implicate you. We'll make sure these items are preserved.

At this very moment, a photo of MM in attendance at a Lars Leijonborg rally, his face contorted in a shout, is on its way via e-mail to somebody's inbox at *Dagens Nyheter*. It's all so perfect.

Ah, Stockholm. I must thank you, as tragic a whore as you are. This entire operation would not have worked anywhere else in the world. Well. Perhaps Japan. This entire operation is exactly what Sweden—the distorted, mongoloid Sweden as epitomized by Stockholm, that is—deserves.

Nowhere else would a public figure like this be unprotected, and completely touchable. In these new times, in this New World, with all of its new threats, there remains this stubborn, bovine inability to adapt.

Where else but here, would any number of able-bodied people stand by and, cowering, watch another human get slaughtered? And do *nothing*. Not out of callousness—out of conditioning.

Nowhere else is *blunda* so deeply ingrained. Out of *risk of embarrassment*.

Oh, but I might look silly. I would draw attention to myself. What if they don't want to be disturbed? What if no one else steps in? What if I'm wearing the wrong shirt? What about this haircut? I'll be the only one, and I'll look like an idiot, overreacting . . . presuming, how dare I think that I of all people can affect a situation like this? No. The officials will handle it. Why, I'd lose my place in line . . .

In the United Kingdom, amongst the Anglo-Saxons, there is a term—the Tall Poppy Syndrome. This is a much more descriptive expression than the Swedish equivalent. And within it is embedded an implied warning. *Grow too tall, and be cut down.*

Jantelagen in its truest form.

So in a funny way, I serve the social order. And thus, the cunt is cut down for having the hubris to aspire toward growth.

On my way out, I pause again in the perfume section. The blonde I'd seen previously steps over to me.

"I came back," I tell her.

"Mmm," she says. "I see that."

"Something for my girlfriend . . ." I raise my eyebrows

slightly, to indicate my doubts that said "girlfriend" will remain so for very much longer.

A quick but knowing look from the lovely salesgirl. "Well," she says, indicating a purple bottle, "this is probably the most popular scent at the moment . . ." She lifts the flask. "*Poison,*" she says.

Any response I might give her is drowned out by the blare of the fire alarm.

ABOUT THE CONTRIBUTORS

Märta Thisner

CAROLINE ÅBERG (translator) grew up in Uppsala, Sweden, and now resides in Bagarmossen, a suburb of Stockholm. She works as an editor and translator from Swedish to English and vice versa. Apart from her solo work, she produces performances and interactive art with her feminist collective ÖFA. When she is not working on books, she spends most of her time reading them.

Marianne Lindberg De Geer

CARL JOHAN DE GEER was born in 1938 and is a film director, photographer, painter, writer, textile designer, and set designer. He lives in Stockholm, has four grown children, three grandchildren, and is married to artist, writer, and director Marianne Lindberg De Geer.

Severe Tennenbaum

UNNI DROUGGE is considered Sweden's leading female cult author, and has generated a wealth of literature as well as a great deal of debate. Her novels have attracted a lot of attention and have found a large readership that has grown with every book. Currently, Unni Drougge is working as a columnist, a lecturer, and a playwright. She is also the editor of a magazine issued by the women's shelter organization Roks.

Inger Edelfeldt

INGER EDELFELDT is an author and artist, born in Stockholm in 1956. She is internationally known for her illustrations for J.R.R. Tolkien's stories in *The 1985 J.R.R. Tolkien Calendar* but in her home country mostly for her books: more than thirty titles in different genres—prose, poetry, works for children and young adults, comic books, and plays. She has received several awards for her work, and currently lives in Stockholm.

Aurora Bergh

CARL-MICHAEL EDENBORG is a publisher, writer, and critic with a PhD in intellectual history. He has written several short stories and novels. His independent Vertigo publishing company has brought out many nonconformist classics, from Marquis de Sade to Samuel Delany. His latest novel, *The Alchemist's Daughter*, was nominated for the prestigious Swedish August Prize in 2014.

Anders Deros

ÅKE EDWARDSON is the author of novels—for adults and young adults—short stories, and plays. His fiction has won numerous awards in Sweden and abroad, he was a finalist for the 2007 *Los Angeles Times* Book Prize, and he is a three-time winner of the Swedish Crime Writers' Academy's Best Swedish Crime Novel award. Edwardson's books have sold over six million copies in twenty-seven languages. When he isn't forced to write, he cooks.

Simon Sarfati

TORBJÖRN ELENSKY has published three novels, two short story collections, a book on Cuba, and an introduction to the writings of Italo Calvino. He also works as a critic and essayist, covering a wide range of topics.

Leif Hansen

INGER FRIMANSSON, one of the most well-known crime writers in Sweden, lives in Södertälje, near Stockholm. She has written nearly forty books in various genres, and her work has been translated into more than a dozen languages. Two of her books have won the Swedish Crime Writers' Academy's Best Swedish Crime Novel award. Her most recent publication is *An Axe for Alice*.

MARTIN HOLMÉN, born in 1974, teaches history and Swedish at a high school in Stockholm. His debut novel *Clinch*, which contains some of the characters from his story in this volume, was published by Albert Bonnier Publishing in October 2015, with subsequent editions coming out in Australia, France, Italy, and the UK. He is currently working on *Out for Count*, the second book in the Harry Kvist trilogy, and the third and final installment, *Slugger*, is due out in 2017.

Monika Manowksa

NATHAN LARSON is an award-winning film composer, musician, producer, and the author of three novels, the latest of which is *The Immune System*. He has made music for many films, including *Boys Don't Cry*, *Margin Call*, and the Swedish films *Stockholm Stories* and *Lilja 4-Ever*. He and his wife, singer Nina Persson, divide their time between New York City and Sweden.

Perry Cohen

RIKA LESSER (translator), poet, educator, and Feldenkrais teacher, has published four volumes of poetry and translations of fifteen collections of poetry or fiction, among them works by Göran Sonnevi and Rainer Maria Rilke. Her honors include the Amy Lowell Poetry Traveling Scholarship, an Ingram Merrill Foundation Award in Poetry, the Harold Morton Landon Translation Award, a Fulbright, two NEA translation grants, and two translation prizes from the Swedish Academy.

MALTE PERSSON is a writer of fiction, poetry, and children's books. He is also a translator, a literary critic, and a magazine columnist. He has lived in Gothenburg and Stockholm, and currently resides in Berlin, Germany. His short story "Fantasy" was published in English by Readux Books.

Michael Pierce

KERRI PIERCE (translator) is a writer and translator living in Rochester, New York. Her published translations span several genres from Dutch, German, Norwegian, Portuguese, Spanish, and Swedish. She was the recipient of a translation fellowship from Dalkey Archive Press in 2009 and holds a PhD in comparative literature from Pennsylvania State University.

ANNA-KARIN SELBERG was born in 1975. She is a philosopher and the author of two novels, *Vit* (*White*) and *Skymning över Al-Omistan* (*Dawn over Al-Omistan*).

Gustaf Rytter

JOHAN THEORIN was born in 1963 in Gothenburg, and now resides in Stockholm. *Echoes from the Dead*, his first novel, has been translated into twenty-five languages and was made into a Swedish feature film in 2013. His second novel, *The Darkest Room*, was voted the Best Swedish Crime Novel in 2008, won the Glass Key award in 2009, and the 2010 CWA International Dagger. A third Öland novel, *The Quarry*, was published in 2011, and a stand-alone suspense novel, *The Asylum*, was published in 2013.